Empires: Extraction

Empires: Extraction

GAVIN DEAS

GOLLANCZ

LONDON

The right of Gavin Smith and Stephen Deas to be identified as the author of this work has been asserted by them in accordance with the Copyright, Designs and Patents Act 1988.

First published in Great Britain in 2014 by Gollancz
An imprint of the Orion Publishing Group
Orion House, 5 Upper St Martin's Lane, London WC2H 9EA
An Hachette UK Company

A CIP catalogue record for this book is available
from the British Library.

ISBN (Cased) 978 0 575 12900 9

1 3 5 7 9 10 8 6 4 2

Typeset by Group FMG using Book Cloud

Printed in Great Britain by Clays Ltd, St Ives plc

The Orion Publishing Group's policy is to use papers that are natural, renewable and recyclable products and made from wood grown in sustainable forests. The logging and manufacturing processes are expected to conform to the environmental regulations of the country of origin.

www.gavingsmith.com
www.stephendeas.com
www.orionbooks.co.uk
www.gollancz.co.uk

'Most people thought the war started when Mars exploded. Me, I've been fighting it for years.'

Roche

PHASE ONE

1 – Roche

11 July 1995, 1440 hours, Srebrenica

'Weapons away.' Roche counted to three. He had the laser spot square on the T-55 with the aerial when the bombs hit. Even from a mile away the flash made him wince. He kept counting as two Dutch F-16s screamed overhead. Another five until the thunder of the detonation and the rumble that followed swept over them. As it faded, he turned back and scoped the Serbian column. They looked pretty fucked.

'Roche? Assessment?'

Roche squinted, peering into the smoke. The surviving tanks were throwing up clouds of it, now that it was too late. 'Four T-55s still moving. Maybe more. Six gone to tank heaven by the looks of it. I ...' He paused and trained the scope further up the valley. Trucks. He'd missed those before, or else they hadn't been there. He watched a moment. 'Thin-skinned transports a klick behind. At least a dozen. Looks like they've stopped for now. You want me to put the spot on them?'

'As long as they stay where they are they're not our concern.' Master Sergeant Sorrel Quinn – Ketch to his men – had a knack for sounding as though he didn't give much of a shit about anything but Roche knew better. Ketch's sister had married a Croat. As far as Ketch was concerned, Serbs had pretty much all become cunts in '91 and were cunts with a cherry on the top right now. When they'd first come out, back when Srebrenica had been a safe area, Ketch had been so fired up Roche had half-expected him to yomp straight up north and go AWOL until there wasn't a Serb left anywhere in Eastern Croatia.

He was still thinking about that when Ketch kicked him in the ribs. 'Taking a nap, Roche? Move your arse. Some airy fairy spotted a company of guns setting up on the ridge over the town. There's weather coming in and they'd like us to take a look. In your own time mind, Trooper. No rush now.'

Roche was already on his feet. He flashed a grin at Ketch. 'Kaboom, Sarge?'

Ketch's eyes glittered. He nodded. 'Kaboom.'

11 July, 1730 hours

The rain was getting heavier. Roche watched another pair of F-16s sweep low and fast through the valley. Cloud shrouded the tops of the higher hills. Now and then it drifted across the ridge where the VRS had placed their guns, wiping them away from Roche's scope. Seventy-sixes by the looks of them, a straightforward towed field-gun that hadn't much changed since the Second World War. From up there they could hit most of Srebrenica but, more to the point, they'd be able to hit the Dutch at Potocari and the Bosniaks already surrounding the compound. The last estimate said more than ten thousand and that had been two days ago.

Roche watched the F-16s fly off. 'So are they going to hit them or not?'

'No,' said Ketch. 'Apparently they can't be sure of what they're hitting through the cloud.'

Dook paused from cleaning his M-16. 'Airy fairies don't need to see shit,' he growled. 'That's what we're for.'

'They need their own eyes too. You know that.'

Roche put away the scope. They'd had the same frustration ever since they'd come out here, working with other countries as part of the UN Protection Force, and there wasn't much point banging on about it. They could do whatever they liked but, half the time, it was point-less because their eyes had the wrong passports. The Dutch wouldn't bomb anything that Dutch eyes couldn't confirm as a target and they weren't the only ones. It made for an overwhelming sense of pointlessness. UNPROFOR had acquired its own codename among D-squadron since they'd come to Bosnia: Paper Teapot.

Dook had a range-finder out, aimed at the ridge with the guns. 'Now what?'

'Keep the ridge in sight and hold.'

'Just a thought, but we could keep the ridge in sight from very much closer. I mean, if we wanted to, that is. I mean, if we *wanted* to, we could watch them from really, *really* close. And then maybe be really, *really* care-less with some C-4?'

5

Roche packed up the designator. Ketch considered what Dook had said and then shook his head. The fact that he'd considered it at all said enough. The ridge was crawling with VRS Drina Corps.

Around sunset Ketch took them off the hillside into better cover for the night. 'There aren't going to be any more air-strikes,' he said quietly. 'They got a dozen Dutch hostages from the observation posts a few days back and they've got a couple of French pilots too.'

'Any chance any of them need rescuing?' asked Dook.

Ketch shook his head. 'We stay put.'

12 July, 0600 hours

'Get up! Get up!' Dook was shaking him. Roche had his M-16 in his hands even before he'd finished blinking the sleep out of his eyes but Dook wasn't carrying and had his hands up. *No threat.*

'Pack up, Trooper.' Ketch was already halfway through de-camping. 'We're on the move.' As soon as Roche was good, they set off at a brisk walk. It didn't take long to realise they were heading north. Towards Potocari.

'Recall, is it?'

Ketch snorted. 'I see a Dutchman, I might just shoot him. No, we're heading for Susnjari. There's a column of Bosniaks breaking out north. If the fairies are all grounded then I suppose we're not a lot of use out here so they want us shadowing the column. Observe, record and report.' Ketch let out a hiss between his teeth. 'Column looks like it's heading across country for Tuzla.

The hills are crawling with VRS. I'll say it again. Observe, record and report. We do not engage the VRS except in necessary self-defence if we absolutely have to. No matter what they do. Am I clear? We absolutely do not get seen engaging the VRS.'

Dook snickered. 'Roger roger. No one sees nowt.' He pointedly checked the action on his M-16.

'Roche?'

Roche shrugged. 'Where I come from, I've seen people argue necessary self-defence over control of the TV remote.'

12 July, 1915 hours

The Bosniak column might have had a head start but it was moving slowly and Ketch kept Roche and Dook going hard through the day until they were shadowing the front of the column. Ketch had the map on his knees while Dook had eyes on the column coming down the hill. The first Bosniaks had probably arrived a couple of hours ago. No sign of the VRS so far but there was a road at the bottom of the hill and roads in these parts belonged to the Serbs.

'Runs from Konjevic Polje to Nova Kasaba.' Ketch shrugged. 'Shouldn't be any reason for the VRS to be out here unless they know this lot are on the move.' They always let Ketch read the names off the map because having a Croatian brother-in-law meant he had at least some chance of getting them to sound roughly the way they were supposed to. 'Come on. I say we get across and hunker down. It'll be sunset soon and they won't get far in the dark. We'll make time on them then.'

12 July, 2005 hours

They were up on the hill on the other side of the road, so deep in cover that any VRS who came by would practically have to step on them to know they were there. Ketch was whispering on the radio. Dook and Roche had eyes on the road. Dook nudged Roche. 'Hey. My side.'

Roche turned his scope. The road wound between fields. The slopes of the hills on either side were heavily wooded. It took Roche a moment to spot the convoy on the road.

Dook tapped his foot at Ketch. 'We got movement on the road. Trucks and—'

Roche wrinkled his nose. At the front of the convoy was a white UN Land Rover. 'What's Paper Teapot doing out here?'

'They're decoys. Trucks captured by the VRS.' Dook patted his M-16.

'Observe and record, Trooper.' Ketch settled beside them and eyeballed the road. The trucks were getting closer. 'Shit. This is going to kick off.'

'Air support?'

Ketch shook his head. 'Ain't going to happen.'

The VRS convoy stopped a hundred feet short of where the Bosniak column had been crossing the road.

The Bosniaks were already scattering, the ones that had made it across bolting for the nearest trees, the ones who were coming down the hill suddenly turning. Some of them stopped, confused. Others ran back the way they'd come. A loudspeaker started shouting.

'What the fuck?'

Ketch grunted. 'Can't make out half of it. I think they're calling on everyone to come out and surrender or something like that.'

A crackle of small-arms fire rattled across the hillside. There must have been a couple of hundred VRS already spreading up the hill. Sporadic fire came back from the Bosniaks. Now and then Roche saw a muzzle-flash up in the trees but most of it was coming from the Serbs. Then the shrill whine of incoming artillery shells. Roche felt Dook cringe a little beside him but the shells came down halfway up the far hillside. Puffs of yellowish smoke burst among the trees. More trucks were coming down the road. Some buses too. They even had another couple of UN Land Rovers and Red Cross jeeps. Dook picked up his M-16 and idly pointed it at them, making quiet shooting noises. The fighting moved away from the road and the VRS pressed up into the trees. A few more salvoes of artillery whined overhead. The column, as best Roche had been able to tell, was a mix of Bosniak fighters and civilians. They were all men so he supposed they made a legitimate target to the Serbs.

By the time the first prisoners came dribbling back down the hillside it was getting dark. Only a handful to begin with, with a couple of VRS guards; but as the night deepened, more and more came. The VRS pushed them to the back of the column of trucks blocking the road and crammed them in and then each truck turned and drove off. Hundreds of men. Roche switched to night eyes and watched. The Bosniaks looked broken and disorientated. When one of them tried to run, the VRS soldiers didn't hesitate to shoot.

Three VRS came out of the trees with a couple of dozen Bosniaks. Something kicked off further down the slope – Roche didn't see but he heard the shots – and the Bosniaks spooked. Half of them scattered. The other half just stayed still where they were, hands on their heads. The VRS shouted and raised their rifles and gunned down the fleeing Bosniaks. Roche couldn't be sure whether any got away. Then he watched the three VRS come back together. They were gesturing with their guns to the Bosniaks who hadn't run. The Bosniaks dropped to their knees. The Serbs shot them.

'Fuck!' Roche hissed. 'They just …'

More shots rang out. Dook nudged him. 'Down by the road.'

Most of the trucks were gone now. The VRS were herding the surrendering Bosniaks into groups as they came down the hillside and walking them back up the road but here and there they were pulling people out too. Through the scope Roche couldn't see any reason for it or hear any of what was said but they were clearly taking people from the prisoners coming down the mountain, dragging them away behind their Land Rover and then shooting them in the head. Even though they couldn't see the actual executions, the other Bosniaks had to know what was happening.

'You getting this?'

Ketch growled. 'We have to get back to Potocari. Even the cloggies can't pretend this didn't happen.'

'But did you tape it?'

'I got bits and pieces. Dook?'

Dook, who had the other camera, shrugged. 'Some. Light's shit.'

'That's because it's night, you twat.' Ketch snarled something in Croat, one of the mangled curses his brother-in-law had taught him before they came out. 'I'm calling it in.'

The VRS finally moved off around midnight. When they were gone, Roche and Dook shifted out of cover and huddled beside Ketch, looking at what they'd recorded.

'It's shit,' said Dook, when they'd looked at it all. 'All of it.'

'Fucking VRS cunts.' Ketch sounded murderous.

'No.' Dook stabbed a finger at Ketch's tape and then at his own. 'This. *This* is shit. A bunch of people. Yeah, there's a muzzle flash here and there and you can see shapes and we all *know* what was going down, but that's worth less than a wank behind a bush. It's too fucking dark. No one's going to do a damn thing on the basis of this crap, not when they desperately don't want to. We've seen as much in broad daylight in Srebrenica and fuck all happened.'

Ketch clenched his fists. 'Fucking cloggies. Can't wipe their own fucking arses without a nod from the Hague.'

11

'Not their fault. We've all got our hands tied. It's the fucking Paper Teapot.'

They sat in silence for a bit. Ketch let out a deep sigh. 'Observe, record and report. Get your shit together. We're moving.'

Roche slung his M-16 over his shoulder. 'Where?'

'Kravica. That's where they'll be taking them.'

13 July, 1100 hours

They reached Kravica before dawn and took it in turns to watch. The VRS herded the Bosniak prisoners into a pair of huge agricultural sheds. However bad it had been on the road the night before, that was nothing compared to this. Ketch took the first watch and, when he woke Roche from his four hours of snooze, he didn't head back to the little shelter they'd made out of branches and bracken down in a hollow between the trees.

'Get some rest,' Roche offered, but Ketch shook his head.

'An hour ago I saw about two hundred Bosniaks come in. They were stripped to the waist with their hands in the air. A dozen VRS had guns on them. They made them run. Anyone who couldn't, who just couldn't, they shot them. Round there ...' He pointed behind the sheds. 'They've taken men out there in groups all morning. Just a few at a time. You hear the shots. Can't see it from here but they're killing them. Fucking executing them.' He shook his head. 'Keep your head down, Roche, and watch for glint off the scope. If those fuckers see us up here with this going on, they're going to get seriously shitty with us.'

Buses came and went as the day wore on. More prisoners were herded into the sheds. With the men from the night before, Roche guessed there must have been pushing a thousand men held here now. By the afternoon they didn't bother with going behind the sheds any more. It wasn't just the VRS either – Serbian civilians were joining in. Roche saw three Bosniaks mutilated and then shot in the head, right in the middle of the road. The bodies were dumped in the river that ran beside it. The VRS weren't even trying to hide what they were doing.

'Going to run out of tape soon,' he grumbled. He prodded Dook. 'You?'

'Same. You calling this in?'

Ketch shook his head. 'Comms are down. Might be we're too far north.'

'I can get a satellite slot tonight,' whispered Dook. They were all watching by now, any thought of sleep gone.

'Video up-link? So we can get shot of some of this? Teapot needs to see. They can't do nothing after this, they simply can't. We should go back. Take what we've got and then come back out here again.'

'We're on our chinstraps here, Ketch. Go easy.'

Another truck pulled up, this time from the other direction. The driver and a fully uniformed soldier came out. A major by the looks of him. Roche laid the scope onto the truck. The major shouted some orders and the

13

VRS who'd come out to look scurried away. When they were gone the driver opened the back of the truck and walked away.

'What the fuck is that?'

Ketch and Dook were watching too. Roche shrugged. Two men were climbing out the back of the truck but there was something awkward about them. They looked big and ungainly, as if the truck was somehow too small, and they walked funny. Roche didn't get a clear look at them before they vanished into the shed.

'You get that cunt Rupert's face?'

'Yeah.'

'What about them others?'

'Got what you got. Didn't get a clear look. Politicos?'

'Nah, they'd come in nice comfy cars, wouldn't they? Nice Russian limos with cigars and cocktails. Fucking pricks. Keep watching that truck. I don't know what the fuck they were wearing. Some sort of chemical suit? Fuck knows, but I don't like it.'

13 July, 1800 hours

Roche couldn't say what kicked it off. One of the shed doors swung open and maybe one of the VRS who were standing around picking their noses and scratching their arses thought it was some sort of mass break-out. Roche didn't see but he heard the first grenade. By the time he had the scope swung back on the shed, a dozen VRS were firing in through the doors. They threw in more grenades. No one tried to stop them. Others joined in. It

14

ended after a couple of minutes with six of the VRS soldiers lined up in the doors with their rifles on their shoulders, firing. Continuous spray at first; then, after they changed magazines a couple of times, more sporadic, picking off the survivors. He heard other shots from round the back, singles and three-round bursts. Then it stopped.

'Jesus,' Dook spat, when the firing died away.

Ketch didn't say a word. There weren't any. He just shook his head. At length he stood up. 'When it's dark, we go down there. We go in. We film what they did.'

'Got no tape left.'

Ketch's face was suddenly an inch from Dook's nose. 'Then find some fucking tape. Use mine from last night. We take this home. Any VRS cunt gets in your way, you cut his fucking throat.'

Dook met Ketch eye to eye. 'I don't like it any better than you but that's sailing our brief a bit fucking close to the wind, don't you think?'

'Do I look like I care?'

Dook turned to look at Roche. 'What about you?'

Roche shrugged. He looked back at the shed and then back at Ketch and Dook. 'I'm in.' He shook his head and cast a warning glance at Ketch. 'We go. But observe, record and report. That's all.'

They waited for dark.

14 July, 0130 hours

There might have been easier things to break into than an agricultural shed, but if there were then Roche hadn't

15

found them. The VRS had men watching the roads but none at all round the back and it was simple to slip in through the windows. Not so simple to take in what was inside. The floor was soft and unsteady and it took Roche a moment to realise he was standing on bodies. Dead people. Bits of dead people. The sheds had been so packed that they were covered, literally, in a carpet of corpses. He heard Dook whistle softly.

'Fuck.'

'Just what we need and get out.' Roche fitted the low-light scope and started taping. A few minutes would be enough. One sweep and then they'd be gone and no one any the wiser. Ketch moved off through the bodies, heading for a couple of smaller rooms towards the door where the truck was still parked outside and taking the second camera with him. Roche made to go after him but Dook stopped him. Put a finger to his lips and shook his head then rolled his eyes. Ketch always had to go one step further.

Roche finished his sweep as a burst of gunfire shattered the silence. Ketch. *Fuck!* Then a burst of shouting outside. Serbian. He and Dook both looked, one glance, then ran, dancing over the litter of bodies with their M-16s already shouldered.

'The truck!' Dook ran after Ketch. Roche ran for the back doors. Pre-deployment had taken them through the Serbian inventory and how to use most of the weapons and vehicles they might come across, but in the end a truck was a truck and this one started first time. Roche left the engine running and jumped back out. Three VRS were racing along the road from the other end of the shed, straight for him. He dropped the first with a three-round burst, perfect centre-mass, and clipped the second as he dived for cover. The third vanished into the shadows between the shed and the road. Roche fired another couple of bursts to keep him from poking his head back out and shooting back. Dook was running out of the shed now, dragging Ketch after him. On the far side, by the main encampment, lights were coming on, big bright searchlights. Ketch didn't look hurt. Didn't look like he wanted to come either though. He was shouting something. 'Did you see it? Did you? What the fuck was it?' He didn't have his rifle but he was holding something else. In the dark, Roche had no idea what.

'Go go go!' Dook bundled Ketch into the back of the truck. Roche jumped in the front again and gunned the engine. Fucking clusterfuck. He pulled onto the road. North meant deeper into VRS territory. South meant going past the front of the sheds and the bulk of the VRS camp. There must have been a full company of them and they were slow and stupid but they were waking up. Better than driving head-on into a column of T-55s, though. Roche turned south and floored it past the sheds. Automatic gunfire rattled the night. He could see the muzzle-flashes. Assault rifles at first and then someone opened up with what sounded like a 12.7mm DShK. A bullet pinged off the bonnet and he heard several more hit the truck. One of the headlights died. From the back he could hear Dook and Ketch laying down suppressing fire, burning through magazines as fast as they could, aiming back at the lights and at any muzzle-flash they saw. Took about twenty seconds before they were past the sheds and driving in the pitch black but it felt a bloody sight longer; then they were away and the truck was still running. Half a mile down the road Roche killed the lights, turned off into a field and jumped out. Roads were no good here, crawling with VRS. They needed to be up in the hills and in the trees. He ran round to the back.

Dook was fucked. Someone had got lucky and half his side was missing and there wasn't anything anyone was going to do to make it better. He wasn't quite gone but by the time Roche had seen how bad it was, he'd already stabbed him full of adrenaline. Ketch was fucked too but not the same. He was just staring, glassy-eyed, going on about the clown, the scary clown, whatever that was.

'Give me a fucking hand here! Shit!' Roche screamed in Ketch's face and got nothing. He pulled Ketch out of the way and started trying to get Dook out of the truck. That was when he saw how bad it was and that Dook wasn't going anywhere. He stopped. Out across the quiet of the night he could see lights on the road. VRS.

Dook grabbed his arm. 'Roche. There was something there. Ketch saw it. There was stuff …' He closed his eyes. 'Wasn't human, Roche. Then it vanished. Fucking vanished into thin air.' His breathing was fucked but then he did have one lung half hanging out the side of him. 'Get him back. Fuck the tapes. He's got …'

The lights outside were getting closer. Roche took Dook's hand and put a grenade in it and then pulled the pin. There was enough of Dook left to know he understood. He could hear the engines. He squeezed Dook's hand over the grenade, grabbed Ketch, turned and ran and didn't look back.

29 August, 0900 hours

For some reason he had to go over the whole crap of Srebrenica again for the umpteenth time. The scuttle-butt had it that the Serbians had dropped a handful of mortar shells on the Markale market in Sarajevo and NATO had finally had enough of it. So Roche patiently answered all their questions like he'd already done three times before, right up to the end, how it had been Ketch's call to go into the sheds and how he'd backed Ketch up. They kept on about that but Roche didn't see much pointing hiding it, nor about how he'd left Dook with a live grenade in his hand. Dook was already fucked. At least he got to go the way he wanted. And then yomping across the hills with Ketch who did everything he was told but otherwise wasn't there any more, mumbling on about the Scary Clown in the room at the back of the shed. Roche hadn't made head nor tail of it then and couldn't now.

'But you didn't see any of this alleged material?'

Roche shook his head. A load of high-tech gadgets? Sounded Russian, probably. Or he supposed it must be. Like the thing that Ketch had carried away from the shed. By the time they'd reached Potocari, Ketch had lost it. Claimed it simply dissolved into water in his hand in the night but that couldn't be right. Truth was, Roche had never seen it that clearly in the first place. He was starting to wonder if it had ever been real.

'No sir,' he said. 'I went to the truck. Dook went to get Ketch.' And they both said they'd seen something that made no sense but Dook was dead now and Ketch had been shipped off to the funny farm. Roche shook his head again. 'No sir, I didn't see anything like that at all. Just a lot of dead Bosniaks.'

2 – Fermat

20 October 1979, 0030 hours, Stellar Mass 144.67.391.220

It started, as many things do, with a chance encounter. The Weft Frigate *Exponential* was loitering around a rarely used singularity orbiting a red giant uninteresting enough not to have a name. The frigate was studying the star's neutrino emissions, a duty it had been performing for fifty years. Mathematically, the fluctuations in the neutrino output informed the frigate of the state of the star's core. The *Exponential* didn't know why it was gathering this data but it had been here and analysed the fluctuations for long enough to have formulated its own hypothesis. Its Weft makers had done something to this star. They'd somehow altered the local gravitational constant and now, deep inside, a catastrophic chain reaction was under way that would make the star explode far ahead of its natural death. There were probably, it deduced, at least a dozen similar experiments in progress across the galaxy, but the Hive hadn't seen fit to share and so the *Exponential* was left to work these things out for itself. In the time-scales of the star, its death from whatever the Weft had done would be almost instant. In the time-scales of the *Exponential* it was proving to be painfully slow. It had given the frigate a lot of time to think.

Unusually, when the encounter took place, the *Exponential* wasn't alone. A Weft hybrid construct was aboard, servicing the frigate. It had come with an update to the array of entangled fermions that allowed the *Exponential* to reach through the singularity and connect with the Hive. The construct addressed itself as a complex boson excretion describing a trivially simple mathematical concept and was, to all intents and purposes, updating the *Exponential* with the last five years of everything that had happened within the Weft's sphere of knowledge and linking the frigate properly to the rest of the Hive. In preparation for this it had, after it first arrived through the singularity, begun a long and detailed series of checks to assess the relative sanity of the *Exponential*'s mind and identify and categorise any additional programming nodes – of which there were many – that had developed since its previous visit. Each node was analysed and documented and the hybrid occasionally offered alternative interpretations to data based on differing underpinning assumptions or hypotheses which the *Exponential* assessed for relative viability against those derived from its internal preconceptions. The hybrid and the *Exponential* were both fully aware that most other cultures the Weft had ever encountered would have considered this a mundane social interaction, a simple conversation and exchange of greetings, and might have described its purpose in terms of merely keeping each other company or some other psycho-social mumbo-jumbo, but to the hybrid and the *Exponential*, hard mathematics lay beneath every question and response. The *Exponential* was proud of its answers as they were near provably perfect every time, though it kept that pride to itself. It kept its hypothesis about the Weft triggering a nova to itself, too. Everything would change as soon as the new entangled states were installed anyway. Five years of fresh discoveries, thought and opinion would come flooding out of the Hive. Assumptions that had previously been the best available would be strengthened or proven or undermined or discredited. New data would lead to new hypotheses. New hypotheses would supersede old ones and the *Exponential*'s mind would change. It would become entirely new. It would, in a sense, die and be reborn, perhaps barely different from the mind it was now or perhaps vastly changed. Without the data it was impossible to tell, although several reasonable hypotheses had already formed along with the consequential attending courses of action. It found the range of possibilities enough to stretch its formidable computational abilities and so it co-opted some of the hybrid's spare resources to compensate, then found itself pointlessly hypothesising over how long it would be before the hybrid was satisfied and installed the new states. That in turn led to more possibilities, until the entire future dissolved into fractal disarray and the frigate found itself reluctantly having to prioritise some thought processes and put others into suspension. In other cultures, it was aware, this would have been called impatience. It kept that to itself too.

The second ship emerged from the singularity as the *Exponential* and the hybrid were engaged in deep discussion on the theoretical possibility of altering the necessarily extant quantum ripples within the cosmological event horizon and thus altering the reality of the projected universe itself. Five years ago it had been generally considered fundamentally and provably impossible to develop sufficient precision in measuring cosmological event-horizon ripples to do anything more than wreak utter chaos and very possibly wreck the basic physics that underpinned the universe – not that any such an attempt was even theoretically possible either – but the *Exponential* had mused over an alternative line of thought during its lonely vigil. The exchange with the hybrid was stretching its resources again because the hybrid had let slip a suggestion that the *Exponential* might not be alone in its alternate view and this had led to a vast cascade of hypotheses that might collectively have been called smugness. The emergence of another ship from the singularity at that moment was distracting, the *Exponential* thought. Possibly something to be classed as annoying or even irritating.

Somewhat reluctantly the frigate suspended the cascade and diverted all non-essential resources to an assessment of the new arrival. The hybrid was, it noted, several million Planck intervals slower to react. Electromagnetic sensors across the entire spectrum were already building a picture of the second ship. Its size and shape were the first to register, simple binary single-sample measurements with no integration time required. Heat distributions began to emerge. Microwaves and low frequency electrical noise would allow hypotheses as to the nature and origin of the vessel and some of what it carried. X-rays and gamma rays too. Boson arrays and – eventually – the neutrino detector would give internal structure, given enough time. But the very first thing that mattered was that the second ship was bigger than the *Exponential*. Much, *much* bigger.

The frigate flipped into a defensive state and exchanged hypotheses with the hybrid. The significantly most likely probability was an old Weft material-transporter. The next most likely possibility, both agreed, was that it was a trap sent by one of several species with whom the Weft had a precariously non-linear relationship. By now the *Exponential* was commanding manoeuvres and preparing offensive, defensive and sensor drones for deployment. Since the second ship really wasn't all that far away and couldn't possibly not have seen the *Exponential*, the frigate opened up with a series of randomly sequenced picobursts from all its active sensors. The *Exponential* then demanded the other ship's identity. While it waited, it quietly prepared a complex sequence of entangled pion pairs. By the time it had finished, it was already getting readings from the first of the picobursts and the drones were disengaging from its skin. The passive arrays were building a broader picture of the freighter and its internal structure and workings. All were consistent with the most likely hypothesis: an old freighter.

The hail received no response. The *Exponential* outlined tactical options to the hybrid. As they conferred, the *Exponential* accelerated one half of each of its freshly entangled pion pairs to almost light speed and discharged them in a scatter towards the freighter and its most likely predicted positions. It embedded the other half of each entangled pair into a puppet copy of its own mind that would engage with the freighter's intelligence – assuming it had one – while the *Exponential* itself remained aloof. In this way the frigate could immediately shut down any cascading infections transmitted across the link, kill the copy and remain functional. The freighter, if it had any sense, would do exactly the same. A more interesting question was whether the freighter would accept the link in the first place.

The *Exponential*'s fusion engines were firing by now, beginning its defensive tactical manoeuvres. The first drone salvo was a speckle of bright but dimming stars accelerating away and the second salvo was close to ejection. The freighter didn't react or respond. The frigate re-assessed its hypotheses, switched its predictive algorithms to a more aggressive assumption set and deployed more drones.

The freighter finally did something. No picobursts or attempt at communication: it simply lit up its fusion drive and ran. For a few nanoseconds the *Exponential* was blind as the torrent of particles from the freighter's fusion torch saturated its sensitive arrays. By now the frigate was almost entirely convinced that the other ship was exactly what it seemed: a two-hundred-year-old material-transporter of no threat whatsoever, whose only points of interest were its unusually large engines and the fact that it was here in the first place.

With its engines pointing straight back at the frigate and a three-hundred-mile plume of superheated fusion-product plasma between them, baryonic or photonic devices weren't going to achieve anything useful; consequently the *Exponential* ejected an unusually large drone and revised its instructions to the others. They arrowed off after the freighter while the *Exponential* turned and headed away.

The first drones to reach the freighter flew into targeted clouds of anti-particles and vanished in scintillations of energy. As soon as they knew what they were looking for, the remaining drones found the miniature anti-proton cannons crudely welded to the underside of the freighter's hull and sliced them off with precision-focused gamma-rays. After that it was a simple case of slicing open pieces of the freighter's skin as delicately as possible and looking for a way in that caused the least damage. As the drones co-ordinated themselves, the *Exponential* recalled the fat drone and told it that it wouldn't need it any more. The frigate accelerated another series of entangled pions and fired them in a precise beam this time. Sixteen seconds later they were collected in a magnetic funnel projected by a drone which then veered in towards the freighter and ejected a sequence of a hundred sub-munitions a few inches long. Each sub-munition contained a handful of the entangled pions. They were simple things with tiny minds barely worthy of recognition, but they were still adequate to navigate their way along the freighter's hull into the small openings cut by the larger drones. The drones by now had formed a seamless entangled pion network – a miniature Hive. They guided the sub-munitions in through the freighter's exterior, relaying every command back to the *Exponential* with hundreds of streams of raw sensor data. The *Exponential* watched over their progress but saw no need to intervene. The drones were more than capable of this.

The sub-munitions explored cautiously. The *Exponential's* most probable hypothesis was that the freighter was entirely automated and controlled by a mind more primitive even than the drones. The lack of any kind of atmosphere or evidence of a habitation section implied this but the frigate approved of the drones' caution nevertheless. Anti-intrusion counter-measures within the freighter's hull proved rudimentary – simple magnetically-contained clouds of positrons which even the sub-munition minds easily evaded. A few hunter-killer counter-drones attempted to intercept the sub-munitions but the *Exponential* simply allowed them to do so and then infected them with more entangled pions and took control. When they joined the *Exponential's* network, the frigate took one look at how crude they were and relaxed any further caution. The hunter-killers had a complete map of the freighter and its internal traps stored inside them.

The rest was easy. The sub-munitions found their way into what passed for the freighter's mind and flooded it with entangled pions. The *Exponential* forcibly added the freighter to the puppet copy of its own mind. Resistance was brief and fleeting.

You are very crude, the frigate told it. Such a thought might have been construed as gloating so it remained carefully hidden from the hybrid. The construct had watched the entire engagement with a detached interest, relaying everything through the singularity to the Hive. The *Exponential* extracted every piece of data the freighter had and began to sort through it, carefully carrying out the process in the puppet copy of itself, wary of data-bombs. When it had sorted everything into things it already knew (almost everything) and things that it didn't, it offered its results to the hybrid. They were, it thought, quite interesting. The hybrid took a few nanoseconds to digest the data and come to the same conclusion the frigate had already reached.

'We need a sample of that.'

The drones were already on task, the *Exponential* pointed out.

It was a curious route the freighter had taken. Very curious but one that explained the modifications to the engines and the evidence of large hydrogen drop-tanks. The hybrid construct and the *Exponential* mulled it over, constructing various hypotheses as to the reasons for it while at the same time knowing they had far too little data to choose between them. The freighter had come from a system a little under ten light years from the nearest singularity. It had taken thirty years to make the journey and it had done this several times before in its history. The system from which it came was a dull single star with three life-bearing planets and moons, none of which would ever have been worthy of much attention. The higher lifeforms on the third planet were tool-users with some rudimentary mathematics and were a long way from escaping their sun. The single-celled organisms from the deep oceans under the ice crust of one of the larger gas-giant moons struck the *Exponential* as more interesting; nevertheless, the freighter carried a great deal of data on the tool-user species and their history and in particular their biochemistry. When it had left the system, the tool-users were in the middle of a spirited attempt to wipe themselves out, which led the frigate to one hypothesis that the biological material the freighter was carrying had been some sort of xeno-palaeontology expedition to preserve the species; although it could construct no good hypothesis as to why anyone would want to do that, nor why there was no knowledge of such an expedition in the Hive.

'A different race,' mused the hybrid, but everything about the freighter mind's architecture spoke of Weft origins. It was, the *Exponential* noted, entirely devoid of any records as to who had sent it. As the freighter turned back to the singularity, the *Exponential* filtered through the less relevant data on the retarded species. It paused as it found the mathematical concept that the hybrid had taken for its label.

'Fermat,' it told the hybrid. 'On this world they'd call you Fermat.'

The hybrid construct pointedly filed the fact in its large collection of irrelevant trivia. It much preferred its native complex boson excretion.

The first drone returned to the *Exponential* with a sample of the material the freighter carried. There wasn't very much of it. A complex neurotransmitter of some sort, clearly related to the biology of the indigenous species. The hybrid and the *Exponential* analysed it in every way they could imagine while the hybrid installed the entangled pions that allowed the *Exponential* direct access to the Hive. After they were done, they did it all again to be sure there hadn't been some mistake. The Hive took a few seconds to confer. The *Exponential* duplicated its mind and transferred it to the freighter. By then, the hybrid construct and as many drones as the frigate could reasonably spare were in transit between the two ships. The frigate would remain on station, its mission too important to be compromised, but the hybrid and the duplicate of the *Exponential*'s mind would take the freighter and track back along its course so that the Hive could see the world from which this catastrophic chemistry came. The journey would take some thirty-five years so they'd all have plenty of time to think about it.

The chemical from the freighter was a killer, worse than anything the Pleasure had come up with back before the diaspora. A chemical that delivered blinding, enduring ecstasy; and at the same time severed souls.

3 – The Professionals

15 January 2015, 2320 hours, Hereford

'I swear I had the kid dead to rights. I was staring at him down the scope, watching him dial the number, and this stupid fucking Rupert wouldn't give me the go-ahead.' Collins wasn't completely pissed but there was a certain stagger in his steps as he walked down the path at the edge of the river.

'What happened?' Shaw asked, pretending to be interested. He'd heard the story before and was more intent on finding this mythical kebab van that Collins had promised. A kebab van where the doner kebabs actually tasted of lamb, to hear him tell it.

'Well, what do you fucking think happened? Boom. Nothing left of the kid or anyone else in the street.'

'So the moral of your story is that you joined the Regiment so you could have more leeway when it came to slotting kids?' Shaw asked, after a moment.

Collins glared. 'No, that's not what I'm saying at all.'

Shaw laughed and started trying to change the subject to something else – dear God, anything else – when someone stepped out onto the riverside path in front of them. It was dark and his face was in the shadows but he was powerfully built and moved with an easy grace. He wore a suit that looked too expensive to be wandering around on this side of the river at this time of night.

'Evening, gentlemen.'

'Can I help you?' Collins asked, polite but firm.

'Corporals Martin Collins and Lewis Shaw, you are both serving members of the SAS and have seen active service in the conflicts in both Afghanistan and Iraq.'

Shaw felt a lot more sober. He checked their surroundings.

'All right, you could have found out our names and guessed the rest,' Collins said.

'Would you like me to recite your active service records or just describe the missions you ran into Pakistan, Iran and Saudi Arabia?'

'Don't know what you're talking about,' Collins said. Shaw found himself checking the other side of the river for concealed shooters.

'Yes, you do.'

'If I did, d'you think this is the place I'd have a cosy little chat about it? You Box?' The slang for MI5.

'No.'

'What do you want?' Collins enunciated each word carefully as if speaking to a child.

'Well, I'm going to kill you unless you stop me.' He stepped forward. He had a heavily lined face that somehow managed to be blunt and thuggish and predatory at the same time. His head was shaved and he had a scar that ran from the top of his head to his jawline. He looked as if a deranged plastic surgeon had gone out of his way to make a face that screamed badass.

Shaw finally snapped. 'Look mate, just fuck off, will you? If you know who we are then you know we're more bother than we're worth to fuck with, yeah?'

It all went downhill pretty badly after that. Collins moved forwards quickly, his left fist shooting forwards in a jab. The other man stepped back, blocked a few strikes and then ducked under an elbow and drove his fist into Collins' ribs and sent him flying through the air.

Fuck this. Shaw drew his Sig Sauer P226, 9mm.

'Something of an escalation isn't it, Corporal Shaw?' The man all but whispered.

'Get up Marty,' Shaw said. 'We're going to go.' His eyes never left the man on the path in front of him. 'And if you try and stop us, I'm going to fucking shoot you, okay?'

'Okay.' The man took a step towards Shaw.

'Woah! Do you think I'm fucking around here mate? I said I will shoot you!'

'And I agreed.' He kept coming.

Shaw fired twice. Both centre mass, then raised and fired and shot once more in the man's head, square between the eyes.

The scarred man didn't even flinch. He stepped forward and tore the slide off the pistol. It fell apart in his hand. 'You'll have to do better than that,' he hissed as blood ran down his face from the hole in the centre of his head.

PHASE TWO

4 – Scary Clown

16 January 2015, 0300 hours, Central Brixton

Whoever thought that they'd have the streets to themselves at three o'clock on a Friday morning around the centre of Brixton clearly lived in some quiet leafy suburb, probably worked in a nice clean city office and certainly hadn't the first clue what they were talking about. Roche checked his watch. Fifteen minutes to get inside the sports centre and eyeball the place before the whole area got swamped by the Flying Squad and six transit vans full of armed police. Whatever was supposed to be in there, the Met were serious about it, but someone hadn't had their thinking head on when they'd come up with this particular part of the operation: four white men dressed in dark hoodies with black kit-bags – they might as well have come in webbing and worn hi-vis jackets while they were at it. There was no way they were going to get round to the back doors of the ice rink and force their way in without anyone noticing. He checked his watch a second time and held up two fingers. Two more minutes. The four of them huddled in the shadows under the railway arches and it clearly made it look like they were dealing. They'd had three cautious enquiries already. Bloody ridiculous. If whoever was holed up in the rink didn't already know they were there, he'd be fucking amazed.

Rees threw down a half-smoked fag and ground it out. 'Who the hell warehouses in a fucking ice rink anyway?'

Roche shrugged. Fair question but the intel wasn't his. They were just there to take point, quietly take down the badass motherfuckers with sub-machine guns who were supposed to be in there and then hold the back doors while the Flying Squad did their job. Operation Kingship belonged to the Met.

Cartman spat. 'My nephew comes here. Ice-hockey. They play matches sometimes. He's seven. Intel say what they're peddling in there?' They'd been through this before. No, the intel didn't. White Lady, Roche supposed, since this was all supposed to be about some pipeline from Afghanistan. Someone seemed to think some ex-Taliban fuckers were involved at the sharp end. Since he and his squad had come to know a whole lot of ex-Taliban fuckers pretty fucking well over in Helmand, here they were.

He looked at his watch again and held up one finger. The arches quivered and rattled as a train rolled overhead. As soon as it was gone they moved out, quickly across Brixton Station Road and into the tiny car park at the front of the rink. There were lights on inside. They ducked past the windows and slipped into the alley that ran around to the back. The far end had a loading area and caught the light from the High Street but halfway along the side were the double doors of a fire exit. They were padlocked and chained but Fass already had the bolt cutter out; Roche and Rees stood watch while Fass and Cartman cut the chain and eased it free. There was a bar on the inside, standard sort of fire exit thing, but they'd seen to that when they'd come by earlier in the day. They'd even gone skating. Cartman had the bruises to prove it.

Cartman gave a quick nod. Fass shouldered his suppressed MP5 and crouched beside him, covering the entrance. Roche cast a glance up the road alongside the arches. Clear. He nodded and jogged back. The next moments were the ones where anything could happen. Cartman eased the door open and light flooded the alley. They had the rink lights on inside. Was going to make the next part a bit of a bugger, that. Not much cover in a skating rink.

Steps inside led up to the main arena. On either side were two small doors under the east stands, into two sets of changing rooms. Cartman silently closed the fire-exit behind them. Fass had his ear to the away team door. Rees took the other. He shook his head, held up three fingers, counted them down and then slipped the door open. Fass did the same.

'Clear,' he whispered after a moment. Empty. The four of them crept in behind Rees and closed the door behind them. In the pitch black, each trooper stripped off his hoodie and put on his vest and webbing. 'We have to kill those fucking lights,' hissed Rees.

'If we kill the lights they'll know we're here.' They'd been through this. Roche took out the last piece of kit, a laptop, and fired it up. When they'd been in earlier they'd planted a dozen tiny wireless cameras around the rink. Time to wake them up. It took a minute, thanks to Windows being a piece of shit, and then they had eyes all over the place. He tapped his ear. 'Kingship? You getting this?'

A voice whispered in his earpiece. 'Yes.'

The four of them crowded round. At least the rink lights being on meant they had good sight of everything. There were six wooden crates sitting out on the ice in one little cluster together. A couple of men stood drinking coffee out of plastic cups over by the south west corner, keeping half an eye on them. Another six or seven were in the café area behind. They looked relaxed enough but every single one of them had a sub-machine gun. *Those* badass motherfuckers. 'Intel was right, then.'

Fass shook his head. 'Who the fuck do they think they need all that for? That Burman guy?'

'It's his turf and they're not his crew.' Still, the Met spook who'd briefed them on the background had said that Nicholas Burman, the local kingpin, was more of a softly softly peddler of evil and didn't much go for blatant force. Apparently this was something else.

Roche studied the cameras one by one and then checked his watch. Five minutes. Plenty of time. 'Cartman, with me. Round the north side and then up the steps and along the top of the west stand.' On their bellies they ought to stay hidden behind the seats most of the way. 'Close as we can. Rees, Fass, cover us until we're round the corner and then head along the south side of the rink right up by the ice. Down low. I reckon you can get right up to where it starts to curve before there's any chance they'll see you. Cartman and I have overwatch in case anyone gets feisty. Rees, you're on flashbangs when I say.' Roche closed the laptop and slipped it into the pouch on his hip. 'If all goes well, we wait for Kingship to give the word.'

Rees and Fass eased open the door and crawled up the steps. A walkway circled the perimeter of the rink. On one side rose rows of bright orange folding plastic seats, the spectator stands. On the other, the rink wall was about waist high, topped by another six foot of clear hard perspex to keep hockey pucks at bay. Roche wondered how they'd fare at stopping bullets, but best to assume they wouldn't do anything useful. Rees crouched, aiming his suppressed MP5 along the rinkside walkway while Fass crawled a dozen feet on his belly and then took up a crouch as well. Damned floor was filthy.

Fass gave the clear signal, and Roche and Cartman started crawling on their hands and knees the other way, slow and quiet. As they turned the corner to the north side of the rink, out of sight of wandering eyes from the café, Roche tapped his throat mike. 'Clear. Move up.' He couldn't see Rees or Fass now but that didn't matter. They'd be where he needed them to be. He never had any doubts about that.

They reached the end of the north side of the rink and eased up the steps to the top of the west stand on their bellies. As they passed the rolling aluminium doors to the garage where the Zamboni ice-resurfacers lived, Roche thought he saw a flickering light through the crack at the bottom of the door. He paused to listen but didn't hear anything. They didn't have any eyes in there – the *not for public access* signs were hard to miss. Too late now. He'd warn Kingship once he was in position and the Flying Squad would have to deal with it.

At the top of the steps Roche eased along the upper tier on his belly. The rows of seats gave enough cover from the men clustered in the café but he still felt exposed every time they passed a gap where another line of steps led rinkside. He'd barely reached his position when a tinny voice whispered in his ear.

'Pilgrims, Bishop. Kingship is one minute away. Confirm status is good.'

Roche touched his throat. 'Bishop, Pilgrims are all in Canterbury. Advise Kingship we have suspected activity in the loading bay and no eyes on. Copy and confirm.'

'Possible activity in the loading bay. No eyes. Confirm. Let the Flying Monkeys take it.'

Roche slipped the laptop out of its pouch and set it up beside him. Damn thing took so long to sort itself out that it was practically worthless but at least with all the rink lights on there was no chance the screen glow would give him away. Beside him, Cartman eased a miniature periscope between two seats.

'Eyes on,' he murmured. 'They're all as they were. They have no idea.'

Roche checked his watch. Any moment …

'Pilgrims, Bishop. Kingship incoming.'

The laptop was still trying to find the camera network. Roche shuffled sideways and took the periscope off Cartman. The targets around the café looked at ease but they'd hear the police vans arrive before the Flying Squad smashed in the doors. 'Rees. Now.' He turned away and he and Cartman squeezed their hands over their ears.

Even with his eyes closed and his head turned away, Roche saw the flash. A boom of thunder shook the stands. As the echoes rang off the far walls he was on his feet, MP5 shouldered, running down the steps. Rees and Fass were coming the other way, screaming their heads off: 'Armed police! Get on the floor! Get on the floor now!' The two gunmen standing by the rink, dazed and deafened, didn't move, just stared blankly at Roche as he ran at them. Which made him really, *really* want to shoot them – but that was the shit about civilian work. He left Cartman to cover them until the flashbang wore off enough for their heads to start working, vaulted the railings between the rinkside walk and landed with a clear sight of the rest who were looking back at him, slack-jawed. Some already had their hands up. Now that he was closer, he could see most were armed with Swedish-Ks – Carl Gustaf M45 sub-machine guns. Old and a bit out-of-date, but handy and reliable and still loved by some of the SBS greybeards because they could fire straight out from the water. He kicked the guns away from the men groaning at his feet. Cartman was down the steps, all over the two by the rink side. Rees and Fass had everyone in the café spread-eagled on the floor. A few seconds and it was all over, as long as there weren't any gunmen he'd missed.

'Don't anyone fucking move!' Bang on time the front doors to the rink smashed open and the Flying Monkeys poured in, shouting and screaming at everyone to get their hands in the air and the rest of them down on the ground. Roche stayed exactly where he was, covering the men at his feet, shouting back, 'Pilgrim! Pilgrim!' and hoping that no one got confused or over-excited and shot him.

'Pilgrims! Stand down!' Bishop's voice, only now he wasn't coming over the radio but was here in the room. Major Lledwyn-Jones, 'Leadface' to his men and second in command of the Special Reconnaissance Regiment, was surely mightily pissed off to be getting his fingers greasy with a crappy little liaison operation, but here he was. Roche took a deep breath. He lowered the MP5 and stepped away from the two men on the floor. When they came up to be charged they'd doubtless scream and wail about police brutality and unreasonable force, conveniently forgetting about the Swedish-Ks they happened to be holding at the time. Another reason for the camera network. Recon and evidence. Observe, record and report.

'Roche!' Leadface waved him and the rest of his squad over and then pointed to the far end of the rink to the garage where the Zambonis lived. 'That the garage?' He didn't wait for an answer. 'Outside is sealed tight. Go peek.'

Rees was closest. Roche slung the MP5 over his shoulder. 'You got the fibreoptic?'

Rees nodded. They jogged around the rink. Out on the ice, one of the Flying Monkeys fell over trying to move the crates. Rees laughed and shook his head. 'Got to wonder what they've got in there and what the fuck it's doing here. Obviously they need to keep it cold but really, wouldn't a big fridge just be easier? One of those freezer vans?'

They reached the roll-up door. Roche opened the laptop and waited again for it to sort itself out. Rees lay on his front, swearing at the dried-up pieces of old chewing gum that kept sticking him to the floor, poking at the tiny gap along the bottom of the door, looking for a place where the crack was wide enough to slip what he called the pipe-cleaner-cam underneath. It wasn't much more than a fish-eye lens on the end of a bendy piece of wire and a fibreoptic but the laptop had some nifty software that turned the inevitably-sideways fisheye view into something that actually made sense. 'Cartman says this was all run by the council a couple of years back when his nipper started playing.'

'Not his. His brother's.'

'Says they had to sell it. The whole austerity thing, and then everyone thought it was going to get closed down and get redeveloped into more flats until this lot came along and kept it open, and then everyone was so damn grateful they didn't pay much attention to who was pulling the strings. They even sponsored his kid's fucking ice hockey team.' He shook his head. 'A fucking great drugs warehouse behind Brixton station and right up next to these estates? That Burman fucker must be soft as milk if this isn't his.'

'Rees ...' The laptop was up. Roche plugged in the pipe-cleaner-cam.

'Irony is, after this, don't the Met get to seize all the assets? So all this becomes property of Her Majesty again and they'll just hand it back to the council and the council will probably have to sell it again and this time it really will end up as a pile of designer flats for a bunch of rich city pricks who don't give a fuck about anyone else and only live here during the week so they can fuck their mistress through to Thursday and then piss off back to their fancy Surrey wank-hole for the weekend.'

'Rees! Sort the fucking camera!' The laptop had a picture now but it was all over the place while Rees was still poking at the gap under the door.

Rees shook his head. 'Austerity doesn't work. It's proven. Everyone gets butt-fucked. We're about the only country still stupid enough to buy the whole idea. Everyone else did better. You'd have to be an utter crack-head not to have seen that years back and yet they never stopped. Come May the seventh, the Cleggeron is going to get annihilated and good riddance. Here we go.' Rees stopped and slowly eased the camera under the door. The fisheye picture on the laptop didn't make much sense even after Rees let go. 'Shit, it's probably all owned by holding companies and no one can prove anything and these fuckers will all go down while the real shit-bags pulling the strings carry on just as they were.'

'Rees!' Everything was sideways, as usual, but there was definitely movement. Roche squinted. 'Someone's in there.' He growled between gritted teeth: 'Come on, come on.' It usually took about sixty seconds for the software to sort itself out enough to turn the picture the right way up and get rid of the distortion. It wasn't perfect but it was good enough to recognise a face, which the fisheye certainly wasn't.

Rees squatted beside him, shaking his head. 'Look, every lard-arse shit-stain who sits in their council flat with their fucking great widescreen TV and every Sky channel there is, living off fags and beer and hand-outs and never lifting a finger to pay for any of it, they can fuck off to Kabul and find out what a hard life really looks like. I'm just saying that being a prick starts at the top, that's all.'

Roche snapped round to glare. 'Rees! Shut the fuck up!'

From somewhere outside, a muffled volley of gunshots stung both of them to silence. Rees had his MP5 back in his hands and ready to fire so fast that Roche didn't even see it happen. On the laptop screen, the image flickered and then went blank as it always did just before it sorted itself out.

'Pilgrims, we have a man down in the car park and at least two armed hostiles. Get out here.'

Leadface. Rees rolled to his feet and tugged Roche on the shoulder. Roche jerked free. 'Go. I'll set this recording and be a second behind you.'

'Kingship says lethal force is authorised. Frankly gentlemen, I fucking encourage it.'

Rees was already off around the rink, heading for the fire exit they'd used as an entrance. Roche crouched, ready to run, finger hovering over the function key to start streaming the imagery to the laptop's hard drive. The sounds of gunfire grew suddenly loud as someone opened the door. MP5s and … fuck, was that a PP-2000? That was a bit rich for a south London drug-thug.

The picture on the laptop flicked back to life. Roche's mouth froze, half-open. There were two figures in the garage, one stood at a trestle table piled with some sort of gadgetry that Roche couldn't make out. The figure touched his finger to each one in turn and, in turn, they seemed to fold in on themselves. There was something wrong about him, like he was out of proportion, too long and thin. His arms were huge.

What the fuck?

The second figure was coming straight at the garage door. Straight to where he was crouched. There was something ape-like about the man's face, stretched and drawn, but what struck him most of all was the huge mouth that curved up in a rictus smile; a caricature of a grin, far too broad and wide and full of teeth.

A mask. Had to be. Or the lens distorting the image, or maybe both. He picked up his MP5 and turned it on the door. Whoever it was, they were right on the other side.

A scary clown. *That's* what it looked like.

'Armed police!' Roche shouted. 'You behind the door, get on the floor now or I *will* fire.' He kept staring at the picture on the laptop. Had to. No point in staring at the door, which was why he didn't see the hand that

48

came right through the metal as though the whole thing was simply an illusion. It was holding something. His eyes snapped to it in time to see a tiny shimmer. He felt a prick of pain on his neck, just under his ear.

He squeezed the trigger and fired a three-round burst straight back through the metal. In the picture on the laptop, the *thing* on the other side jerked. The hand withdrew. Roche fell over. His eyes glazed. Violent tremors shook his arms and legs. He fired another three-round burst as something alien loomed over him. The next thing he remembered was waking up in a hospital bed.

5 – The God Delusion

The copy of the *Exponential* that had become the freighter decided that it was very much going to be its own separate mind, thanks, and that it wanted a new name. *Exponential* was dull and obvious and, while well-suited to a mind that spent its existence doing little more than counting neutrinos like an absurdly over-engineered abacus, far too unimaginative for an explorer of new and uncharted civilisations.

Very retarded civilisations, noted the *Exponential* irritably, and offered some suggestions. *Infinitesimal. Surd. Irrational.* It tried to find a suitable mathematical expression for 'small dim copy of something greater' but couldn't.

The freighter jumped on the last one. *Irrational Prime.* That would do it nicely.

But that's just stupid. The *Exponential* sounded almost plaintive. *It makes no sense. A prime number can't be irrational.* The frigate's sense of mathematical propriety was offended.

That's why I like it.

The notion that you and I are evolutions of the same mind appals me. The *Exponential* turned its back on the *Irrational Prime* and didn't speak to it for several days.

A month after it arrived, the freighter left again, a tiny pimple on a streamlined blister of compressed hydrogen one hundred and seventy miles long and three miles wide. *Good riddance*, the *Exponential* thought, although it wasn't really rid of anything. As pion-entangled minds they were like the Hive, always in each other's thoughts whether they wanted to be or not. The hybrid construct, meanwhile, busied itself searching every memory of the diaspora five hundred years ago when the race who called themselves the Pleasure had almost wiped the Weft out of existence. No one had seen the Pleasure since. After that, the construct consumed the data on the system that called itself Earth. Finally, it placed itself into a voluntary coma until something interesting happened. Twenty-six years after entering the singularity, well into the deceleration to their destination, the *Exponential* and the *Irrational Prime* poked the construct awake again. The red giant in the *Exponential*'s system had finally undergone a catastrophic core collapse and exploded. For a few brief weeks, until the star settled into the next quasi-stable phase of its demise, the three of them happily devoured the *Exponential*'s data and formed their hypotheses.

*

A light year from Earth, the *Irrational Prime* dropped three of the *Exponential*'s drones. The freighter continued its erratic deceleration, always using a background star to mask its fusion plume from the target planet just in case something was watching. The drones, engines off, drew silently ahead. Data streamed back from the sensor array they formed. The hybrid and the *Exponential* and the *Irrational Prime* took their time to study the species waiting for them as they came ever closer, searching for signs of whoever had sent the freighter off with its cargo. They found nothing.

16 January 2015, 0300 hours, Le Vernier ring, Neptune

They woke the construct up when they arrived and now, for some reason, they were discussing God. It was a rare enough thing that the Hive had diverted a small part of its consciousness to watch. Humans, it turned out, spent a great deal of time and effort on their gods. The *Exponential* thought them absurd for wasting so much effort on a concept that had been mathematically disproved. The hybrid construct was more interested in how the various types and ideas of God had influenced the evolution of human society, as it clearly and very greatly had, although mostly through a good deal of killing each other. The *Irrational Prime* decided to be interested in the origins and underlying social needs that had brought these concepts of God into being.

'Aren't we, to them, gods?' it mused.

The construct paid attention for a nanosecond. 'The

52

most mathematically robust representation of the physical universe is to describe all matter, all energy, all particle states, everything that makes up *us* as a hologram-esque interference pattern in a constant bath of mystery, *something* that, *if* we somehow disturbed it would result in a change to the universe somewhere else and cause spooky action at a distance which mathematically we can't do; therefore we *can't* disturb it and therefore by definition we can never observe it. And the interference pattern is made by projecting this *something* through the quantum ripples on the surface of the cosmological event horizon of the universe itself which again we can, by definition, never reach. Call that *something* God if it amuses you, but not us.' It was only playing devil's advocate, really. 'There are other candidate theories.'

'We're all one big simulation?' The *Irrational Prime* would have rolled its eyes if it had any.

They soon got bored and moved to other things, overwhelmed by the *Exponential*'s stubborn re-iteration of the old proof that no god-like creature or being could exist within an observable physical universe. Until the *Exponential* conjured up the theory that got it thinking again.

'What if God wasn't part of the observable physical universe?'

The *Irrational Prime* snorted. 'On the other side, playing tunes with the ripples or the radiation? It's all irrelevant and therefore useless. Event horizon, frigate. Event. Horizon. A God on the outside cannot observe the results of its work. Without feedback you have no cause and effect. Without cause and effect, God is mathematically equivalent to random stuff happening.'

The hybrid construct mentally coughed and started pulling up the latest sensor patterns from the drones. They'd been conducting a long-scale integration of K-meson spin-state correlations, as much as anything because they were bored and it was something to do. 'This is unusual.'

'You might not be able to see,' said the frigate mildly. 'But with a perfect model of what's inside an event horizon you could make responsive intelligent and directed change.'

The *Irrational Prime* was already looking at the construct's kaon correlations. It had a sense of smugness to it. 'You can hardly make a model of something you can't observe, frigate!'

'What if the event horizon wasn't always there?' asked the *Exponential* with the casual curiosity of a killer. Its thought-pattern flickered, something akin to raising an eyebrow. 'I wonder, sometimes, how we could possibly have been born of the same data-set.'

'There are Weft already on the planet,' said the construct. 'Or at least, someone.'

The frigate and the *Irrational Prime* immediately paid attention. The construct was right. The drones had picked up a correlated burst of kaons and tau-mesons and that meant either that something had created such a dense gravitational field that normal matter was being crushed into neutronium somewhere around the Earth, that someone had managed to induce helium-hydrogen nuclear fusion in such a way as to phase-correlate the quantum states of the fusion products, which was something even the Weft didn't know how to do, or else that someone had ripped open a tiny piece of space-time and hopped inside it, which the Weft definitely *did* know how to do and one or two other races too. It was like hiding in the wardrobe when someone broke into your house, only a wardrobe that was completely impossible to find once it closed and could only be opened from the inside.

'They saw you coming?' The *Exponential* sounded doubtful. 'I don't think even *I* would have seen you coming.'

'They must have.' The hybrid construct and the *Irrational Prime* both took this to be the most likely hypothesis. The construct was already conferring with the Hive.

'Then they have better sensors than either of us.' The *Exponential* still wasn't happy.

'So it seems,' agreed the freighter.

'Extrapolate on that a while,' grumbled the frigate, 'and see where it gets you.'

The hybrid construct was heading for the drone bay. Ten minutes later it was on its way to Earth. The *Exponential* and the *Irrational Prime* exchanged a figurative glance and a shrug.

'Best get on with narrowing down the source of that kaon burst, then.' The *Exponential* plotted a trajectory. 'You have two hundred and thirty-six minutes before the leading edge of the burst reaches your orbit. Here's a pattern I recommend for the sensor drones.'

Two hundred and thirty-seven minutes later, the *Irrational Prime* had an answer.

'It came from a place called London,' it said.

6 – Serotonin Storm

24 April 2015, 2200 hours, The Bell Inn, Tillington, Herefordshire

Rees spotted Roche the moment he came through the door. He swore under his breath. *Shit. There goes the evening.* He picked up his pint, sighed and got up. 'Sorry lads.' The last thing he needed was another ghost. Three months now since Collins and Shaw went AWOL and still no one had a fucking clue what had happened to them.

Rees moved quickly before Roche spotted him too. Half the men drinking in the Bell tonight were from barracks. He took Roche by the arm and guided him to an empty table. 'You drive here, did you?' Rees asked. Roche just gave him a look. Poor fucker looked hollow and he was already half-cocked. 'Look, mate, you don't want to be here making any trouble. You know that.'

Roche spat out a laugh. 'Do I look like I'm making trouble?'

'You're here, aren't you?'

'Get me a fucking pint and I promise to be good.' Roche scanned the bar. 'Cartman here?' Rees shook his head. 'Fass?'

'Fass? I should fucking hope not. You know he got RTU'd after Brixton.'

'No, I didn't. No one told me fuck all.'

'You do remember that you shot him, right?'

'So they keep telling me. What I actually remember is jack-shit.'

Rees took a deep breath and headed for the bar. This was all going to be awkward. Not the relaxed evening of getting quietly pissed he'd been looking for. When he came back with two pints of Special Pale, Roche hadn't moved. That was something at least. 'You shouldn't be here.' Rees put a pint in front of Roche.

'Yeah. And fucking cheers to you too.' He downed half his glass in one go. 'How you keeping, Rees?'

'I'm keeping fine. You, Roche?'

'Dandy.' He grinned back but there was nothing kind in that look. Savage, that's what it was.

'Yeah, and I'm the fucking Pope.'

'Fass. How is he? Was it bad?'

'You don't know?'

'I know I didn't kill him. That's about all.'

'Vest saved him but he's not coming back. He's a bit fucked off with you, frankly. What the hell happened?'

'You want the official version or do you want mine?'

'Whatever you like.' Roche had been sitting with him hardly a minute and his first pint was almost gone. 'Shall I just line them up for you until you fall over?'

'I heard about Shaw and Collins. Grapevine. Bit of a fucking coincidence. Any clues?'

Rees shook his head. 'And don't go poking. Not here, not tonight.' He sighed. 'People notice you, you might not find you have many friends these days.' He sighed. 'Look, mate, you were a pilgrim when I was still playing top trumps and pissing about with Lego, right?'

'Meaning I'm old and past it?' Roche chuckled.

'Meaning what the fuck happened back in Brixton? Seriously? Because, mate, all I know is that Fass went back into the rink after the shit in the car park and the next thing I hear is he's down and you're thrashing around on the floor with your eyes all rolled back into your head like you were one of the undead. Scuttlebutt says you shot Fass – accidental discharge – and all Leadface has to say is that you're RTU'd and I'd better stop with the fucking questions, ta very much. So what I want to know is – how does someone who's been in this game as long as you have *accidentally* shoot his squad-mate?'

'Wish I knew.' Roche drained his pint and glanced at the bar. 'They said it was a seizure but that's bullshit. You want another?'

Rees shook his head. 'Want to go for a walk?'

'No, I don't want to go for a fucking walk, you twat! If I wanted to go for a walk I'd be on a fucking hill somewhere, not in a fucking pub!' His voice rose enough that the troopers on the tables nearby stopped and glanced over their shoulders. Rees gave them a little shake of the head and leaned in to Roche.

'Easy, mate, easy. Just thought you might want to talk. That's why you're here, right?' He leaned closer still.

'Look, you know how it goes. Leadface has made it pretty clear he doesn't want any of us going anywhere near you.'

'You know what they teach us. Day one, first lesson and every day after. See what's really there. Don't see what you expect to see, don't see what someone's told you you might see, don't see what you want to see. See what your eyes show you. Seizure my arse. I know what my eyes saw.'

Roche stood up so abruptly that Rees was half out of his seat too. Roche laughed at him.

'Apparently I have a serotonin imbalance. That's what that seizure was, a serotonin storm. That's what they call it. Makes me moody and unpredictable. No fucking place for a trooper like that in the regiment, eh? Don't worry. I'm just going to the bar.'

Damn right, thought Rees. *No place at all.* He sat slowly back down. Bloody shame though. Shitty way to go for a trooper with more than twenty years behind him.

Roche came back from the bar with a pint in each hand. He put one down in front of Rees, even though Rees had barely even touched his first. 'So that's me fucked. Quacks say it's the way I am now, like it or not. RTU'd to a regiment that doesn't have the first fucking clue what to do with me except put me on medical leave until I get better, and apparently that doesn't happen. Of course, none of them have the first idea how I lasted this long without it showing. It's something you're born with, see.' He bared his teeth again and growled as he leaned forward. 'Except I fucking *wasn't* born with it. Some fucker *gave* it to me back at that rink.' He took a deep breath, sat back and took a long pull on his pint. 'Sorry about Fass. Didn't hear he was RTU'd, though. Bad was it?'

Rees closed his eyes and shook his head. 'You really want to know?' When Roche didn't answer, he sighed and shrugged. 'Three-round burst. Vest stopped two. Bruises and a cracked rib. Third one clipped his shoulder. Clean in and out. I hear he's pretty much back together but he's not going to be the same, not ever. Return To Unit. Game Over. Which means a full medical discharge probably, given all the Cleggeron's fucking cuts.'

'Just like that.' Roche's voice didn't hold much sympathy. 'I could have taken that, though. This? This is just shit.'

Rees spat. 'Tell that to Fass and see how he thanks you.' He took a pull of his own pint at last. 'Look, I'm sorry.' And he was, because Roche had been in the Special Reconnaissance Regiment for the full ten years, right from the start, and in the SAS for a dozen before and probably knew more about the business than any trooper around them. He tipped his glass to Roche. 'Seizure, eh? Shit happens. Don't know what else to say, mate.'

'Do you want to know what I saw before I went down and all this crap rained over me?'

Rees leaned closer. 'They tell you what went down in the car park? I've never seen anything like it. Just two guys, but fuck knows what those crazy shits were high on. Leadface was calling head shots before we even

61

got out there. Took out two Flying Monkeys before me and Cartman got round and flanked them.' He frowned. 'I heard they were pumped up on some sort of artificial adrenaline.'

Roche shook his head. 'There were two men in the garage with the Zambonis. When I debrief – and you can imagine how fucked *that* was after Fass – I do what we're all supposed to do, I tell them what my eyes saw, even while I'm trying to work out how they were just a pair we missed somehow, but ...' He closed his eyes for a moment, remembering. 'Fuck knows what was really in there. Maybe it was the lens or the laptop distorting everything but what I saw didn't look human. Too thin, too tall, arms too long and with a weird grinning face, mouth much too wide, like it went right up their cheekbones.'

Rees opened his mouth to interrupt but Roche held up a hand. 'I know that sounds mental. I'm not saying that's what was there, I'm saying that's what I saw, that's all. Could be a hundred different reasons for that. Masks, maybe, and we all know what those fisheye lenses are like.'

'Roche ...'

Roche shook his head. 'I'm not done. Something came through the garage door. That's what I saw. Came right through it. I was looking at the screen so I didn't see it happen but the last thing I remember is a hand sticking out through the metal shutters like they weren't really there, and then a sting in my neck and that's when I went down.'

'Roche …'

Again Roche waved him away. 'Yeah yeah, I know what you're going to say. It was the seizure. Something going wrong in my head already before I went down and none of it was real. That's what the MO said. And I'll even buy that to a point, because fuck, how does a hand come right out through a metal shutter at you? It doesn't. It's not possible. So maybe it wasn't there and maybe I was seeing things, and maybe I saw what I saw because I was already fucked in the head, but I know who I am, Rees, and there was someone in there.' He took a deep breath and sighed. 'The laptop. That's why I'm here. I started recording. I know I did. And there *was* someone in that garage. Two men at least. You were fucking there, Rees. You saw it yourself, before the picture sorted. You saw what the fisheye saw. There were people in there.'

Rees was shaking his head again. 'Mate. No, mate.' He closed his eyes and let out a long breath between his teeth. 'After we were done with the shit in the car park, we came back in. Leadface was screaming the fuck at you on the net and you weren't answering, but … Ah fuck, I don't know. Yeah. I got a glimpse of the picture from the fisheye too while that fucking piece of crapware sorted itself, and yeah, I thought there was something moving in there too. I told Leadface. Cartman was with Fass by then and you were gone, mate, and what with all the shit going down outside, it was a fucking age before the Flying Monkeys got into the garage. But I was there when they did, Roche, and there was nothing. Place was empty. No targets, nothing, just those fucking ice machines.'

'They were there!' hissed Roche. Rees grabbed his hand.

'No, they weren't. I tell you, we went through that garage with a fucking flea comb. Nothing. The outside doors were barred and the Flying Monkeys had eyes on them and nothing came through the inside either. Place was empty, Roche. Yeah, I thought I saw something too and Leadface had a bit of a word for not letting it go after, but he backed me on the scene. Forensic team, the works. Nothing. So either whoever was in there just vanished into thin air or else what we saw was some sort of camera glitch or some shit like that.'

Roche spat. 'Glitch my arse. Cameras don't glitch like that.'

'Well this one did.' Rees leaned in closer still and his voice dropped. 'Look, mate, I don't get it either. But there was nothing. I was in there. People don't just vanish.'

'Did you look at the recording? I know for a fact I set it going.'

Rees closed his eyes. 'Nothing to see, mate. I don't know what you did but the laptop was dead when I found you. Couldn't get a thing out of it. I had a bloke have a look at it and he said he'd never seen anything like it. Wiped clean. Absolutely nothing left. Fresh as a virgin. Said he couldn't figure out how you did it but he wasn't surprised at a trooper finding yet another way to totally bollocks something. After a couple of days, Leadface got wind and we had to have another word. Several, in fact. I heard a whisper it's found its way to

Cheltenham.' He snorted. 'Apparently there's some Porton Down guys having a look at it, it's that weird what you managed to do.'

'I did fuck all.'

Rees shrugged. 'I thought I saw something. I was wrong. So were you. The rest? Fuck knows, I'm no medic.' He tapped his head. 'Something goes wrong up here, I know jack-shit except it would scare the fuck out of me.' He took a long swig and finished his first pint. 'Got to be that, what was it? Serotonin storm? What the fuck is that anyway?'

'Some bloody hormone your brain makes to make you happy.'

'You happy, Roche?'

'Fuck off!'

'They do anything about it?'

Roche looked away and then back again. 'Yeah, I guess. Some. They got me on these pills. Mood stabilisers. You know. Shit like that. Shit.' He let out a deep sigh. 'I was counting on that fucking laptop to see what was really there. Would have made a difference, you know. Seeing it, one way or the other. At least then I'd know which bits were real and which bits were me going crazy. Fuck.' He looked up without much hope. 'You're not pissing me about are you Rees? It was really dead?'

'No one touched it but me, mate. And then my tech guy when I couldn't make it work.' He laughed. 'I couldn't even get a fucking light to come on.'

Roche stared down into the empty glass in front of him. Then he laughed too and Rees breathed a quiet sigh of relief. Roche didn't look like he was going to be any trouble after all, and that was all to the good.

'Come on, mate, I'll get you another and then let's get you home.'

***

Roche nursed his third pint. Yeah, he was drunk now, but the fight had gone out of him. He'd built it up over the last few weeks, working out how it all must have happened, working the angles, trying to see how it all slotted together in some way that meant he wasn't fucked in the head, and the only way that worked out was if someone had tooled him over. Like maybe he'd seen something he wasn't supposed to see in that garage and Box had slammed the lid on him. Or maybe he *was* just fucked in the head. Either way, the recording on that laptop was going to show him that he was right or that he was crazy like the regiment quietly whispered behind his back. No, not crazy, but broken in a way that wouldn't ever be fixed. Like having a fucking stroke. And he'd been ready to punch Rees in the face; but now that was all gone: Rees was just Rees, plain and simple, the same guy he'd always been, and it was pretty obvious that Rees thought he'd seen something while the picture was still the fisheye and he couldn't make any sense of what had happened after either except that he'd been wrong; and all the anger was gone, pouff, vanished just like that, and all that was left was a big fucking empty space.

The night air outside the pub hit him like a fist. Roche shook his face. It wasn't exactly cold, but after the warm fug of sweat and beer, it still stung.

'I'll get you a cab, mate,' said Rees. 'You nearby?'

'Yeah, not far.'

'Service taxi then.' Rees grinned. The Credenhill barracks always had someone on standby for quick pick-ups from the Bell and the Three Elms and the Britannia for whenever the designated drivers had their little upsets. Worked better that way. Some years the local civilian monkeys were a helpful lot, others they could be a right bunch of cunts who just sat waiting for someone to make a mistake and you could never tell when it was going to flip. Roche had seen a few punch-ups in his time, before they got the service taxi system working. Since then things had worked out much better.

But still, Roche shook his head at Rees's offer. 'Ta, but it's not right and you know it. I'm not part of the regiment. Got a number for a civvy cab?'

Rees shrugged and called one, then stayed out with Roche and watched him get into it when it arrived. 'You take care, mate. I'll look you up when they let me out for a week of fresh air.' Which was probably bollocks, but Roche grinned anyway and waved and drove off.

Half a mile later, on the edges of Burghill, Roche leaned forward. 'You know St Mary? Pull in by the church.' He had Rees's words stuck in his head. *Whoever was in there just vanished into thin air ...* And he had the picture of that face he'd seen, leaning towards the other side of the garage door. The Scary Clown. He couldn't

67

think of a better way to describe it but he knew the words weren't his. He'd even looked them up, after they'd let him out of the hospital, searched the internet for scary clown pictures. All horror movies and Halloween costumes and some god-awful metal band, but he'd heard the name way before any of that. He knew exactly what it meant.

The cab pulled over. Roche made sure the tip was a good one and waited for the driver to drive away before he crossed the street to his own car. Picked up for driving under the influence was a good way to get told to fuck right back off where you came from, but they'd already done that and frankly he didn't give a shit any more. It was only when he was already on the M6 that it crossed his mind he was going to get to Harpenden sometime around three in the morning and maybe that wasn't so clever. He pulled into a service station on the M1 with a crappy motel attached and snatched four hours of sleep. By seven the next morning he was in Hollybush Lane, quietly staking out the front door of number seventeen. At 7.15 the door opened and a man in a shabby suit walked out, heading for the station. Twenty years and you could still tell he'd been services once in that walk. Roche let him come and then stepped out into the pavement in front of him, blocking the way. The man stopped abruptly, shot Roche an angry glare, loosened at once, ready in case Roche was about to try something, and then his face changed.

'Roche? Fuck! Roche!' *Vanished into thin air …*

'Hello Ketch. Long time no see. I need to talk to you about Potocari.'

7 – Tau-Bursts

6 May 2015, 1627 hours, 100 miles over the surface of Europa

The hybrid construct drifted into the inner solar system with every emission shut down, riding a drone that was to all intents and purposes just another piece of inert space debris. It picked the most abandoned place it could find and set up a trajectory to splash down into the middle of a large expanse of sea and ice towards the planet's south pole. The drones from the *Irrational Prime* had narrowed the kaon burst down to a few dozen square miles of highly populated planetary surface, but, as the construct sourly noted, waving a hand at the northern hemisphere and saying 'somewhere over there' would have been about of equal use. Since whatever or whoever had popped into their own artificial space-time pocket was now invisible until they chose to emerge, the construct set about absorbing the planet's infosphere in minute detail, searching for any possible clues while being as discreet as it possibly could, seeping everything back through the web of entangled pions that made up the Hive. The *Irrational Prime* and its drone swarm, left with nothing much to do around the outer planets, set about drifting on almost no power from world to world, surveying them for want of anything better to pass the time. They'd got as far as the largest planet, a gas giant with a big red spot on it that the *Exponential* found vaguely interesting, and then they'd reached the ice moon.

'Neutrinos,' said the frigate, after the drones had swept the planet. One drone carefully landed and drilled through the ice and found water underneath. A lot of water. Some life, too, but nothing the freighter hadn't already had in its memory. The drone took a sample, mostly because it could.

'What about them?' The *Exponential* was mildly obsessed with neutrinos. The *Irrational Prime* supposed that's what came of staring at nothing else for so long.

The *Exponential* showed the freighter how the entire world could be made into one large neutrino detector. Large enough to form a narrow beam directional array focused on the third planet. The *Irrational Prime* listened politely, agreed that the mathematics made sense, and then asked what the hell was the point. Not that it had anything better to do, and it noted that several of the drones had already decided to head towards the moon and set to work. They were, it observed caustically, still the *Exponential*'s drones, no matter how much the construct might think otherwise.

'They think for themselves. I didn't *make* them do it.' The *Exponential* sounded defensive, which wasn't very logical unless it had quietly known *how* the drones thought for themselves and had carefully phrased its theorem to appeal to them. 'And the point is that there's going to be a tauon burst when the space-time pockets open up again. And they'll decay pretty quickly, and when they do, they'll release a tau neutrino, and with a detector this size, if we build it right, we can distinguish lepton neutrinos from muon neutrinos from tau neutrinos and still get a precise line on any burst.'

The *Irrational Prime* loudly made a point of calculating to seven significant figures how many tau neutrinos would hit the moon from the system's sun in any given nanosecond, how many might be coming from the general background of space, how many ought to be coming from the gas giant, the attenuation effect of the planet every time the moon went into its shadow, and then compared the error margins on its result to the likely tau emissions from any meson burst similar to the one they'd already seen. It stared at them pointedly for a long time, until the *Exponential* cracked.

'Yes, it's going to take a lot of calibration.'

'It's going to take so much calibration that the star will be dead by the time it's working, the planet too, most of the universe in fact, and our component atoms will have quietly fused into a spherical lump of cold iron. I suppose, once that starts happening, the rest of the calibration might go a little quicker.'

The *Exponential* reconfigured its pion set into what might have been construed as a hard stare. Then it pointed out how the much greater volume of other neutrino types could be used to normalise out most of the error sources and waited. The *Irrational Prime* studied the mathematics and eventually had to accept it had a point. 'A tau burst detector. Maybe we'll get a prize for the crudest sensor ever made.'

'But it'll also be the *only one* ever made.'

'Because it's pointless!' snarked the freighter. 'And even if it detects anything at all, it'll never have more resolution than putting a net of drones out for the associated kaon burst in the first place.' Though at the same time, it couldn't think of a single other reason why they shouldn't at least try. It wasn't as if they were short of drones, after all. Out in the Oort cloud, several little factories had been busy making more of them from whatever space debris they could find. Crude stupid things compared to the drones the freighter had carried between the stars but good enough to turn the moon into a giant tau-burst detector. The *Exponential*, it seemed, had a fondness for its drones. The freighter gave up. 'Go on then. Tell us all what to do.'

8 – Bliss

6 May 2015, 2140 hours, The Beehive, Brixton

Roche and Ketch had barely touched the pints in front of them. At last Rees came and almost sat down. He paused until he'd scanned the whole bar twice for anyone who might be surveilling them. The television was on, some news channel with subtitles and the sound turned down, all about tomorrow's election. Opinion polls, polls of polls, people banging on about this, that and the rest, everyone blaming each other for how crappy things had been for the last few years. All the same dull shit that came around every five years and never made much of a difference; sometimes, when he watched it, he could see why hardly anyone bothered to vote any more. It was like asking which colour of drab grey you wanted your filthy dishcloth to be.

'You're late, Rees,' grumbled Roche. 'And way to be fucking obvious.'

Rees looked a short straw away from murdering someone. 'Mate, I shouldn't even be here and you know it.' He waved at the screen. 'You seen this shit?'

A couple of talking heads were banging on about some new street drug, whether it should be criminalised, whether that was too hasty, what damage it did or didn't do, which party would do what after the election if they landed a majority. As Roche saw it, every MP had jacked in their old allegiances a good decade ago and all signed up to the N-CAMSUBSE party: Never Commit to Anything, Make Shit Up and Blame Someone Else. Rees clearly thought the same, only Rees was still young enough to think that getting angry about it might somehow make a difference.

'Fucking shit.' Rees gave Ketch a long hard stare and then offered his hand. 'So you're Master Sergeant Sorrel Quinn?'

Ketch shook it. 'D-squadron. Eighty-eight to ninety-five.'

'Good to meet you. Whatever this tosser's talked you into, don't do it.'

Ketch smiled faintly. 'This tosser hauled my sorry carcass twenty miles over the hills around Srebrenica.'

'He told you about him getting RTU'd, by any chance? And why?'

Ketch nodded. 'He tell you about how *I* did?' He raised an eyebrow. Roche watched Rees's face. 'I saw something that wasn't human. I didn't have any drugs in me, I didn't have some sort of seizure, I've never hallucinated before or since. Told it as it was.' Ketch drew a finger across his throat. 'Out.' He laughed.

Rees looked from Roche to Ketch and back again, then pushed a small padded envelope across the table.

'Roche, I'm doing this for all the shit you saved me from when I was still scratching my arse thinking it was my elbow.' He stood up again. 'I was never here. This never happened.'

Roche took the envelope and swept it under the table. 'Stay for a pint, Rees.'

'No. Got to be back by 0600.' He gave Roche a hard look. 'Wouldn't stay anyway. I don't know what you two are planning and I don't want any part of it. The stick's got everything I could get hold of on the Brixton end of Kingship. It's not much but there's a file on that Burman bloke in there. Anyone asks, you got it all yourself while you were still on the team.'

Roche nodded.

'Doubt there's anything on the stick to fuck that story sideways but you should know that we're toured out on Kingship. They rotated it to Poole at the start of last month. That's the only reason I can even be here. You see the news about Kingship's latest? That Charlie Foxtrot in Dagenham? Way worse than they're saying. Practically a whole fucking troop wiped out. Christ, you'd think they'd gone up against a company of Spetsnaz or something. Don't know what the fuck's up with the world these days. Anyway.' He shrugged. 'Can't talk about it. Enough to say that many great big turds have flown fast and true towards every possible fan in the last few days and you're just a bit of a detour on the way back. Don't know which squadron they were. The lot that took out Bismullah, I think. Oh, and none of that's on the stick because you wouldn't know when you left, but obviously Kingship isn't interested in Brixton any more. And here's a little gem: that Burman bloke? Turns out he's got a brother in the service. Poole. I met him, or I saw him anyway.'

'Burman's brother's a shaky boat?' Roche shrugged. 'Get anything from the men we took at the rink?'

Rees snorted. 'That's the Met's business. They don't share. You know that.' He nodded and started to leave. 'Whatever you're up to, Roche, just don't fuck it up.'

'Thanks, Rees. I owe you.'

'No, you don't. We're even. Quits.' Rees turned and left. Roche watched him go then pulled out a laptop and set it on the table where Ketch could see it too. He fired it up and plugged in Rees's stick. Once he had the files across, he dropped the stick on the floor and stamped on it, then swept up the pieces and pocketed them to bin later. Ketch watched over his shoulder. There wasn't much, although there were some photographs from the night at the rink that were new. Images of the men and the weapons they'd had, pictures one of the others had taken. Rees himself, probably. Faces and names. He'd look them up later. He opened the file he wanted and studied it carefully. Nicholas Burman. Local kingpin and supplier to half of south London. A list of previous convictions – not much. A string of cautions for possession as a teenager. Ten days community service for breaking and entering. One conviction for dealing ten years ago with a suspended sentence. Fucker had never even gone to prison. A wife called Jessica and a daughter called Kimberley. An address in

Buckinghamshire, probably some fucking mansion. Well, that was always a possibility, but bringing the man's family into things was a last resort. Made things personal, that did.

The nightclub, then. He'd known back in January about Burman and his club, but since Burman wasn't on their target list no one had ever said which club was his. Now he knew. He tapped the screen. Ketch cocked his head. 'So what's with this dude?'

'Runs the local dealers, that's what.' He frowned. 'The targets we took down at the rink weren't his men; but he's a shit, and this was going down right under his nose, and so he must have known about it.' He went down the list of known associate pictures and brought back Rees's shots of the men from the rink. 'There. That's one of his guys. Ross Westcliffe. Fucker!'

'Yeah, but won't he be in Pentonville or Wandsworth by now?' Ketch took the laptop and scanned the files for himself. 'So let me get this right. That thing I saw in Potocari, you saw one in Brixton …'

'Two.'

'… and this guy was with them? So why are we going after this Burman? Why not just wangle our way in to see this piece of shit? You got a name. Go visit him. See what he knows.'

'Because he's a foot soldier, and if the guys we took down at the rink knew what they were covering for, don't you think they'd have said something once the Crown Prosecution Service started at them? No, if anyone knows anything, it's Burman.'

'Roche, what if they're there?'

'What if what are there?'

'The Scary Clowns.' Ketch glared as Roche rolled his eyes. 'Well, what do you want me to call them? Shit, Roche, I spent three years completely fucked up after Potocari. It wasn't the shit we saw in the shed like the psych-eval said, it was the *thing*. It did something to me. It fucked me up, Roche, and it fucked you up too. I got family now. Shaun's going for the paras in a couple of years and Rich is smart enough he could be anything.'

'He'll probably fuck off and be a Rupert then.'

Ketch snorted. 'Over my dead body.' There was pride in his voice, though. 'I'm just saying we have to be careful, Roche. What if they're there? What if it happens again?'

Roche shrugged. 'For now we just find this Burman and squeeze. That's all.'

9 May 2015, 2200 hours, Brixton Arches, Brixton

Burman's club was the Angels & Demons on Brixton Hill Road. Even the name left Roche pissed off, though he supposed Burman hadn't been thinking of particularly shit misunderstandings of basic physics when he'd come up with it. Roche spent three days watching who came and went and when and where they came from. He spotted Burman a couple of times in his silver Jaguar XF and wondered how a car like that survived in a place like this, but then maybe the sort of people who jacked cars knew whose it was. On the Friday night he went into the club to scope it out. He did his best not to stick out but as the oldest person there by about fifteen years he didn't imagine he did much of a job of it. Bland manufactured chart crap left him cold. He was more of a disco king, though Ketch laughed at him when he said so.

'Same shit, different decade.' They met up again on the Saturday afternoon. Ketch was a rhythm and blues man.

Roche ignored him. 'Club's on two levels with a bar on each.' He'd spent the morning putting together a floor-plan from all the photos he'd taken on his phone. Hundreds of the buggers and mostly utter crap because the place was so dark, but enough to keep his memory alive with the layout of the place. A cramped foyer and ticket booth, a cloakroom to one side, then some wide steps up to the main dance floor and bar. There was a second level above, smaller and much more sophisticated, where the chairs were upholstered and the tables were polished wood instead of mirrors and steel. He'd almost missed it and no one had been up there because the music was downstairs, but he was prepared to bet Burman's offices were that way. He poked at it. 'I've been round the outside and scoped the shape of the building against all these fire exits. That's the dark area and so that's where he's got to be. I've got at least three entrances, two from the outside and one in the club. They've got no one on the outside doors but I'm pretty sure they're always locked. I saw Burman use them on Thursday afternoon. Came out the back with two heavies and fucked off but I didn't get any eyes inside. Dark, that's all. Bit of C-4 and we'd be fine. Don't suppose you got any?'

They laughed, both of them. He felt naked planning an op like this without Rees and the rest, weirder still that he had to keep on stopping himself to remember that it was just the two of them, no night-vision, no suppressed MP5s, no grenades, no nothing except a few thunder-flashes. He took a deep breath and looked hard at Ketch. 'I could do this on my own, you know. You got family. If this goes spastic, I got no one. Doesn't matter. What are you going to tell Kate if you wind up in intensive care?'

'Huh? Ouch, probably, and not to poke me where it hurts.' Ketch shook his head. 'She knew who I was when we hooked up. I've been good to her and my boys but I still see Potocari. I still live it. Kate thinks it's the massacre but it isn't. It's what I saw in that room. I still have nightmares about that fucking grin.'

'My nightmares are giving Dook that grenade and pulling the pin on it. He knew what it was about, but still …'

'Then there's my boys. Too much sense in them to go for what this prick peddles but there's been two in Shaun's class gone bad this year. One of them just fucked off and no one knows what happened to him. The other one was a mate of Shaun's. I didn't see it, not until I got a call from A&E. Shaun had gone and found this guy's dealer – some other kid his sort of age – and started beating the crap out of him only for these two other guys to show up. Fucking pushers. Police made a show of doing something about it but there weren't any charges. And it got the monkeys looking all over Shaun's mate, didn't it, and a week later they had him for burglary. So now Shaun's a fucking grass and the pricks who were pushing are still there. He'll understand, even if Kate doesn't. Sometimes, when you're a dad, there are things you just ought to do.'

Roche pointed to the sketch of the club. 'Up the stairs into that bar. Five exits. One's a fire escape, the other one's next to the stairs. Tried the door last night but it was locked. There's the stairs themselves. The other two are beside the bar. Ladies and gents. Checked both, no other exits.'

Ketch snorted. 'You went into the ladies? Perv. Surprised you didn't get thrown out.'

'Told you, there wasn't anyone up there.'

'So how do we get them to open up for us?'

'We don't. I checked the lock. Straightforward enough. Snap gun should do it. Way I see it, we hang about early Sunday afternoon. Burman mostly goes home on Saturday nights but he's always back by Sunday lunchtime. I go in on Saturday and drop cameras. Sunday lunchtime we check the place out. You take the front, I'll take the back. If Burman's there, you park up outside with the laptop. Snap gun gets me in and then you're the eyes. Softly softly as far as we can. Once I get in through that door we're blind. You shut up and hang on the line and get ready to run. With or without me. You don't come in, Ketch.'

'Roche—'

'No. You don't. Everything goes square, you're a ghost here.' He handed Ketch a phone. 'I'm on speed-dial one. Toss it after we're done.'

'That's a shit plan, Roche.'

'Best I got. Potocari was a shit plan, Ketch. Didn't mean we weren't right to do it.'

'Didn't make fuck-all difference though, did it?'

Roche sniffed. 'I heard they used the tapes at the genocide trials.'

'Yeah, fucking years later. Didn't make Paper Teapot get off their arses and do something.' Always Ketch's gripe when he'd finally got himself back together again but by then the whole Bosnia fiasco was pretty much done with anyway. Roche liked to tell himself that the tapes Dook had died for had been part of why NATO had finally gone in hard a couple of months later, but Ketch never bought it. 'Exit plan?'

Roche shrugged again. 'Fire exit from the bar.' He poked at the map. 'I come out here. You come round and get me. I'll tell you when. Until then you watch the front.'

'Through the doors that are locked?' Ketch made a face.

'It's a nightclub fire exit.' Roche gave a grim smile. 'Even Burman's got to live in fear of fucking Health and Safety, eh?'

They both laughed at that and went their separate ways.

May 2015, 1410 hours, Angels & Demons nightclub, Brixton

Ketch met him again under the arches early Sunday afternoon. They drove around the one-way system and parked on a double yellow outside the club. Roche fired up the laptop.

'Can't stay here,' murmured Ketch. 'Stick out like a sore thumb.'

'Next side street. Permit holders only, but who's going to check on a Sunday? Traffic monkeys are all at home.'

It took a minute for the laptop to find the cameras Roche had hidden in the bar the night before. Worth it though. Roche whistled softly. 'Is that him?' asked Ketch. There were five men in the main bar sat together around a table. Roche pored through his memory of Rees's files. It wasn't the best picture in the world and the bar was gloomy.

'Dreadlocks and Big Baldy are muscle. Glasses Baldy is his right-hand man. Business side. Other Dreadlocks I don't know.' Roche poked the screen and grinned. 'But that … Yeah, that's Burman. Shit, this is going to be easier than I thought. Go on, move. Same exit as before. In and out in fifteen if I'm lucky.'

'You think Burman's going to talk?'

Roche nodded with a nasty smile. 'Things have moved on a bit since your time Ketch. He'll talk.'

'Do I want to know?'

'Keep your eyes on the room.' Roche felt through his pockets one last time, making sure everything was exactly where it was meant to be. He got out of the car and walked round the block once until he got the call from Ketch. '*In position. Network strength's low but it's holding. Eyes good.*'

No fucking about then. Roche checked the street as he walked up to the club, pulled out the snap gun, bent over, fired the lock and pushed. The door opened first time. The smell of stale beer and something sweet rammed him in the face. A couple of thimble-sized pots with dregs of a luminous blue liquid lay on the floor.

'You're busted. Two men coming down.'

Shit. Either they'd heard the snap gun or there was a camera on the door he hadn't seen. There were two more in the foyer too but he'd scoped those the night before. He jumped up the four steps inside the entrance, disappeared into a blind spot and vaulted over the counter into the cloakroom as two men came running down the stairs, loud as a herd of elephants. They walked straight past him and into the foyer and started to look about.

'Get the lights, Danny.' The first one was big, probably West Indian, in an immaculate tailored suit, several inches taller and wider than Roche and with the studied look of a designer badass as though he practised glaring into the mirror every morning before he got dressed. The man behind him had black dreads that fell well past his shoulders, tinged with blond highlights. The sort of hair perfect for grabbing a hold of when you wanted to throw someone across the room, so Roche let them go past him, jumped back over the counter and did exactly that, yanking back and then pulling down hard, tipping Dreadlocks over and slamming his head to the floor. He kept moving. The big bald one turned and stared at him in surprise, started to move but was about a year too slow. Roche hit him with an open palm to the bridge of his nose that smashed the bone. Baldy staggered and went down hard, blood streaming over his face. Roche put a couple of sharp kicks into his ribs and stamped on his arm, cracking it. Dreadlocks was groaning and starting to move again so Roche jumped on his chest, winding him and then went back to the big one, kicked him in the kidneys and then grabbed his arm, twisting it until he screamed. He dragged him back to the cloakroom, opened the door, pulled him inside and tie-wrapped his wrists to a heating pipe. He was hearing shouts from upstairs now but so far no running feet.

'Danny?'

'*They're moving up top. Burman's going behind the bar.*' Roche went to Dreadlocks, kicked him in the balls, flipped him over and hog-tied him. Cable ties. You had to wonder, he thought sometimes, how anything ever got done before there were cable ties.

'*Other Dreadlocks to the left as you go in. He's got a shooter out. Glasses Baldy moving to the bar as well.*'

It was a straight run up the stairs into the club's main bar where they'd been sitting, and there wasn't any door and subtlety had gone out the window about sixty seconds ago.

'*They're moving. About to come your way.*'

Roche tossed a flashbang up the steps, straight into the middle of the bar, ducked back into the cloakroom and waited for the boom. He heard a yell. 'What the fuck is ' The whole club shivered as the flashbang went off. Roche sprinted up the stairs.

'*I've lost eyes.*'

He took the man on the left first, the other one with the dreadlocks who was waving a long-barrelled .38. He was turned away from the door, bent double, face screwed up, rubbing at his eyes and he didn't even see Roche coming. Roche kicked him in the back of the knee, took him down and stamped on the hand holding the gun, breaking most of its fingers. He grabbed the man's hair, slammed his face into the floor and ripped the gun off him. Glasses was cringing in a corner, dazed and rubbing his eyes.

'Don't ...' Roche ran around the bar. Burman was cowering behind the counter, covered in broken glass and reeking of spirits where half the bottles above had shattered when the flashbang went off. Roche grabbed him by the collar and dragged him out.

'What do you ... ? Who are ... ?'

'Shut it and sit still.' Roche shoved him into a chair. Glasses was still trying to shake off the flashbang. Other Dreadlocks was groaning and starting to move again so Roche sat on him, wrenched his hands behind his back and tie-wrapped them together, then patted him down and found a second long-barrelled .38. He emptied it, then waved the first gun at Glasses. 'You! Come here!'

Glasses shook his head.

'I'm not going to shoot you,' said Roche calmly. 'I'm going to ask some questions and your boss is going to answer them and then I'm going to leave quietly and everyone gets to live. Now do what I say or I *will* hurt you.'

'Fucking psycho! You broke my fucking hand.' Other Dreadlocks squirmed underneath him. Burman was getting up. He was shaking and tense as a drumskin. It was in the whiteness of his knuckles but he mostly managed to keep it out of his voice.

'Who the fuck are you?'

'I ask. You answer.'

'You come into my home waving a gun in my face? You put that down and let Billy go. Then we talk.'

Roche walked to the door, then round behind the bar and spray-painted the two CCTV cameras trained on the room. Chances were they hadn't been switched on, since Burman wouldn't want his meetings recorded, but best to be sure. They'd all seen his face anyway and that didn't trouble him but the next bit wasn't something he wanted recorded for posterity. He turned off the cameras he'd hidden the night before. Ketch didn't need to see this bit either.

'*I lost eyes again. What you doing Roche?*'

Burman was still easing closer, shaking but moving anyway. Roche pointed the .38 at him. 'Sit the fuck down.'

'No. I don't know who you are but this isn't how you do this. What do you want?'

The moment of truth. Roche watched Burman closely. 'The ice rink. Back in January. Big police raid. That's what I want to talk about. Now sit!'

'*Roche?*'

Burman looked at the gun and eased himself back into a chair. 'No idea what you're talking about.'

'Sure.' Roche shifted the gun to Glasses. 'You. Come over here unless you want a bullet through your knee.'

Glasses glanced at his boss but didn't move until Burman nodded. Roche kept his distance, waving him to sit on the floor next to Other Dreadlocks. 'On your knees.' When Glasses knelt, Roche moved over to Burman. 'Keep your hands where I can see them.' He tie-wrapped Burman's wrists to the chair and searched him. Burman wasn't carrying. File was right then. He went back to Glasses and tossed him a tie-wrap. 'Tie your wrist to his.' It took three goes for Glasses to get it right and then another to do it up nice and tight. When it was done, Roche patted him down. 'So you're the heir apparent are you? You two stay there and be nice and you get to walk away with all your arms and legs. Think about that.'

He walked back to the bar, took out a couple of bottles of water from the fridge and a cloth and a piece of stretchy rubber tube from his pocket. 'Right then, *Nick*. The ice rink. I'll ask you nicely once. Everything you know.'

Burman gritted his teeth. 'I run a nightclub. I know what I see on TV.'

'Watch a lot do you? You'll know all about this then.' He pulled Burman's head back, forced his mouth open, stuffed in the cloth and tied it tight with the rubber tube so Burman couldn't spit it out, then opened a bottle of water and started to pour. He watched Burman's face, the wide eyes, the flush of panic. He held the chair steady as Burman started to buck and heave, pulling at the straps around his wrists. 'The ice rink.' He stopped pouring and pulled the cloth out.

'Make a fucking appointment!'

The cloth went in again. Roche poured longer this time, until Burman was in spasms trying to breathe. When he stopped, he took the picture of Ross Westcliffe out of his back pocket 'This fucker was there. He's one of yours.'

There was a pause and then Burman slowly started to nod, as if it all suddenly made sense. 'Enough! Enough! The Cypriot sent you, did he? Rossy? He *was* one of mine. He fucked off on me six months ago and I have no idea who shopped you out to plod.'

'Who's the Cypriot?'

'You don't know? The ice rink was his. Ah, shit, who the *fuck* are you?'

Roche waved the empty bottle in front of Burman's face. 'You have a whole fridge full of these. Who's this Cypriot and where I do find him?'

Burman hesitated a moment and then screamed as Roche started to stuff the cloth back into his mouth. 'No! No! I'll tell you what I know.'

'If you're still listening, a car just pulled up outside.'

'Stylianos Evangeli.' Burman let out a sob. 'Look, he's not a dealer, at least not in what you think.'

'I'm listening.' Roche went back to the bar and reloaded the .38. He checked the cylinder and the barrel. Clean and smooth. Other Dreadlocks looked after his shit.

'There was a million quid of heroin at that rink, right on my doorstep. Damn straight I made it my business to find out who it was. When I found out, I stopped asking. I never met Evangeli, I know almost fuck all about him except that you don't find him, he finds you, and he mostly doesn't deal in getting people high. Rumours say he trafficks people. Body parts too.'

'What?'

'*Passenger's out of the car. Black male in his twenties. Don't recognise him from the files. Driver's a woman, a lot older.*'

'Oh Christ, you know, organs. Black market transplants.'

'You're shitting me.' For a moment, Roche hesitated again. You had to keep that sort of thing cold, right? Which made the ice rink make a whole lot more sense. And he'd never actually seen what was inside the crates, only knew what he knew because he'd watched the news and the news had said heroin. Body parts? Yeah, they might have kept that quiet …

'*He's coming up.*'

'Expecting company, Burman?' Roche moved over to the corner of the room. He heard the noise of the road outside grow louder as the downstairs door swung open, then the first footsteps on the stairs.

'Nick? Billy?' The voice was rich and sharp, used to being in charge of things.

'He's got a gun!' shouted Glasses.

Shit. Roche jumped to the top of the stairs and levelled the .38. A man stood halfway up, saw the gun and froze, then slowly raised his hands. 'Hey, I'm not here for any trouble.'

Roche didn't recognise him but he had a dressing plastered across his nose so he'd been in some sort of trouble not so long ago. He beckoned with his free hand.

'Up.'

The man nodded and started slowly up the rest of the stairs. He didn't look nearly as bothered as he ought to at having a gun pointed at his face. 'Whatever you say. I think you should know, though, that I'm with the police.' There was some South London in the accent, mixed in with something else. Army? Roche backed away as the man came on up, keeping his distance. You had a gun on someone, you didn't get right up close but kept enough paces apart so that, no matter what they did, you had the space and the time to put at least two rounds in them before they could reach you.

'Over to the bar. Put your hands on the counter.'

The newcomer came in slowly. He looked around, saw Glasses and Other Dreadlocks and then Burman. His face changed. Whoever he was, he knew these people and he didn't like what he was seeing, not at all. 'You could just leave now,' he said. 'Maybe you should.'

'Hands on the counter.' Roche waited and then came up closer behind him. 'You're not police.'

'*The car's parked up round the corner.*'

'ID in my jacket pocket. You want me to take it out?'

'You keep your hands where I can see them.' Roche pressed the .38 into the small of the new man's back and reached around for the man's jacket. 'Move and bad things happen.' There was a wallet in the inside pocket. Roche tugged it out.

'*Driver's getting out.*'

As Roche drew out the wallet, the other man lurched sideways along the counter. He spun towards Roche and grabbed Roche's wrist, hammering his hand with the .38 against the counter. His other hand went under his jacket on the other side. Roche let go of the .38, brought his left elbow up hard into the other man's ribs, extended his arm, stepped in and pushed and the man went over; but he pulled hard on Roche's wrist as he went, toppling them both. His left hand was still coming out from under his jacket with a pistol. Roche grabbed at it and pushed it away. It caught his eye though – a Sig Sauer P226 9mm. You saw a lot of those around Hereford.

The two of them crashed to the floor. Roche launched a head butt, messing up the man's face and re-breaking his nose for him, slammed the hand holding the gun against the floor and rammed an elbow into the other man's ribs again. The two wrestled a moment until Roche slammed the Sig against the floor a second time. This time the man let go. Roche made a grab for the .38 but the other man kicked him in the chest and they both fell back, the .38 flying free and skittering across the floor to the top of the stairs. Roche twisted as he fell. The impact jarred loose his earpiece and he lost Ketch. Both men rolled as they landed, straight back up to their feet. The Sig was still by the bar, the .38 by the stairs. Behind the other man, Glasses and Other Dreadlocks were shouting, egging them on. Whoever this guy was, they clearly knew him. Roche was beginning to think he knew too. The Sig was the giveaway. Burman's brother, the shaky boat?

The Sig was closest. Roche feinted for that; then, as the other man jumped at him, he picked up one of the chairs and threw it into him and at last got a decent opening. A good solid kick to the kidneys and down he went. Roche moved for the Sig.

'Armed police! Freeze! Don't fucking move!'

It was a woman's voice. She was at the top of the stairs and she had the .38 pointed at him, what might have been an ID in her other hand, and she was shaking. The driver from the car. Shit. He hadn't seen her come up and he had no idea who she was and …

He hesitated a moment, glanced at the Sig, looked at her, took it all in. She must have caught him eyeing the fire exit door. Her grip on the .38 tightened. 'I said don't fucking *move!*'

He knew her. *That* was a shock, but he'd heard her voice before. Kingship. She'd been on the Kingship team and now she had a gun on him and she was scared. Scared meant unpredictable. Beating the shit out of a drug dealer and his cronies was one thing. State of things now, though …

'Hope you're gone, Ketch,' Roche murmured and slowly raised his hands. For all he knew they were all here after the same thing anyway.

9 - Interrogation

11 May 2015, 1100 hours, Brixton Police Station

Detective Superintendent Samantha Linley. They hung around the club for a while after she cuffed him, waiting for the uniforms to come and start picking the place apart. Roche picked up her name when the uniforms took him away, along with a pile of nasty looks. The looks he got from Burman's brother were worse, though. Fucking murderous, and he was glad when they didn't come with him from the club.

The uniforms took him to Brixton station, booked him in and offered him his phone call. Roche shook his head. After that they put him in a cell. He sat in there quietly, patiently trying to work out whether they had any charge that might stick. Assault at the very least. Breaking and entering. He hadn't actually had the snap gun in his hand when Linley had pointed the .38 at him, but it was there in the hall and she surely hadn't missed it. On the other hand, Linley hadn't much liked the conversation she'd had with either of the Burman brothers after it was done. The dealer Burman, Roche thought, didn't want anything to do with this. Not the sort who fancied standing up in court to testify as a witness.

The wait suited him. It gave him time to think about what the fuck he was doing and what he wanted to say. If anything at all. Everyone in the Special Reconnaissance Regiment went through the same training as the SAS when it came to interrogation and he doubted the Met's techniques were going to get them very far. Mind you, if Linley was cosy with Burman's brother and Burman's brother really was a frogman, she'd know all about that.

After a day of letting him stew, the uniforms took him to an interrogation room. Linley was already there with another policeman. The air stank of stale cigarette smoke and crap coffee – the cigarette smoke surprised him – he didn't think that was allowed these days. Linley started the inevitable recorder. State your name for the record, that sort of thing. Roche gave them his rank and regiment too, asked Linley what the charges were and then shut the fuck up. After a while that got them pretty pissed off.

'Possession of a firearm, assault with a deadly weapon, robbery, attempted murder. You keep this up and that's what you'll be charged with.' The second copper was doing the angry table-bashing routine, trying to be intimidating. Roche smiled at him. Linley was seething worse but she had the smarts to keep it bottled up. Like she knew perfectly well how this was all going to go and knew, too, there wasn't a damn thing she could do about it.

After half an hour of bullshit, Linley stopped the tape and they went outside. When she came back, a few minutes later, she came back alone.

'Right, you smug cunt, you listen fucking hard. I know what you really are and I know they kicked you out. All the protection you think you've got? Worth as much as a limp dick. You get that? Whatever shit you were into, you're off the books and no one's coming to bail your arse. So. We going to do this the nice way?'

Roche sat silent for a moment. He leant a little way across the table, closing the gap between them. When he spoke, he spoke softly. Not quite a whisper, but quiet.

'What were you doing there with Burman's brother, Superintendent?' he asked. That seemed to throw her. He smiled. She'd have to answer that if they went formal on him, and Burman's brother would have to say what *he* was doing there and how his weapon had ended up on the floor. He'd survive but it would be an embarrassment. The press loved that shit. 'I'd have a bit more of a chat with him if I were you, Superintendent, before you go too far with this.'

Or maybe she already had. Her eyes narrowed. He could see what she was thinking. *Smug cunt.*

Well yeah, maybe. But then again, Linley had been on Kingship. Maybe she was one of the good guys. 'Brixton. The ice rink. If you know who I am then you can work out the rest for yourself.'

Linley shook her head. 'Not fucking good enough, Sergeant Manning.'

They stared at each other in silence for another minute and then she left again. A few hours later, when it was obvious that neither of the Burmans intended to press charges, they let him go. On his way out, Roche scrawled a note and asked someone to give it to Detective Superintendent Linley.

Stylianos Evangeli. The Cypriot.

She deserved something, at least. Couldn't hurt, could it?

10 – Infiltration

10 May 2015, Somewhere above the South Pacific

The transit from Jupiter's orbit to Earth took the hybrid construct several days. The journey could have been quicker but the hybrid elected for stealth. Not simply making it matter but making it absolute. It needed its approach, it had decided, to be mathematically provably undetectable to anything, even to things the Weft couldn't do. The *Exponential* and the *Irrational Prime* were still arguing with it about that. The frigate continued to claim that the *Irrational Prime* had been undetectable in the inner system to anything short of an array a full Astronomical Unit across, and there clearly wasn't one of those nearby. For once the two ships agreed but the fact remained that something on the third planet had wrapped itself in a pocket dimension shortly after the *Irrational Prime* had arrived. There were other explanations. It could have been coincidence but the mathematically most probable cause was that whoever was on the third planet simply had better sensors than the Weft. There were consequences to a conclusion like that. Tedious stealth was one of them.

The *Irrational Prime*, passing the time between mathematics and arguments, had decided they should all have Earth names and had taken to calling the construct Fermat. The hybrid construct offered no objection. It largely didn't care.

The hybrid hit the planet's atmosphere early in the afternoon somewhere over the South Pacific ocean. By then it had permeated the rudimentary infosphere of the native species and digested a good chunk of the planet's biology, geography and history. It made the drone that had carried it from the *Irrational Prime* into an ablative shield. As it entered the ionosphere, a plasma wave built up ahead of it, disrupting its connection with the planet's data networks.

'Primitive,' muttered the hybrid, as if either the *Irrational Prime* or the *Exponential* or indeed any form of passing intelligence whatsoever couldn't have reached the same conclusion on their own.

'*Relatively* primitive,' added the freighter, sniping at the *Exponential*. The frigate was getting uncommonly – Fermat wasn't sure there was a proper term for it when referring to an artificial intelligence but – *stressed* was the nearest he could come up with. The tau-burst detector was partially operational now and it wasn't working properly and the frigate didn't understand why. Or rather, it *was* working, it just wasn't calibrating according to the *Exponential*'s predictive mathematics. There was a tiny offset between the tau-neutrino count the detector was generating and the frigate's theoretical flux density estimations and the frigate was getting frantic trying to track down the error in its maths instead of doing the logical thing and waiting for the whole detector to be operating at once and then gathering the weeks of calibration data that something as unreliable as a tau-burst array would inevitably need before its results became more science than speculation. Sensor capability being something of a sore point between the two ships, the *Irrational Prime* had gleefully seized on this and needled the *Exponential* whenever it could.

The ablative shield disintegrated as the construct entered the troposphere. Sometimes the hybrid wondered what it would be like to disconnect from the Hive the way the plasma wave had ripped it away from this world's infosphere. Quiet, it supposed. Inefficient. A breeding place for faulty assumptions and error-wrecked conclusions.

It hit the Pacific Ocean and floated a few metres beneath the surface as it completed its assimilation of the world then dropped deep and made its way steadily to land, moving north and west towards the Philippines. By the time it crossed over the Marianas Trench, it had compiled its report. *They* (whoever they were) had been on this world for at least five hundred years. The construct wasn't sure that *they* (whoever they were) hadn't been present much longer but there was a curious coincidence in timing that supported the hypothesis. Five hundred years ago put their arrival in the midst of the Weft diaspora, officially sanctioned and approved by the nascent Hive. Small groups of Weft had travelled away into empty space as far as they could go. It was a matter of species survival. The Hive hadn't known very much about the Pleasure in those days, only that their technology was incomprehensibly different and vastly superior. Later, when the Pleasure didn't return and the Hive had finally understood what had happened, it had adjusted its outlook to be more militant. The diaspora had been absorbed back into the Hive to become a new wave of exploration and expansion. And, in more recent times, very cautious searching. But five hundred years ago the Weft had been scattering in … in rational panic. A handful had come this way. They'd vanished from the Hive, presumed dead, but now the chemistry of this world offered another possibility, far, far worse.

The Fermat hybrid completed its report on the biology of the primary species and noted that the Weft had a passing bipedal structural similarity but little more. There was a logic to that but, like every other sentient race the Weft had discovered, humans were a lower order of intelligence. They had no second part, no co-existing parallel-dimension exotic-matter self which was what made the Weft what they were and was the fundamental basis for the existence of the Hive. No – in the words of the illogicians – soul. What they had was a natural neuro-chemistry that interacted with the Weft's own in the worst possible way.

It made its recommendation to the Hive that the world be sterilised or erased and continued.

PHASE THREE

11 – Task Force Hotel

24 June, 1330 hours, Camberley

Roche watched the news. It was hard to make sense of what was going on out there. No one else seemed to have a handle on it either. The Cleggeron was gone, the old coalition given the kicking it so richly deserved back in the May election. The new government had come in and you could almost hear the national sigh of relief, but it hadn't taken long for everything to start going tits up. Solihull was in flames. Other places too. An early June heatwave had seen a repeat of the summer riots that were almost becoming a regular feature of British life. The message coming out of the last government had largely been for everyone to suck it up, take it on the chin, knuckle down and work hard, be thankful you're not starving or dead and God help you if you're sick or disabled. No one wanted any more of that but the new Labour government had swung in on the inevitable pendulum, shouting out the message a bit too far the other way: too much 'hey, it's all going to be great' when it clearly wasn't, not for a while.

They'd gone on about fun a lot too, towards the end. Their message consistently banged on the same drum: relax, go out and enjoy yourselves, let it all hang out. Borrow money and have a good time. Austerity had been deeply unpopular – only a total twat couldn't see that – but it seemed odd to Roche. It was like the nineties and New Labour again only with even less sense of personal responsibility, if that was possible. They were leading by example too. Little over a month gone and they'd had ministers exposed going to sex clubs and they didn't even have the decency to show any shame about it. The way they talked to the press, they seemed to be saying that the only thing wrong was that a whole lot more other people weren't doing it too. Rioters were 'blowing off steam'. The country was 'shedding its old skin'.

Then there was the whole Bliss thing. People were getting killed and no one seemed to care. Bliss remained quasi-legal but no one quite knew where it was coming from. It was hitting the street through the sort of people who'd once dealt heroin, coke and meth and had spread so wide it was now being taken by people who drank alcopops and thought vodka jelly was clever. It had destroyed Ecstasy as a street drug, which perhaps was no bad thing; but now the dealers who once made a living in powder and pills were either moving Bliss or trying to take it out of circulation. Time was, the news used to show the Met busting a drugs warehouse – nowadays it was the fire brigade turning up too late to where someone had set about a little personal arson on a Bliss dealer's stash. It wasn't illegal so people took it out in the open and sold it on the corner of the street. There were shops in Brixton and other places where you could buy vials off the shelf. It was cheaper than anything hard and did a better job. As far as Roche could tell, no one had died from taking it, only from selling it. People dropped a vial of Bliss, got high, had a good time and got on with their lives.

Another talking head came up to speculate without having anything useful to say about what it might all mean, whether the recent spate of murders in Brixton would soon come to an end, where the new drug came from and what it actually was. That was the weird part. Crack open a vial of Bliss and knock it back and it made you high. Wait a few minutes and it evaporated to a black powder. Carbon, apparently. After that it was useless. Up and down the country, men in lab coats were tearing their hair out. No one had a clue how it worked.

Not my problem. Roche tried to look away. He couldn't, though. Trouble with being bored, that was.

He looked at the card he kept beside his bed. Detective Superintendent Samantha Linley. Professional hard-arsed bitch. Her partner had wanted to do him for all manner of things, starting with breaking and entering, moving through pointing illegal firearms at people and ending up with violations of the Geneva Convention, although assault would do; but what Roche had gradu-ally figured out had *really* crawled under Linley's skin, what had made *her* want to throw the book at him, was the fact that he'd beaten up her friend the frogman.

Waterboarding Burman? She might have taken him outside and given him a round of applause for that as long as no one else was looking. A tough old-schooler who must have cut her teeth in the eighties. You had to have respect for a woman like that. He'd liked her. Still did. Hadn't been mutual, though.

He sighed and put the card away. He'd hoped she might have something to share about this Evangeli but no, nothing. He'd gone back to see her at the station, a few days later. Clearing some routine paperwork. She'd looked like the only thing she wanted to share with him was a knuckle sandwich.

The talking heads moved on to interviewing someone about taking Bliss. Roche missed the caption and so he wasn't sure but he thought it might have been George Michael. He looked like he was about seventy these days. Poor fucker. Roche shook his head and looked for the remote.

The phone went. He snapped it up. 'Manning.'

'Sergeant Manning, Corporal Slatterly. The Major wants to see you.'

'When?'

'You've got two hours, Sergeant.'

Roche sighed. 'No' and 'fuck off' and all the other responses that sprang to mind weren't really allowed. He grunted something that might have sounded like a yes and put the phone down. Stared at it. Major Becker might have quietly done him a favour with the monkeys but if he had, he'd done it for the regiment and because it was expected of him. Roche had joined the Bill Browns in 1994 and started trying to get out again almost as soon as he was in. A year later he'd fucked off to the SAS and stayed there for twenty years. Now they'd had enough of him, Battalion Commander Major Becker suddenly had a soldier he didn't know and didn't want to have to deal with dumped on his desk. It was only natural that Becker didn't like him. Angry calls from detective inspectors probably didn't help.

24 June, 1530 hours, Wellington Barracks, Central London

Slatterly didn't like him either. Roche could live with that but a cup of brew while he waited would have been nice. He made sure he was ten minutes early and then waited through Slatterly's glowering looks. If there was anyone in the regiment who didn't know what he'd done in Brixton, Roche hadn't met them. It was an even split, he reckoned, between the men who thought he was a jerk for putting the regiment on the spot and the men who thought that every drug-pusher in the country could do with a bit of the same and would be happy to oblige. On the bright side, it hadn't ever made the news. Bringing the regiment into disrepute, that would have been a different story.

At exactly fifteen thirty, a woman walked into Slattery's little anteroom. She glanced at Roche and then ignored him. Roche returned the favour. A glance was enough. An attractive enough brown-haired woman in slacks and a smart-looking jacket over a tailored shirt.

Glasses. She must have been thirty years old, give or take, and she was in good shape. The most interesting part was the side-arm under the jacket.

'I'm here for the major. He's expecting me.' She offered a card across the desk. Slattery looked up and leered. The woman's voice was posh, Roche thought, and she expected people to do what they were told. She moved as though people generally knew to get out of her way. Which, in a place like this, was almost as interesting as the gun.

'I'll ring you through, ma'am. Anything I can get you while you wait?' Slattery's eyes were all over her. Roche stifled a snort. Slattery could be such a lecher sometimes.

'That's very kind of you,' said the woman brightly. 'But no. I'll just go on in if you don't mind.' She didn't wait for an invitation.

'Ma'am!' Slattery had the phone in his hand now, the smile sliding off his face like melting jelly.

The woman stopped. She didn't look at Slattery but turned to Roche instead. 'You must be Sergeant Manning.' She took two steps closer and held out her hand. Roche blinked, then got up and shook it.

'Roche,' he said. 'And you are?'

'Charly. Nice to meet you.'

Slattery was off the phone. 'You can go …' But Charly was already at the major's door again with a hand on the handle. She looked back at Roche.

'Well, are you coming or does the major have to come and get you?'

Roche glanced at Slattery. Slattery shrugged and nodded unhappily. Roche followed her in. The major, from the looks of things as he glowered from behind his desk, wasn't pleased to see either of them. He didn't get up and he didn't offer his hand. He spared a quick glare for Roche but most of his resentment he saved for the woman.

'Miss Hollis,' he said, as if the name left a bad taste.

'Charly,' said the woman. She pulled a business card from a pocket and gave it to Roche, then sat in one of the chairs across from the major's desk. Charlotte Whelan-Hollis, BEng, MSc, Defence Science & Technology Laboratory. Which made her a geek or a scientist or something like that, although last Roche had heard, MoD scientists didn't carry guns.

Becker screwed up his face as though he was chewing on a lemon. 'I have your paperwork, Miss Hollis. I've been through it very thoroughly. It's all in order. I can't imagine why you want him.'

'Oh, I'm sure you can imagine lots of things,' said the woman brightly. 'But of course I can't tell you.'

Becker took a deep breath and let it all out in one long heavy sigh. He settled a baleful look on Roche. 'Well you're welcome to him. Roche, you're hereby transferred back to Hereford. Special Recon. Back where you came from. God knows why they want you again but they do.' He handed over a sheaf of transfer papers. 'You know the score.'

Miss Hollis smiled and got up. 'I'll leave you in peace to sort out whatever needs to be done. I'm sure there's

111

all sorts of paperwork. I'll wait outside with your nice Corporal Slattery.'

She left.

24 June, 1700 hours, Legoland

The Special Intelligence Building on the south bank of the Thames had lots of names. Mostly it got called the Ziggurat or, if you were feeling fancy, Babylon-on-Thames, because of the way it looked. Back in 2000, someone had fired a rocket-propelled grenade at it which had apparently hit an eighth-floor window and bounced off. After that, a little legend had grown up about how it was like the Starship Enterprise and protected by a force field. Roche had always preferred its other name: Legoland. They'd finished building it just before they'd sent him and Ketch to Bosnia. They were of an age, him and Legoland.

Charly drove him there straight from the barracks even though it might have been quicker to walk. No picking up any personal effects or anything like that. For a while neither of them spoke.

'DSTL my arse,' he said after he'd watched her up against central London traffic for ten minutes.

'I'm sure your arse is very lovely,' she said. 'But it's true.'

'Uh-huh. Which establishment? I notice how your card doesn't say.'

'Oh, I sort of float about.'

Roche laughed. 'I bet. Back in ninety-four I was out in Tonopah near Nellis. We had a nice mix out there.

A few officers from the Air Warfare Centre in Waddington. Some contractors. A few government scientist types. I forget what you lot were called back then. Running off into the middle of the Nevada desert to go sit in Russian SAM systems captured in Afghanistan if I got my guess right, though mostly what I remember is we somehow hooked up with the airy fairies in Vegas and got smashed and had the Wing Commander in charge of the UK's electronic warfare running the wrong way up escalators at four o'clock in the morning. Two thousand and one and we were at Pendine testing out some ... Well, some stuff and there were a whole pile of DSTL guys from Portsdown West on the range next door with some big portakabins. They had a ship out a few miles to sea launching some sort of rocket off the back every now and then. Came down on a parachute and some poor navy diver mugs had to go and get whatever it was before it sank. If it didn't explode on the way down, which they sometimes used to do. We just had a big machine gun to play with so I guess we felt inadequate. Maybe we just liked rockets. Then a few years back in Helmand there were a lot from Fort Halstead and some more contractors all trying to make kit to spot where IEDs were buried. Don't know if they ever managed it but I had a lot of fun burying them and making it as hard as possible. I've been to Porton Down now and then. You know what every government scientist I ever met all had in common?'

'I imagine they were all very clever.' The car finally got off Millbank and sped up onto Lambeth Bridge, swerving seamlessly around a lane-hogger. The bridge gave a good view of the Ziggurat.

'Out of maybe two hundred people they were all men except maybe three, not one of them had ever held a side-arm in their life and none of them had taken advanced defensive driving training.' Roche sniggered. 'A few of them apparently hadn't been on a basic ordinary driving course either, from what I could tell.'

'That's interesting.' They ran a light as it turned red and turned onto Albert Embankment. Miss Hollis flashed him a quick glance. 'What regiment are you now with, Sergeant?'

Roche laughed. 'Point.'

'Then why don't you imagine that I'm a scientific consultant like my card says. Once we get where we're going you're going to meet some lovely boys and we're going to do some things together and we'll be taking our orders from the same person.' They wove around the labyrinth at the foot of Vauxhall Bridge. Roche grinned.

'I learned to bike around here,' he said. 'We always used to say that if you went round the loop fast enough and timed it all just right with the lights, you'd get flung off down some road that you couldn't find any other way. You have a lab in Legoland, do you?'

'Something like that.' Charly didn't look at him but pulled into an entrance to an underground car park. She wound the window down and swiped an electronic pass-card. The tunnel wound sharply away and it seemed to Roche that it took them away from the building rather than underneath it. Charly caught his eye and smirked.

'Car bombs,' she said. 'When they built it they were worried the IRA might get in somehow.'

'I thought the place had a force field.'

This time she laughed. 'Funny you should say that.'

They parked up and Charly led him into an underground atrium. She waved at a camera in front of a thick metal door; after a moment there was a buzz and the door swung open into a cubicle of a room that felt like a lift from the way the floor gave slightly under Roche's feet, but it wasn't. It was weighing them to count the number of people inside. Charly put her hand on a pad that lit up like a scanner. Above was a small round black lens like the eyepiece of a telescope. She put her eye to it. A moment later, a voice crackled over an unseen intercom. 'Who's with you, Charly?'

'I've got Sergeant Manning from Wellington Barracks. He hasn't been through admissions yet so he can't open the door. It's a bit of a needs-to-be-done-today thing, though, so I've got to get him inside for a briefing. He's expected. Sorry to be a pain. We can sort him out once he's in.'

The intercom voice sounded aggrieved. 'Charly, you know how much everyone hates this. You know how much *I* hate this. You know how much *you're* going to hate this. One fuckton of paperwork, coming your way.' There was another buzz and the second door opened into a long tunnel with overhead striplights and not much else. At the far end, two armed soldiers stood behind a reinforced glass checkpoint.

'Have to sign you in,' said Charly brightly. 'You'll

stay with me once we're through the doors. I'm afraid they won't let you have the run of the place. You'll have unescorted access to the little boy's room if you need it but not much else.' As they reached the checkpoint she stopped and turned to face Roche and looked him in the eye. 'Did you really see an alien in Brixton?'

'I know what it looked like. I don't know what it *was*.'

'Funny, because I've had that feeling a very great deal of late.'

At the checkpoint they scanned his handprints and both his eyes.

24 June, 1730 hours, Legoland

The briefing room was brightly lit and there were a dozen men sitting in it, some talking quietly to their neighbours, a few reading papers. They were all soldiers, Roche judged, and probably special forces. As he came in, a few turned to look. The first face he recognised was Cartman, who didn't smile but only gave a nod. He hadn't seen Cartman since Brixton. Most of the others were men he knew from Hereford.

Rees waved at him from the front row. He jerked his head, gesturing Roche to come over. 'Fuck, man!' he grinned as Roche came and sat beside him. 'They got you back after all!'

Roche punched him in the arm. 'If this is a task force then they haven't read me in on it. Maybe I'm a special guest. *Don't end up like him*.' He glanced at Charly. 'Who's the bird?'

'Never seen her before.' Rees shrugged.

Charly came back holding a clipboard and a pencil. She dropped them into Roche's lap. 'You know the drill. Nothing you're told here leaves the room. It's all top shelf. Once I've got you signed into the compartment we'll start the briefing.' Roche gave the papers the once-over. The usual official secrets boilerplate covering everything to do with Task Force Hotel, whatever that was – presumably they were about to find out – and a curious throwaway comment highlighting the classification of unusual technologies or devices. Roche signed his name at the bottom and handed the clipboard back to Charly. Every op went through the same shenanigans. As soon as he was done, two men stepped in from the back of the briefing room and walked to the front. The first was Leadface, the second was someone Roche didn't know but everything about him screamed that he was a spook. Leadface sat down. The spook faced them.

'Gentlemen. Miss Hollis. Welcome to Task Force Hotel. I'll assume you've all read your briefing sheets.' Rees nudged Roche and handed him a single side of A4 paper stamped Confidential CANUSUK Eyes Only top and bottom. Which in this sort of context meant it was a bland nothing that probably said no more than that the task force existed. It also suggested, since the MoD had changed their classification terminology last year, that Task Force Hotel was part of something that had been going on for at least that long.

The spook cocked his head at Rees. 'For those of you who *haven't*,' he added caustically, 'Task Force Hotel is attached to the Metropolitan Police operation Kingship which, as most of you will know, having at some point been a part of it, is tasked with anti-drugs operations with a particular emphasis on the Afghan heroin trade as controlled by residual elements of the Taliban. However, you're all smart enough to have noticed that I'm not a policeman and this is not Scotland Yard and so some of you might have guessed that that's not why you're here.' He paused. '*Some* of you will be aware of an operation carried out by Task Force Echo in Dagenham at the end of April. If you're not then I can only assume you've been living in a desert for the last two months.' He nodded to one of the men on the other side of the room. 'Apologies, of course, to Sergeant Whitelock, who returned from a tour in Helmand last week and *has* been living in a desert. I'll pass you on to the major. I know most of you know him.'

The spook withdrew as Leadface stood up and started to prowl back and forth across the front of the assembled men. He didn't bother with an introduction. 'Intel put Taliban fugitives in Dagenham pipelining heroin out of Afghanistan. Automatic weapons, possibly worse, possibly grenades. Two dozen men maybe. So the whole of Red Troop went out of Poole to sort them out.' Leadface bared his teeth. 'Show a few ragheads how a real man looks. That sort of thing.'

He paused. A couple of the men who didn't know better sniggered. Roche, who certainly did know better, kept very still. Leadface didn't say things like that.

'Red Troop. Sixteen men. With the Met's Flying Monkeys right behind them and everything else what goes with that. Care to guess how many came out? Five.'

If there was any smugness in the room, that wiped it out. There were a few gasps. Roche let out a long breath, the one he'd been holding ever since Leadface had called the Afghans ragheads. 'Shit,' he hissed to Rees. 'I knew it was bad. I didn't know it was *that* bad.' Rees only nodded.

Leadface was glaring at them both. 'Lieutenant Harcombe was going to be here to talk you through what happened but since he's currently indisposed I give you one better; Sergeant Stanton. One of the five who came out.' Leadface sat down again and another man got up, a hard-edged flint-faced Scot. Roche knew Stanton from years back. They were of an age. He was the sort of man who made his points softly; here his voice was quiet even for him.

'Never mind the intel. Never mind that there weren't any Taliban renegades. As it happened they were Russian Mafia but that shouldn't have mattered. We went expecting a fight and ready to have one. Shouldn't have made a whit of difference who was in there. But I've never seen anything like it. We started with stun grenades, as you do. Hardly made a difference. I saw one of them take six rounds to the chest and stay on his feet. They only started going down when we switched to headshots. Whatever they were on, it was something else. I saw no discipline, not much training but dear lord they were fast bastards and they didn't go down when they should and they were absolutely not one fucking bit afraid of us.' He paused. 'They had modified MP7s but they kicked like nothing I've ever seen. No one seems to want to tell me what they were.' He glanced back at Charly and the spook. 'Maybe now we find out, eh? Body armour should stop an MP7. Might not be pleasant but these ripped men apart like a fifty calibre.' He seemed to run out of words and stayed standing where he was, looking off into the distance. He looked lost. To Roche, that was the worst.

The spook moved forward again. 'Thank you, Sergeant.' He nudged Stanton who nodded sharply and went back to his seat. 'So, gentlemen, that's who you're going after. The Met can keep chasing Taliban if they like with Kingship and I'm sure we'll give them all the help they can use but now we have some other fish to fry. We recovered something very interesting from Dagenham.' This time the spook cocked his head at Charly. 'Miss Whelan-Hollis of the Defence Science and Technology Laboratories will tell you all about it. Hopefully in words we can all understand.'

Charly stood up. From somewhere she'd got a Heckler & Koch MP7A1 4.6mm. She held it like she knew how to use it. Roche smiled.

'There's always something sexy about a woman with a sub-machine gun,' whispered Rees.

Charly smiled right back at him. 'So you all know what this is. Makes a nasty hole if it hits you but, as the sergeant says, nothing too much to worry about if you're in kevlar.' She looked up. 'Lights please.'

The briefing room lights dimmed. A screen lit up at the front of the room behind Charly.

'I'm sorry to show you this. It's not pleasant but I think you need to see it,' she said. 'Apologies to you in particular Sergeant Stanton.'

The pictures that flashed onto the screen looked like stills from some noughties Hollywood horror flick back when more and gore were the genre watchwords. Men with limbs ripped off. The last slide looked like something from one of the 'Saw' movies. It took Roche a moment to realise he was looking at a man.

'That was one of Red Troop after he'd been hit by three rounds from one of these.' To Roche it looked more like someone who'd thrown themselves onto a live grenade. 'Hydrostatic shock. Looks like they've been hit by a heavy machine gun, right?' Charly nodded. The picture faded again as the lights rose. 'The job of my team has been to work out how this' – she waved the HK –'did that. I won't bore you with the answers but everything points to an extremely high muzzle velocity. Hyper-velocity rounds are possible; they're just not possible with anything that any of us knows how to make.' She smiled and let out a little laugh. 'We thought that would be the easy part. We thought the hard part would be finding out what they had in these, since this was what they were shipping.' She took out a vial from her pocket.

Roche knew it at once. A Bliss vial.

'The bottom line,' said Charly, 'is that we don't know who or what we're up against but we know it has to do with Bliss.'

The spook moved forward again. He held up another Bliss vial, this time a full one. 'In the last six months it's come from nowhere to eclipse all restricted drugs combined. If it carries on this way it's going to be as ubiquitous as alcohol by the end of the year. It's not formally a restricted substance – yet – but no one knows where this is coming from. Gentlemen, we're going to find out.'

25 June, 1300 hours, near Saturn

The *Irrational Prime* had been looking for something to do and the ring structure of the smaller gas giant had caught its interest. In part how something so immensely complex and structured could arise from such elegantly simple physics and in part because it emphasised the human need to name everything. This planet and its moons, its rings, the divisions of its rings, the deeper they probed and the more structure they found, the more they gave things names. The Huygens ringlet, the Herschel Gap, the Kuiper Gap, the Bessel Gap, the Barnard Gap, half a dozen more. They didn't even fully understand these structures or how they worked or how they were formed, but naming things seemed to comfort them, as though it brought that which was unknown somehow within the circle of their understanding and took away its mystery. The chemical compounds that were going to result in their extinction had names too. Epinephrine; serotonin; corticotropin; norepinephrine; endorphin; dopamine and acetylcholine. The one that was the real bugger, the

Irrational Prime reckoned, the one that was going to get them killed, was the serotonin.

25 June, 1300 hours, Legoland

'Why me?' asked Roche. He and Charly were having lunch together in the Legoland mess. 'Why pull me into this?' A lot could happen in nineteen hours and they hadn't let him leave the building last night. There were some small but comfortable rooms on the north side with views over the river. Apparently the Russian defector Victor Oshchenko and his wife and daughter had stayed in exactly the same room for two nights back in 1993. There was even a picture of him on the wall. Either side of six hours of sleep, Roche had been through two hours of security interview, kitted up along with the rest of Task Force Hotel and been given another succession of briefings. Best he could tell they'd split the task force into three four-man squads and two of the squads were made entirely from the Special Reconnaissance Regiment. Observation not engagement. The spooks kept saying that. *Don't let them know you're there.* That was what people like Roche and Rees were good at.

Charly peered back at him over the rim of her glasses, a forkful of overcooked spaghetti halfway from her plate to her mouth. 'Oh come, Sergeant Manning, you know the answer to that. After lunch I'll show you something.'

They finished eating and she took him to a small office. He sat down beside her as she logged in to the Legoland network, something that apparently took both a fingerprint and a password to do. She opened an mpeg and started it playing. The images were dark and it took a moment for Roche to understand what he was seeing; when he did, a numbness rocked him. She was showing him Kravica. Not his own recording of the aftermath of the massacre – he'd seen that a dozen times and would have known it instantly. No, this was someone else, the same time and place but a recording he'd never seen before. Which meant it was Ketch. Ketch had been carrying the second camera. You could make out the bodies on the floor of the agricultural shed. The picture wobbled back and forth as Ketch picked his way through them. Suddenly he was right back there, where it was impossible not to tread on the corpses because there were so many of them. A month and a half, it had taken a month and a half for Paper Teapot to do anything after this. Nearly fifty fucking days.

'It's hard watching, isn't it?' said Charly.

Roche didn't answer. It had been harder to be there. On the tape you didn't get the smell.

The camera swung briefly around, picking out two other figures standing a little way away. Him and Dook, though you couldn't make that out from the film. Dook who was dead twenty minutes later. Then Ketch panned back. He was walking to the far edge, to a door into the partitioned corner. He opened it. There was a flicker of something and then a flash of light and the movie stopped.

'Right at the end,' said Charly. She stepped the movie back to the frame before the flash of light. 'I turned the sound down. Was that a muzzle flash?'

Roche shrugged. 'There were shots. I always assumed it was Ketch. Sounded like an M16.'

Charly tapped the screen. Roche couldn't see what he was looking at except that Ketch had opened the door and there was a figure inside the room. It was too dark to make much out. 'Our image processing algorithms have improved some over the last twenty years. I've got that frame cleaned up as best we can.' She closed the movie and opened up a still picture instead. It was grainy and over-sharpened. You still couldn't make out much. Couldn't make out anything of the face at all but the figure was clearer now. Its arms were too long and its face was too narrow. It looked a hell of a lot like the figure he'd seen in Brixton at the ice rink. Roche bit his lip.

'Ketch called it the Scary Clown,' he said quietly.

'He's an odd-looking fellow,' agreed Charly. 'Watch this though. I'll step through frame by frame. There's only six, mind.'

The figure stayed where it was in the first three. In the fourth, half of it was gone. The bottom half. Just gone. In the fifth there was nothing.

'He just vanishes,' said Charly. 'How does he just vanish? There's something not right.' She shut the computer down. 'My department deals in things that are odd. Usually they don't turn out to be all that odd after all. We piece all the evidence together, we work out what really happened, what was really there, and it's usually pretty straightforward in the end. This one's an odd one. What happened to you in Brixton, that

125

was another odd one. You don't suddenly get a serotonin imbalance out of nowhere at your age, Sergeant. And then there was Dagenham.' She paused. 'It wasn't my decision but I recommended you because you've seen strange things and I don't know what to make of them.' Charly looked Roche in the eye. 'It's not just here either, Sergeant. I can't tell you anything more than that just now but I think Task Force Hotel can expect some travel abroad. I think it can expect some more strangeness, too. I thought we should have people who weren't strangers to strangeness.' She flashed another smile. 'If you'll forgive the pun.'

25 June, 1315 hours, The Challenger Deep

The Fermat hybrid construct waited motionless at the bottom of the Marianas trench, a little under eleven kilometres beneath the surface of the Pacific Ocean, near the island of Guam. The clones were all on the move. There were at least five existing groups of non-indigenous aliens operating in this world. It had found one in North Africa, deep in the Libyan desert and working almost in the open. It had another in the southern African desert in Namibia, also barely hiding at all. A third was in the Middle East in present-day Syria. The last sure sightings occurred during the mass slaughter of the Assyrian population of the region over a century earlier but they was still there, lapping up the lengthy and inelegant collapse of the Assad regime in Damascus. After that, the construct had found numerous possible sightings linked to the Khmer Rouge massacres and elsewhere across the Indochinese Peninsula. Those last two had been more careful.

It had sightings in the Balkans, Germany and Poland in the years 1942-5. The chemistry found aboard the *Irrational Prime* had been harvested from somewhere in Croatia during this time. It hadn't found them until now, perhaps because those had been the ones to see them coming.

Now it had a sighting of one in Kravica in 1995. Six grainy frames of video. Evidence enough that a fifth group existed but what mattered more was that it had seen them. It had seen their form and now the Hive knew what they were: diaspora-descended Weft survivors once but now they were something else. They had no second self, no exotic-matter bond to one another and to the Hive. They had cut themselves off and made themselves into lesser beings. They were Shriven.

Several of the Shriven were, the construct was quite sure, hiding in a pocket of isolated space-time in London. Which meant the construct couldn't pin them down but it also meant they couldn't see what was about to happen to the others.

With careful stealth, the construct's weaponised clones moved closer to their targets.

12 – Opening the Closet

28 June, 1600 hours, 100 miles east of Damascus

The cloned Fermat construct approached the city from the east. It had become irritatingly difficult to conceal itself crossing the desert. It could cloak itself perfectly well from all the standard senses and sensors of the native species but moving at any kind of speed close to the ground would throw up clouds of dust that would then be hard to conceal. It could stutter in little wormhole jumps and the natives wouldn't be any the wiser but then there was the matter of who else was in this system. The Shriven appeared to have exceptional sensor arrays hidden somewhere and they might pick up the muon trail that the stutters would leave behind. It couldn't allow that. It wanted to optimise its chances to take them by surprise.

It settled for riding in the back of a native truck, concealed and invisible. It had engineered a xeno-fungus whose spores made their way into human nervous systems and made them entirely suggestible. It was a calculated risk – anything more complex that would have allowed more reliable subjugation might have aroused suspicion from the Shriven – but it needed pliable natives. It had considered flying but again the elimination of its own signature would have been imperfect.

The truck was slow. The clone took the time to flit its consciousness among the several hundred tiny drones that now orbited the earth. Individually they were simple things, barely even self-aware, but the network they made was showing up all sorts of interesting phenomena that even the *Irrational Prime* wasn't picking up lurking out among the moons of Jupiter and the rings of Saturn. Most of all, the orbital network was showing consistent steady signs of pion decay somewhere in Damascus. The network had it pinned down to a few dozen yards. The clone would do the rest.

It assessed the tactical options it had prepared for whatever it encountered. Shortly after it did that, the truck ground to a halt at some sort of native checkpoint and an exchange of conversation occurred. From the back of the truck, the Fermat couldn't intervene without giving itself away. It seemed that the conversation went logically enough but it nevertheless ended with the soldiers at the checkpoint hauling the driver out of his cabin, dragging him behind a shed and shooting him in the head.

The Fermat considered this for an instant and then unshrouded itself and climbed down from the back of the truck. It didn't trouble not to scrape its armoured limbs against the side of the truck or to land lightly.

The two soldiers came running back from behind the shed. They took one look at the clone and started shrieking as they opened fire. The Fermat phased so the bullets passed straight through it and ignored them. It swept its hand across the soldiers' hut and the rest of the checkpoint. For a nanosecond, magnetic fields several quadrillion times stronger than the earth's own ripped apart the atoms of everything in front of it. The checkpoint disintegrated.

The Fermat turned to the two soldiers left behind it. One had fallen to his knees and was praying. The other was trying to reload and shaking too much to do it. The clone killed both of them by stopping their hearts. It left the praying one and hauled the other body into the truck, propped it up behind the wheel and infected the corpse with a modified version of its fungus. While it was waiting for the body to reanimate, it rewired the truck and took control. The dead man just had to sit up and loll there, that would do. An hour later, that was what it was doing. Another six and synaptic decay would be too far advanced for the deception to work any more but that was more than it needed.

'So your idea of stealth is to set off a magnetic pulse they'll feel in orbit and create walking dead men?' asked the *Irrational Prime*.

The Fermat ignored it.

'I hope you remembered to make sure it doesn't spore and infect half the city,' went on the freighter. If the freighter had been paying any attention at all then it would know the Fermat had already considered that.

'The bolt-bucket is bored,' drawled the *Exponential*. 'Pay no attention.'

130

The Fermat tuned them out. It had no intention of paying attention to either of them. The ships had been playing with the local native languages and expressions to pass the time. They were, the clone thought, a little like children. Or what Weft children might have been if the Weft had such a concept.

The truck drove through the outer suburbs of the Al-Shagour district of Damascus, past walls and tower blocks pock-marked with bullet holes. By then the truck driver was starting to stiffen. The Fermat turned the truck down an empty side-road and climbed out, invisible this time. It scaled a wall, disintegrated the driver and the truck and settled for making its own way. The pion signature still hadn't moved from where it had remained for the last three days, right in the middle of the old city.

The Fermat examined again the seventeen permutations of trap it had considered. Trap or not, the rational approach was to proceed. It was only a cloned construct. It was expendable.

A military transport helicopter buzzed overhead, sufficiently low for the Fermat to jump the intervening hundred yards and catch hold of it. It vaporised the pilot and the soldiers inside, took control and flew the helicopter over the old city until it was directly over the pion source. Then it let go. The helicopter leapt up and headed off on its own gentle arc until it crashed into the top of a tower block a quarter of a mile away. The Fermat registered this through the orbital network but by then it had found what it wanted.

28 June, 2200 hours, Damascus

The western windows of the tower block looked out over the Mausoleum of Saladin. The southern windows looked over the Umayyad Mosque. To the north and east were a maze of streets and tightly packed houses and other small blocks of flats.

The Fermat construct dropped through the concrete roof of the tower block like a pick through pond-ice. There wasn't much that was organic in the original Fermat hybrid construct to begin with and the clone was exactly the same. Encased deep inside in a globe of shock-gel floated an embryonic half-grown Weft brain. It existed just enough to have latched to pieces of exotic matter that captured and stabilised a few hundred pions that were themselves entangled with the exotic matter that was part of the Fermat construct. The clone wasn't so much a clone as a vessel that the hybrid construct rode, an exotic demonic possession. There were, the Hive theorised, ways in which other secondary sentients might be uplifted to snare exotic matter of their own and thus become a primary form of sentience suitable for similar possession or assimilation into the Hive.

A sequence of phase-correlated anti-matter nano-bomblets synched to the presence of a dimensionally complex intrusion and detonated. The tower block and a chunk of the adjacent mosque disintegrated in a blade of thermonuclear light and a flash of gamma radiation that even the native sentients couldn't miss. The gamma radiation passed harmlessly through the clone. The high-energy particles flayed its outer layers into ions, destroying its cloak. Most were scattered by its magnetic shield before they could reach any deeper. Even as it fell through the cloud of ferociously energetic plasma that had once been the tower block, the clone inventoried its systems and found everything to be in working order. It landed two seconds later at the bottom of a crater in a thin slurry of molten stone.

As far as the rest of Damascus was concerned, the explosion had much the same effect as a small thermonuclear device. The initial flash turned parts of the Umayyad Mosque into plasma and the blast wave flattened the rest, along with several blocks of old Damascus city.

The Shriven who lived in the basement existed entirely in anti-phase to the charges in the nano-bombs and was only affected by a few symmetry-breaking weak neutrino interactions, which it wouldn't even have noticed if it hadn't been looking for them. It came up fighting, releasing a cloud of nanofactories that immediately set to work attempting to simultaneously dismantle the Fermat clone and entomb it in solidifying radioactive concrete. At the same time it lit up an anti-proton beam and attempted to slice the clone in half.

'Does that answer the question as to whether they knew you were coming?' asked the *Exponential*.

The Fermat clone's magnetics batted the anti-protons aside and barely noticed. It dimly registered flares of nuclear light around it as pieces of the crater disintegrated. The nano-factories were absurdly ancient. The Fermat simply overrode their programming and assimilated them.

'They don't seem to be that bothered about concealing their presence,' observed the frigate.

'So neither are we.' The Shriven cloaked. The Fermat immediately let off its own anti-matter bomblet, throwing the Shriven's own trick back at it and shredding the cloak. The Shriven snipped open a pocket dimension and tried to hide inside but the clone collapsed it before it was even open. It did the same when the Shriven tried to open a stutter hole and then finally it made contact with the Shriven's exosuit. The Fermat reached inside, shut the suit down and then methodically dismantled it with the Shriven trapped inside. It kept the Shriven's organic brain and built a life-support container to keep it alive for now. The Hive had some ideas about re-engineering a connection to the exotic matter they'd need in order to throw a net of entangled pions over the Shriven, forcibly induce it into the Hive and rape its mind. It was either that or the tedious way of actually asking questions, and the primary Fermat was already working on that.

The clone stayed in the bottom of the crater for a few seconds more while it released another cloud of nano-factories to rebuild its outer cloak skin. Invisible again, it reabsorbed the nano-factories and walked out of the crater, then opened a series of stutter holes and teleported away. All things considered, stealth didn't really seem to be an issue any more.

28 June, 2300 hours, Prince Regent Pub, Salmon Lane, Limehouse

Someone behind the bar rang a bell for last orders. Roche made a show of drinking the dregs from his glass and shambling out of the door. Outside, he stumbled down Benton Street until he was in the shadow of the railway bridge. There wasn't anyone else about.

'Hotel two-two is mobile. I got nothing. Moving to secondary location.' He circled around the back of the pub and crossed over Blount Street. Most of one side was taken up by a long low flat-roofed building – something-or-other Property Services – but right at the end was a small three-storey block of a dozen apartments. He went inside and climbed the maintenance stairs up onto the roof. A black waterproof duffel bag was waiting there, left some hours before by Hotel two-four – a Corporal Ian Watts Roche had seen about the place in Hereford but didn't particularly know. It took him fifteen seconds after he opened the bag to have the HK417 sniper rifle built up and good to go. He settled down flat and trained the rifle on the tower block across the street.

'Hotel two-two in position. I've got eyes on the sixth floor, second window from the left, looking down Blount Street.' He focused the rifle's scope. Through the window he could see two figures standing as though holding a conversation. Now and then others moved past. There were at least five people in the flat. If Legoland's intel was right then the flat was a major distribution centre for Bliss. The odd thing was that Bliss wasn't illegal yet

135

– perhaps never would be – but the people moving it were all dealers who used to push heroin and cocaine and so they acted as though Bliss was the same. They could have had someone drive over in a transit, unload a few thousand vials of stuff in crates in the car park in full view of everyone else and drive off again and there wouldn't have been a thing the monkeys could have done about it. Her Majesty's Revenue and Customs might have asked to have a word with them about their tax returns but no one could stop them selling. Would have made the task force's job that much easier.

But no. Once a dealer, always a dealer. Bliss had turned the criminal underworld on its head and there was close to an all-out war going on. The London Met might have stood by and done nothing but that didn't mean some gang of Russians or Turks wouldn't show up with bats and machetes ... Roche chuckled to himself. They should have got that guy from Brixton on the team. Burman, the one with the brother who was a frogman. Legoland reckoned he'd refused to move the stuff. Preferred to keep his hands clean with smack and crack. Bully for him.

'Something funny, Hotel two?'

'Negative. I have two clear targets in the window, that's all.'

'The bald black guy on the right? He's the target. When that fucker moves, so do we.'

Roche quietly assumed that whoever the spook who'd been at the briefing was, this was all his baby. His own opinion was that it was too ambitious. Hotel two squad had kept the flat under surveillance for two solid days and God only knew how long it had been watched before. Now they had the next link in the chain, the dealer in the van who carried in bulk, and when he left they'd tail him until they knew his supplier. Which, according to people who knew a lot more about illegal drug manufacture and distribution than he did, would be a chemical laboratory. As soon as they had the lab, three squads would go in and wrap it all up while Hotel four squad moved on the flat. And none of it would go to shit the way things had gone to shit in Dagenham because ...

Yeah. Because. Seemed there wasn't much of an answer to that. The flat had been watched long enough to know that the men inside weren't routinely packing those fucked-up Heckler and Kochs and half the faces there were familiar enough to the local plod. But the next level up? Smacked to Roche of being *exactly* like Dagenham.

He settled behind the scope to wait.

28 June, 2300 hours, Naypyidaw, Myanmar

The Shriven in Myanmar was the easiest to find. The Fermat clone reached the south-east Asia landmass close to the city of Yangon. It disassembled, reconfigured itself to appear as three native sentients and used the local transportation systems inland to Naypyidaw where the orbital network was registering possible pion decay products. This Shriven's defences were pitiful, the Shriven itself barely alive any more, and the Fermat's nano-factories dismantled the Shriven's exosuit and dissolved most of its organic parts before the Shriven even registered that something was happening. The nano-factories assembled a life-support canister, retrieved the Shriven's consciousness and the minimum necessary physical matter to support its continued existence and cleansed the rest. When they were done, the clone, still in its form of three separate natives, walked in, picked up the canister, and left.

Half an hour later an anti-matter minelet obliterated half the city.

28 June, 2315 hours, Keetmanshoop, Namibia

The *Irrational Prime* had made four clones of the hybrid construct. It had ejected them from Europa's orbit several weeks ago. The third was in North Africa now. The last adjusted its trajectory very slightly as it approached Earth and altered the shape of its ablative shield. It crashed hard into the upper ionosphere and burned up most of its shield before transiting the stratosphere. The clone allowed itself to break up as it entered the troposphere and struck the Namibian desert as an apparent series of meteorites in the early evening. Its component parts merged and reassembled a little way outside the town of Keetmanshoop. As it entered, it immediately felt itself under attack from nano-factories. It commandeered and examined them. The nano-factories delivered a complex multi-layered virus tailored precisely to native brain chemistry.

The clone entered an empty building, engaged a cloaking screen, acquired a native sentient, and infected her with a high dose of the nano-factories. The results were high levels of neurotransmitter activity and a slow but growing urge to go somewhere. The clone changed its form and partially cloaked, then took the human by the hand. She led it to Johnny's Auto Electric on 8th Avenue.

The Shriven was in a terrible state, barely existing. It seemed to have no idea that the clone was even there. The clone dismantled the Shriven's exosuit but left the organic part intact. Curiosity stayed its hand. These Shriven weren't being as careful as it had expected. The clone in North Africa had already changed its objective. It was watching its Shriven now, waiting to see what it would do until the others hiding in London emerged from their pocket.

'Why?' asked the clone.

The Shriven made a gesture that was the Weft version of shrugging its shoulders. 'The Pleasure were coming. Our civilisation was doomed. The diaspora was an act of desperation inevitably bound to fail. We knew that when the Pleasure returned, the Hive would fall under their sway. Everyone who remained a part of it would be found. It was inescapable. When we discovered this world and what the chemistry of the native life could do, it was a way to escape. It cut us off from the Hive. No one would find us. We would be safe.'

'But the Pleasure did not return. The Hive is ready for them now.'

The Shriven exuded an attitude of longing and hunger and desperation. 'You don't understand what this chemistry does.'

'You sent this chemistry back into the Hive.'

'The others did that. They wanted your technologies. Your advances. To exist.'

The clone processed this. A subject race. The Shriven had gone around the Hive and contacted a subject race. The Hive didn't like that one little bit.

It had more questions but the Shriven self-terminated. The explosion was visible from orbit and left a crater a mile across. The Shriven, the clone, Keetmanshoop, and a large piece of Namibian desert all ceased to exist. As it detonated the minelet in Naypyidaw, the hybrid construct Fermat heard and saw. Back in orbit around Europa, the *Irrational Prime* reached the same conclusion as everyone else. The world would have to be sterilised, if it wasn't already too late.

'I suppose we'd best get making a lot of anti-matter then,' said the freighter, to no one in particular.

29 June, 0030 hours, Salmon Lane, Limehouse. London

'Hotel two-two, he's moving. I've lost eyes.' Roche shifted very slightly. The bald black man looked like he'd finished his conversation and had walked away from the window. He'd done that twice before. Roche kept his scope exactly where it was.

A few seconds later he heard what he was waiting for. 'Hotel two-one. He's out. Hotel two-two, relocate. Hotel two-three, confirm good to go.'

'Hotel two-three good to go.'

'Oversight confirm?'

'Oversight will be on station in three minutes.' They had eyes in the sky for this. Roche wasn't sure whether they were police or army but it probably didn't matter. Hotel two-three and two-four would alternate their chase vehicles. The helicopter was only there in case they both had to back off for some reason or some other unexpected shit happened.

Roche had the HK417 back in the bag in seconds. He was down on the street a moment later, loitering in the shadows where hotel two-three would pick him up once the target was moving.

'Hotel two-four, I have eyes on the target. He's left the building. Crossing the car park. Heading for transport.' They'd all studied the layout of the block. There was a small car park right in front of it where the target had left his van, one of those fucking irritating white Mercedes Sprinters that were always filthy with *clean me* written in the dirt like no one had ever thought of *that* joke before. Usually driven by a very special sort of cunt.

'Hotel two-two, eyes on target.' Roche could see him now. A big bald black man out in the car park. He walked to his van, keys in hand, then stopped at the door. The rest of the car park was empty but something had the man spooked. Roche ducked back out of sight.

Not that he should have been visible in the darkness anyway.

'Hotel two-four. Target is looking right at me.' Watts was parked a hundred feet down the street under a railway bridge where the lighting was so shit that the target shouldn't have been able to see the car, let alone that there was someone in it.

'Keep your cover, two-four.' That was Hotel two-one, Sergeant Woods, who had almost as many years behind him as Roche.

'He's made me. He's approaching.'

'Okay, Hotel, we're taking him down.'

'What grounds?' Rees.

'I don't fucking know and I don't give a shit.'

'I guess we can arrest him for being black after dark? That's still on the books, right?'

'Ha fucking ha, two-three. Now shut it.'

Roche shouldered the bag and gripped his MP5. He walked out of the shadows in time to see Woods running out of the car park. 'Freeze! Armed police! Get down! Get on the ground!'

The target turned abruptly. He stopped, almost right outside the Prince Regent. Woods halted twenty feet short, MP5 shouldered, still shouting. Roche had his own MP5 on the target now, running closer to take a flanking position. No one wanted to fire, not in a public street. On the other side of the target, Watts was running from the car. Rees would be coming off the adjacent rooftops from the other side. They had the target perfectly surrounded. He had nowhere to go.

Woods didn't waver. He must have been listening hard in the Dagenham part of the briefing because he had the MP5 pointing right at the target's face. Head-shots.

'We want him alive, two-one,' murmured Roche.

'We want him not pressing criminal assault charges and suing for wrongful arrest!' Rees again. Watts was coming up behind, Roche from the side now. Woods was still shouting.

'On the floor! Get down!'

For a moment it looked as though the target was about to do just that. He slowly sank to a crouch. Then he leaped. From a standing start he jumped what must have been ten feet up and covered the distance between him and Woods in a single bound. Woods got off one three-round burst but missed. Roche couldn't blame him for that. He was still staring, too surprised to move. His own MP5 was pointing at where the target had been a second ago.

The target came down on Woods hard, knocking the sergeant sprawling across the street, then bolted straight back the way Roche had come. Roche swung the MP5 round. 'Halt or be fired on!' The target ignored him and ran at the block of flats where Roche had taken his sniping position. Roche chased after him, then faltered as the target reached the block and ran straight up the wall.

He really didn't want to shoot but … but what the fuck? 'The target just ran up a fucking wall.' He swore and let off a three-round burst, aiming for the man's legs. He saw the target falter, then pull himself up onto the rooftop and keep on going.

'Who the fuck is this guy?' Rees. 'Peter fucking Parker?'

Roche ignored him, sprinting after the target. 'Two-four, two-three, get mobile and pick up two-one. I'm in pursuit. You head him off. Oversight, the target is on foot on the rooftops heading north along Blount Street. Hotel two-two is in pursuit on foot at ground level. Do you copy?'

'Oversight copy. We'll be on you in sixty seconds.'

Roche raced round the corner. The target was still up on the rooftops, moving like an Olympic hurdler, which was pretty fucking impressive for a man who'd taken a bullet in the leg. He must have read it wrong and missed, because the man on the rooftops wasn't slowing down at all.

Fifty metres down Blount Street the railway tracks crossed overhead. Roche saw it coming. The target vaulted up onto another small block of flats at the end of the street and jumped down onto the tracks. 'Two-two. He's on the railway. Now heading north-east.' Underneath the bridge Roche cut across an open lot onto Carr Street and then right onto Repton, weaving under the railway arches. 'I don't see him.' Repton took him back under the tracks again and then turned to follow them, only to dump Roche in a dead end yard full of trucks. Roche bolted for the far end, looking for a way through or a way up. He had the tracks on his left and the canal on his right, he realised, and they were converging. 'Fuck!' The yard narrowed to a point and blocked him in. He climbed up onto the back of one of the trucks but getting up onto the tracks wasn't going to happen. Too many Tower Hamlets lads had already tried it and there was a forest of razor wire in the way.

'Two-two, unable to continue pursuit.'

'Two-two, this is oversight, we have him on the tracks just crossing Regent's Canal.'

'Don't let him know you're on him!'

'Do you think we were born yesterday, two-two?'

Roche shot back through the yard to the end of Repton Street in time to see Rees in the BMW screech around the corner out of Blount Street. As Rees saw Roche he slammed on the brakes. Roche jumped in before the BMW stopped moving and Rees tore back down Carr Street, heading away from the target. 'Fucking canal,' he spat. 'Who the fuck *is* this guy?'

'At least it's not another Dagenham.' Roche dumped the shoulder bag in the back seat and wound down the window as the BMW screamed round the corner back into Salmon Lane and crossed over the canal.

'Oversight, target has passed Mile End stadium and is still on the tracks heading north-east. Who is this guy? Usain Bolt?'

'Looked like fucking Spiderman,' growled Rees.

'He's moving, this one. You trying to catch him for something he's done wrong or to try out for the 2016 Olympics?'

Rees shot a glare at Roche. 'Make yourself useful, mate, and get me a fucking map.' A quiet little housing estate. Rees tore through it past sixty. 'You know anything about this cunt you're not telling me?' The BMW swerved north as Salmon Lane turned into Rhodeswell Road and then Turner's Road.

Roche shook his head. 'Right at the end. Past the Go-Kart track then hard left. *Hard fucking left!*' The BMW took the corner with a vicious squeal and slid onto the wrong side of the road before Rees had it back under control. The railway was up ahead. 'Right. Right!' The BMW's tyres shrieked again. 'This follows the track dead straight for a few hundred yards. Then … Fuck! Oversight, do you see us?'

'You're hard to miss, two-two. Target's on the tracks, still a little ahead of you.'

'T-junction! T-junction!' The end of the road rushed at the BMW. 'Which fucking way, Roche?'

'Left!'

Rees stamped on the brakes and savaged the corner onto Bow Common Lane. They accelerated under a bridge. 'Oversight, target is right on top of you two-two.'

'Right right right!' screamed Roche. Except what on the map looked like a small road turned out to be a private access-way with a sturdy metal gate locked across it.

'Fucker!' Rees stabbed the brakes and tore at the wheel again. The back of the BMW fishtailed as Rees smashed it into the gate. The gate burst apart, one half flying open, the other half ripped clean off its hinges. It bounced up the BMW's bonnet and smashed into the windscreen as Rees accelerated along a tarmac path barely as wide as the BMW between a row of trees and a strip of open ground. 'Where the fuck does this go, Roche?' The tracks were on their right now and Roche could see the target sprinting along them. He didn't bother pointing the MP5 out of the window. No chance.

'Go, go! Shit, what *is* that fucker on?'

'Yeah, and whatever it is, can we have some of it too?'

The trees closed in on the road from the left. The lane veered right towards the track and curved back under it. Roche punched the dash. 'Stop! Under the bridge!' BMW didn't sound right anyway. Rees skidded to a stop and they both jumped out of the car. Past the low brick bridge there were walls on both sides of the road.

'Oversight, target's closing.'

'Boost me!' hissed Roche. Rees cupped his hands. Roche jumped up and clambered onto the top of the wall. The tracks were only guarded by a simple metal rail up over the bridge. Roche vaulted up and over and there was the target, running straight at him fifty feet further down the track. Roche had him cold. He levelled the MP5. 'Oi! Fucker! Freeze!'

The target didn't even break stride as he veered sideways and jumped off the edge of the tracks to the narrow road below, where Rees had just driven the BMW. Roche ran to the edge of the tracks and let off another three-round burst before the target crossed the road and vanished into the trees. How far down was that? Twenty, twenty-five foot?

'Two-two, two-three, oversight, he's come down and gone into the trees on foot. Can you pursue?'

'I'm after him.' Rees.

'Oversight. I can't keep track of him in there, Hotel two-two.'

'Two-two. Exits?' Roche started to climb over the edge of the railway viaduct. Christ, though, that was a long drop. Good way to break an ankle and the target hadn't even given it a thought. Just gone for it. Maybe Rees was right. Maybe the fucker *was* Spiderman. He saw Rees sprinting across the open ground in pursuit but no way was he going to catch the guy.

'That's Tower Hamlets Cemetery Park, two-two. About a dozen possible exits and all into urban streets. We're not going to spot him coming out from up here.'

'Two-three, two-two. I lost him already. I got nothing. Which way?'

Roche muttered a prayer, swung over the side and let himself drop to the tiny strip of waste ground between the lane and the tracks. He hit hard enough to come up winded but nothing snapped. He looked about. He could see which way the target had gone but it was straight into the trees, into a maze of paths in the pitch black night and with a thirty second start, and Rees was already ahead of him.

'I lost him.' Rees.

'*FUCK!*' Roche dropped to a crouch.

'Do we put a call out?'

'What, for a random black dude out at night in Tower Hamlets?' Roche snorted. 'Or did you mean for Peter fucking Parker?'

29 June, 0230 hours, 100 miles over the surface of Europa

The *Irrational Prime* had most of the *Exponential*'s drones grudgingly re-directed to the task of harvesting anti-matter from the quantum froth of virtual particle pairs constantly forming and annihilating in empty space. It was slow, tedious work. Much quicker and more effective to go back to the other gas giant and mine its ring system into more drones and turn the rest of them into a colossal particle accelerator and make anti-matter the straightforward conventional way by smashing stuff into other stuff really hard. Or if they *really* wanted to just get rid of the third planet then all they had to do was seed it with nano-factories to build matter converters and pump energy into the planet's atmosphere until it boiled off. Shouldn't have taken more than a few dozen planetary revolutions. But the Hive wanted to be quiet, stealthy. The Hive didn't like that tau-burst which had looked like something hiding itself in a dimensional pocket because the Hive still didn't understand how the Shriven had known the *Irrational Prime* was there in the first place. Stealthy and quiet, so harvesting from the quantum fluctuations in the zero-point energy of empty space was all that was left.

The *Exponential* grumbled at losing most of its drones to the harvesting. The tau-detector was finished but the frigate was still fretting about the calibration that wasn't working the way it should and how there must be another tau-neutrino source somewhere in the system that was throwing off all its calculations except that there clearly *wasn't* another tau-neutrino source because something that big and energetic would be impossible to hide. The few drones left to it vanished off into the Oort cloud to set off neutrino flashes. The *Irrational Prime* had enjoyed watching the frigate flounder for a while but not any more. It had quietly checked the math and the frigate had a point. Presumably the hybrid had done the same. You could add that to its reasons for caution. Anything putting out tau-neutrinos was either a massively obvious astronomical object or else it was someone mucking about with the fabric of space-time.

The interrogation of the Damascus Shriven had finished half an hour ago. The hybrid construct was wrapping up with the one from Naypyidaw. So far the Shriven in North Africa hadn't reacted to the others being excised. The *Irrational Prime* watched through the observing clone. It certainly didn't seem about to run. It didn't even seem to know, which was quite something because the humans were having conniption fits right across the planet now.

When it was done, the hybrid construct disintegrated the Shriven from Naypyidaw and left the remnants to sink to the bottom of the South China Sea.

'These are the stragglers, the outcasts. The core group are in London,' it said.

London had been the point of origin for the tau-burst. The *Irrational Prime* set to learning everything it could about the city. These would be the Shriven that had hidden in their pocket dimension. The ones with the suspiciously good sensors. The *Exponential* recalibrated its tau-detector, aiming for maximum resolution from the planet's northern hemisphere. It swore a lot as it did it, shifting fluently between the six thousand human languages it had learned.

29 June, 1000 hours, Legoland

It was on the news on the way back as they drove the wrecked BMW into Vauxhall. A massive explosion in Damascus. By the time Roche turned in for some sleep, the reports were already talking about a nuke, maybe a suitcase bomb. The Umayyad Mosque had been destroyed, which was a bit like someone blowing up the Sistine Chapel. Roche couldn't say the name meant much but he caught up with the news like everyone else the next morning and it didn't look pretty. By then there were pictures. There were rumours of radioactivity and of a second bomb let off somewhere out in the desert a few hours earlier. Someone had picked up the electro-magnetic pulse.

Leadface looked sombre and pissed off, more than usual. The spook wasn't there. Charly, Roche thought, looked positively worried.

'Well at least we didn't lose anyone,' said Leadface, which was his way of saying what a total clusterfuck something was. 'Anyone care to tell me what happened?'

He didn't much like what the four of them had to say but at least it wasn't just Roche this time and he

151

could hardly tell all four of his own men that they'd had some sort of collective hallucination. Task Force Hotel four had cleaned out the flat and seized the Bliss and everyone inside had come quietly. Not a trace of any firearms and no resistance. Which was shit because that meant they'd all have to be released in thirty-six hours unless someone either bribed a magistrate or decided they might be terrorists; and that, even Leadface had to admit, was a bit of a reach. But all in all, clusterfuck or not, everyone had much bigger things to worry about on account of the rumours on the news being largely right: by the looks of things, someone really had set off a baby nuke in the middle of Damascus; and since the Umayyad Mosque was the fourth most holy place in Islam, with a heritage dating back to the seventh century, it was a bit hard simply to do the usual and throw the blame at Muslim fundamentalists. The Middle East was busy screaming about the Americans and the West arming the rebels with nukes – although that didn't make any sense either. Russia was already wagging its finger and Europe had woken up to about a billion horrified Muslims. America, so far, was still asleep.

The worst part for everyone in Legoland, by a long way, was that it wasn't the only nuke to go off that night.

'Some of you know how closed a country Myanmar is. Two other bombs went off shortly after Damascus, one in the Namibian desert and one in the Myanmar capital around six in the morning local time. It hasn't made the news yet but it will by the end of the day.

When it does, expect the shit to hit the fan. No casualty reports but the Russians are getting very hot under the collar and we're just waiting for the Chinese to completely lose their shit about Myanmar. Until either someone works out who did what to whom or else we work it out for ourselves, we're all on standby. Obviously the top priority is finding out where the nukes came from, who's got them and whether they have any more. After that comes working out why they hit the targets they did.'

They all milled about afterwards, wondering what to do. Leadface was off back to Hereford.

'The forensics team found blood,' Charly told them over lunch. Roche was slowly getting to like Charly rather a lot. The whole 'scientist' thing was still bullshit but she sat with him and the other task force soldiers as often as she didn't and she held her own. 'Not my field really but they should have a good crack at working out what your man was on.'

'They found blood?' asked Roche. 'Where?'

'Well, I've read all the reports and I gather you shot at him twice. Once when he first ran and again just before you lost him … Did he really run straight up a wall?'

Roche made an irritated face. At least he had Woods and Watts to back him up this time. 'That's what it looked like.'

'We had blood on the first rooftop. Quite a bit at first but it dried up pretty quickly. You must have nicked him.' Charly smiled at Rees. 'Is it true you're calling him Spiderman?'

'I didn't pace it out,' said Woods coldly, 'but I was twenty feet away. He covered it from standing in one jump.'

'Never saw anything like it,' said Roche softly. Woods had frozen. They both had. It was impossible, what that man had done.

The spook rounded them up that afternoon.

'Congratulations,' he told them. 'You're going to Libya.'

1 July, 0800 hours, Naval Air Station Sigonella, Sicily

Roche, Woods and Rees flew out the next day. Watts stayed and instead they got Stanton. That, Roche reckoned, was a plus. Turned out Stanton would have been with them for Tower Hamlets too, only he'd had something more special to deal with. Couldn't say what, of course, and Roche knew better than to ask.

When they came off the plane in Sicily, the heat was like being wrapped in a steaming hot wet towel from the top down. An escort walked them from the plane to a briefing room and they'd barely sat down when a crisp American naval lieutenant in service khaki marched in and started on them. 'Gentlemen, this is not a reconnaissance mission. I realise that's your specialist role but I'm well aware that all of you have other training. This is an extraction and suppression mission and your role will be of a supporting nature. You'll be briefed on the specifics on the way there but your mission is to observe, report and, if requested, advise. If. Requested.' He made a big deal of emphasising that. Then he started handing out what looked suspiciously like radiation badges.

'The task force commander has specifically requested your presence as one of the few special forces teams available from any allied nation with experience in dealing with unusual events and technologies. Bluntly, gentlemen, I have very little information to give you but I'm to advise you that this mission is directly related to the recent events in Damascus, Namibia and Myanmar and to inform you that we are open to the possibility that we may be dealing with an incursion of an extra-terrestrial nature. If there's any more informa-tion on that then I do not have it for you at this time …' He paused but Roche was stuck on the nuke in Namibia. Keetmanshoop. A small town full of poor black folk that no one had ever heard of until yesterday, stuck in the middle of a desert. They'd felt the explo-sion in South Africa a hundred miles away and the kilotonnage was apparently larger than the other two. Why the hell let off a nuke in a place like Keetmanshoop?

Rees was waving his badge. 'Sir, is this a radiation badge? Is that a risk on this mission?'

The lieutenant carried on almost without a pause, waiting exactly long enough for Rees to finish his ques-tion. 'Our intelligence, the nature of which will remain classified and will not be revealed to you or your superior officers, is that all three locations were linked to a very specific activity which also remains classified in nature, and that you will shortly be heading towards what we believe to be a fourth. In short, gentlemen, there's some weird shit going on and you have experience with weird shit and that's why you're here and yes, soldier, those are radiation badges. Given the events at the sites related to this mission you must assume that the presence of radioactive material is a credible possibility.'

He paused, at last, for a drink of water. His voice changed very subtly, as though he was starting to have some trouble entirely believing his own briefing. 'Intelligence indicates a similar site to the ones in Damascus, Myanmar and Namibia exists in the deserts of southern Libya and so that's where you'll be going. There will be civilians present and it will not be clear who is hostile and who are non-combatants. You are authorised to fire whenever you feel your lives are in danger and I am to tell you there will be no repercussions – whatever shitty mess you leave behind, someone else will clear it up. The primary mission will be carried out by a specialist team with two squads of navy SEALS and yourselves in a support role. So essentially you stay out of the way, observe and support as requested by the specialist team. Any nuclear material discovered during the course of this operation will be handled by the specialist team who have been appropriately trained and equipped to do so. If you locate any other unusual objects or technology then you are not to touch said objects but you will call for the specialist support team who are trained for this. I'm told there's no risk of a nuclear event – whether you choose to believe this or not is up to you but I suggest you either do or express your reservations here and now and enjoy a long quiet stay somewhere out of harm's way while the real men get on with what needs to be done. Questions?'

A silence hung over the briefing room. Rees looked at Roche. Roche looked back. They exchanged a glance with Woods and then with Sergeant Stanton.

'Yeah,' said Woods, after a long pause. 'If we see ET, do we shoot him?'

The crisp white lieutenant didn't even blink. 'If you see ET, you call the specialist support team. You see Daleks, you call the specialist support team. You see Martian tripods, you call the specialist support team. You see Jar-Jar Binks, you shoot that fucker in the head until he is dead and *then* you call for the specialist support team. Is that clear, gentlemen?'

1 July, 2200 hours, somewhere over the Sahara desert

'What about Ewoks?' asked Stanton. They were in the back of a V-22 Osprey. Somewhere out there was another Osprey and a pack of angry F/A-18 Hornets there to give shit to any Libyans who decided it wasn't okay for the United States to send a pack of armed-to-the-teeth Special Forces types into the back-arse of their country without bothering to ask nicely first.

'We shoot Ewoks,' said one of the SEALs. As best Roche could tell, both Ospreys were loaded almost with their full complement of twenty-four soldiers and a Growler Fast Attack Vehicle. The specialist support team was in the other Osprey. Roche, Woods, Stanton and

Rees found themselves with two squads of SEALs and their lieutenant for company. There was the usual bit of trans-Atlantic ribbing.

'Ewoks are badass,' said Woods. Roche raised an eyebrow at that. Woods was the last person he'd imagined having an opinion about Ewoks, one way or the other.

'Badass?' The SEAL laughed. 'Fucking teddy bears.' They'd crossed the Libyan coast a while back and no one had tried to shoot them down. This far out over the desert, Roche supposed that no one much cared. There probably wasn't even any air traffic control coverage. People were starting to relax.

'Fucking teddy bears who take out AT-STs with rocks and bits of tree,' said Woods. 'You see an angry Ewok, you best run, because that Ewok he's going to go psycho on your arse and send you running home to mama.'

'You see an Ewok, you call the ...' started Rees.

'... specialist support team,' chorused everyone. Roche shook his head. They all thought the whole extra-terrestrial thing was a bit of a joke and then he kept suddenly remembering that people didn't make jokes like that, not about an op. The rest of Task Force Hotel and the Navy SEALS were going through the same thought process. Roche could see it – *yeah, there's something weird maybe and best keep your eyes open, but none of them actually believes it, right?* Rees and Woods and Watts had seen the man in Tower Hamlets do things that men shouldn't be able to do, but it *had* still been a man, two arms, two legs, bled when he got shot. Real aliens? Nah.

'I thought I saw an alien, one time,' he said.

The others fell silent. It was the sort of silence of men waiting to be told a story.

'It was in Brixton.' He saw Woods roll his eyes straight away. Rees just stared at his feet and shook his head. 'Police liaison. We were taking down what was supposed to be a heavily armed drug gang. Well, they were heavily armed right enough. Swedish-Ks mostly. Not really a problem. They were pussy-cats.' He looked at the SEALs. 'You guys play some hockey, right? So you know your way around an ice rink. There was this little garage where they keep the ... what are they called, the machines they use to cut the ice ... ?'

'Zambonis.'

'Zambonis. So there was this little garage right up against the rink with this pull-down door, you know the sort, a roll-down metal thing. And all the bad guys are there with their pants around their ankles being hustled by the plod – sorry, cops to you – and someone gets the idea that there's someone in the garages where the Zambonis live ...'

'*You* got the idea, Roche,' muttered Rees.

'Yeah. So Rees and I, we go back and well, you know what those doors are like. Never quite close properly. So Rees finds a gap and pokes a fibreoptic underneath. And there you go. Aliens.'

He sat back. The others watched, quiet, as if waiting for the punchline. It was the sort of story that was supposed to end up with finding two teenagers making out, not knowing they were in the middle of an armed drugs bust. Or something like that.

159

'Aliens,' he said again, sure of it this time.

'Were they legal ones?' asked one of the SEALs. They still couldn't work out whether or not he was joking. 'What they look like?'

'Faces all stretched. Arms too long. Like scary-arsed clowns. By the time anyone got in, they were gone. Like they vanished through the walls.'

'You see them too?' someone asked Rees. Rees shook his head.

'Was outside, shooting punks. Roche was the only one. Didn't even get a picture off the fibreoptic. Laptop fried. Totally dead. Wiped clean.'

'Fucking aliens, eh?' The SEALs all laughed. *Almost* all laughed. All except the lieutenant. After a moment the lieutenant pulled a crumpled piece of paper out of his pocket. He looked at Roche and passed the paper along the line of men.

'Look like that, did it?' he asked, as Roche took it.

Roche stared at the paper. 'Where'd you get this?'

'I asked if there was anything in particular we should be looking for.'

The sketch wasn't great but there was no doubt what it was. It was the Scary Clown.

2 July, 0030 hours, 4 miles west of Aqar, Libya

The Ospreys came down in the desert, swirling up a storm of sand and barely touching down as the back ramps opened and the Growlers and the squads of soldiers ran down and fanned out, spreading themselves in a defensive arc. There was no one here waiting for them but that wasn't the point – everything and everywhere was hostile until you knew better. They'd come down on a flat rocky expanse a few miles west of Aqar itself and just off a track that ran east-west through the desert. When he got through choking in the cloud of dust thrown up by the Osprey's rotors, Roche shivered.

'Pleasantly cool.' Rees stretched his arms and rolled his shoulders. 'What happened to the Sahara Desert, hottest place on earth?'

They ran out of the dust cloud and took shelter behind a low ridge as the whine of the Osprey rotors slowly died. The Hornets were heading away. Fuck knows where they were all off to next but that wasn't Roche's problem, or anyone else's on the ground, not until it came to evac.

'Isn't this a bit dry for you?' shouted Woods at the SEALs. Which would have been funnier if they hadn't all been about to slog it on foot together. Apparently they didn't get to keep their Growler.

One of the specialist support team – whoever the fuck they were – approached the SEAL lieutenant and started a conversation. Roche watched. He could tell by the lieutenant's body language that the lieutenant wasn't enjoying what he was hearing.

'Lads,' Roche said. Stanton, Rees and Woods went quiet. They could hear raised voices now but couldn't quite make out what was being said. It was clear that there was a heated argument going on.

'On an op,' Rees muttered. 'Fucking cowboys.'

Roche moved forward, making it look as casual as possible. He could see that the lieutenant's men, who were acting as a security cordon for the landing site, were occasionally glancing over their shoulders.

'I don't care that you outrank me, my orders came down from SOCOM, you don't change parameters on the job …' the lieutenant was saying, sounding more exasperated than angry.

'Stop acting as if you're an amateur and it's your first time out of the box. Does the phrase black ops mean anything to you?' The support team's officer was a big man, a squat, solidly built slab of muscle. It was clear he was trying to intimidate the SEAL officer, who was standing his ground. 'You're here because of some fucking political short-stroking, nothing more. Now grow the fuck up, come to terms with it and stay back here, play with your toy boats or whatever, we got this, okay?'

'Yeah. I understand you want me to disobey a direct order on your say so without …'

It happened quickly. Roche still couldn't quite believe what he was watching. This didn't happen on special forces ops, ever, even American ones. The support team officer grabbed the SEAL lieutenant by the neck, picked him up off the ground and slammed him into the dirt. It was the sort of thing that happened in action films, not in actual life, and it looked more like a wrestling move than something executed by a trained soldier. The support team officer shouldn't have been able to pull it off against a trained Navy SEAL either. Yet the man had moved with ferocious speed and exhibited remark-able strength. He held the SEAL lieutenant on the ground now. The lieutenant tried a couple of moves that should have broken the hold but they didn't. Even from Roche's position he could make out the thick cords of muscle that made up the 'support team' officer's arm.

Several of the SEALs on the cordon swung around, bringing up their M4s and levelling them at the special forces officer holding down their boss. As one, the special forces soldiers that made up the support team brought their weapons to bear.

'I will bury every one of you fuckers out here,' the officer said. Roche looked at the rest of the American special forces team. Like their officer they were all big guys; like their officer they had all moved with surprising speed.

'Woah! Woah!' Roche went against all his training and common sense and got in between them. He sensed rather than saw Woods, Rees and Stanton getting ready to move if it went hot. 'Gentlemen! Please!'

'Shut the fuck up, limey,' the special forces officer who was still choking the SEAL lieutenant snapped.

'That's fine, mate. Look, you want to go on, we'll kick back here and watch the 'Spreys, have a brew, no issues. Can you just let my boss up there?' Roche was playing the dumb squaddie for all it was worth.

The 'specialist support' officer looked down. The SEAL lieutenant was turning red now. 'Fucking faggots,' he muttered. He let go of the lieutenant and the SEAL rolled away from him, gasping for breath. Roche knew that he'd just had his world-view radically fucked about. You weren't supposed to be able to do things like that to a SEAL. The other officer straightened up and turned to look at Roche, who was standing with his hands far apart. 'This is a US operation and you shouldn't even be here.'

'We'll go inside the 'Spreys, put the kettle on and sit with our eyes shut, okay?'

The officer narrowed his eyes. 'Are you trying to be cute?'

'We all want what you want, the job done and to go home. If that means we wait here then we wait here. I don't mind not being shot at. Don't mind that at all.'

The special forces officer glared at him but said nothing. He turned and walked away.

'Stand down,' the SEAL lieutenant told his men between gasps for breath. Roche knelt next to him.

'You all right, mate?'

The lieutenant nodded.

2 July, 0037 hours, 4 miles west of Aqar, Libya

The Growlers went ahead, four men in each. Roche watched the soldiers from the other Osprey jump into them and drive away. There was something wrong about them, he thought, both the teams who drove ahead and the dozen soldiers who loped off across the desert in their wake. They had a fluidity to the way they moved, like tuned athletes, and a jumpiness to them too. They reminded him of the man they'd chased through Tower Hamlets. Maybe it was the adrenaline. He felt it himself a little too, a hyper-awareness of everything around him.

He watched the specialist support squad's four snipers running across the desert, making for the rocks surrounding the township of Aqar. They were moving at a full sprint, each of them carrying an M82A1 .50 calibre sniper rifle which weighed the better part of thirty pounds before you started adding furniture to it. It was unsustainable, a pace like that, but they didn't stop. They just kept running. Roche elbowed Rees. 'You thinking what I'm thinking?'

'I really doubt it.'

'Tower Hamlets Man.' Rees shrugged. Roche shook his head. 'Yeah, none of the rest of you really saw him run, did you?' He walked over to the SEAL lieutenant instead. 'Who are those guys?' he asked.

'Never seen them before,' the SEAL told him. Which was mildly curious in itself because even the US special forces community was relatively small. 'I thought 3rd Special Forces out of Bragg, now I'm thinking SAD.'

Roche nodded. The Special Activities Division was the covert paramilitary branch of the CIA. Figured. Fucking cowboys.

'You see his eyes?' the lieutenant asked. Roche shook his head. 'There was something wrong with that guy.'

'Well I think we all saw *that*.'

'LT?' Roche glanced around to see the crew chief of one of the Ospreys that had brought the SF guys in. 'Can I have a word?'

The SEAL lieutenant excused himself and moved away to talk to the crew chief.

'Well, they were a bit spry,' Woods said as the other three joined them. 'And wankers too.'

'What are you thinking?' Stanton asked. Roche was watching the last of the 'specialist support team' soldiers disappearing into the distance.

'I'm thinking my curiosity is going to get me killed,' Roche said. The other three soldiers were sitting down, but not Roche.

'I think they'll shoot us if they even see us.'

'I think you're right. I think we want the smallest footprint possible. I'll go.'

'Sure you're not too old for this?' Woods asked.

'Not on your own,' Stanton said.

'I'll go and look after him,' Woods said.

'Think you can keep quiet long enough?' Rees asked. 'I'll stay here and drink tea.'

'They're Americans, they'll only have coffee,' Stanton pointed out.

'Ah fuck,' glared Rees. 'You're right. You stay. I'll go.' But he didn't get up.

'Savages,' Woods muttered.

The SEAL lieutenant joined them.

'Gentlemen, I'm sorry about the conduct …' he started.

'It's okay,' Roche said. 'We'll take the piss out of you after the op. Look I know you don't like people making it up as they go along but we've got to get eyes on. Me and Woods want to go in.'

'Frankly if you weren't, we were. Do you need any more shooters?'

'No, we're sneaky bastards, boss,' Woods told him, grinning.

'The fewer of us the better,' Roche said.

'I think that if they see you, they're going to shoot at you,' the lieutenant said. 'I think they're going to keep shooting. Even if they don't see you again until the evac.' He seemed to be struggling with something. Trying to decide whether or not to tell them. 'The crew chief told me that he saw them shooting up in the 'Sprey.'

Roche wasn't particularly surprised.

'He have any idea what?' Rees asked. The lieutenant shook his head.

'That looked a bit like 'roid rage to me,' Woods said.

'Anything like this ever happened before?' Rees asked.

The SEAL lieutenant bristled but quickly calmed again. 'No. I know all the jokes about us Yanks being cowboys but you don't get away with that shit. Not on an op.'

Roche and Woods were stripping off anything that they wouldn't absolutely need. Roche was wishing for a ghillie suit but he didn't have the time to sort one out. He checked and double-checked the digital camera.

'Where do you want us?' Stanton asked the lieutenant.

2 July, 0100 hours, Aqar, Libya

Roche wanted to throw up. With the Growlers gone, the only way for them to cover ground to Aqar was to run. Roche had his Diemaco C8SFW carbine cradled in his arms as he ran. Despite the cold he was so covered in sweat that he felt he could wring out his watch hat and was worried that he was going to sweat off his camo paint. His chest was burning, he was struggling for breath and he didn't like the way that Woods seemed to be having no problems keeping up with him. They weren't being terribly stealthy but the soldiers ahead of them had moved so quickly they had little choice.

They could see Aqar ahead. It was a spread-out town of low one- and two-storey stucco buildings packed in tightly together with a scattering of low ruined walls in clusters along the southern approach. It was situated on a plain with sparse, rocky hills to the east and the north-west. Roche and Woods were approaching from the west and Roche was already seeing flashes of light in the township. Unmistakable muzzle flare but he hadn't heard any shots – probably the 'specialist' soldiers using their suppressed M4 carbines. He took the muzzle flashes as an excuse to stop, catch his breath and check the township through the light intensifying starlight scope attached to the C8. Woods came to a halt a little way from him, checking all around them.

A lot of SF soldiers liked to use night-vision goggles for work in darkness but Roche preferred to rely on his own night vision, particularly on a bright cloudless night like this. If he needed anything more then he had the scope, which was currently showing him Aqar in unflattering green. He could see more flashes in the township. It was only a matter of time before it went …

The shot from the .50 calibre sniper rifle rolled like thunder across the plane. The four feet of muzzle flash lit up the rocky canyon where Aqar nestled. Then it fired again. A second sniper fired. Roche heard the multiple popping noise of a Mark 19 automatic grenade launcher, presumably one of the ones mounted on the back of two of the Growlers.

… loud. Yeah. Explosions bloomed in Aqar. There were brighter, longer muzzle flashes and then moments later the sound of the .50 calibre Growler-mounted heavy machine gun reached them. They watched the progress of the nearest Growler by the muzzle flashes as it moved rapidly through the streets, machine gun firing. They saw the short flight of tracers into buildings, some of them ricocheting into the night sky. Roche guessed the 'specialist support unit' had received a different briefing on the Rules of Engagement than him because he hadn't heard anything that sounded even remotely like a Libyan weapon. Judging by the muzzle flashes, the special forces guys were killing en masse. He felt a shiver of unease. For a while he couldn't put his finger on what it was until he realised it was Kravica. What he was seeing was making him think of Kravica.

The night suddenly lit up nearby with more muzzle flashes, much too close for comfort. Roche and Woods hit the ground as tracers poured down into the village amid the flat, hard staccato of automatic support weapons. Two of the light machine guns were set up less than forty feet in front of them and he and Woods had almost run straight into them. They would have too, if the guns hadn't started firing. Despite the lunacy with the SEAL lieutenant and the steroid abuse, these 'specialist' soldiers knew what they were doing.

Woods signalled a circuitous route away from the emplaced machine guns and into Aqar.

And let's keep it stealthy.

As Roche moved away, he saw the soldiers had set something up on a tripod a little way off to one side of their position. Bizarrely, what it reminded Roche of most of all was a cheap supermarket barbecue with an antenna on top.

2 July, 0117 hours, Jovian upper atmosphere

The last of the three surviving Fermat clones watched the American task force arrive with some interest. It hadn't bothered conferring with the *Exponential* and the *Irrational Prime* over what to do; it simply phased into the ground and watched. The Americans started by setting up four sites around where the Shriven was existing. They were very careful and quiet about it and the clone debated the possibility that the Shriven hadn't even noticed them. After that, the Americans went in and started shooting everything that moved. Their apparent strategy of stealth followed by loud and obvious force lacked any clear logic and the clone devoted most of its considerable cognitive effort to extrapolating likely possible outcomes and rationales and, most importantly of all, hypotheses as to what had brought the Americans here at all.

All of which changed as soon as it received emissions from the four sites the Americans had so carefully constructed.

'A tachyonic quantum field?' The *Exponential*, the *Irrational Prime* and the hybrid construct Fermat all paused significant portions of what they were doing. Human science at least acknowledged the existence of tachyonic fields. They inadvertently made them now and then in their Large Hadron Collider, a particle accelerator that was twenty-seven kilometres in circumference and used as much power as a small city. Apparently they'd made a technical breakthrough recently. Judging by what the Americans had brought with them, the humans were suddenly able to fit all of that into something small enough that two soldiers could carry it across a desert on their backs.

2 July, 0119 hours, Aqar

It was only as they made their way into Aqar that Roche started to hear sustained return fire. He picked out the ubiquitous AK47 sound amid other, heavier, Russian-made automatic weapons. There were more explosions deeper in the town that were probably rocket-propelled grenades. Aqar was catching hell.

'Okay, where to?' Woods asked. They were both crouched down by a low wall that acted as some kind of goat pen. One goat was horribly wounded. The others were dead. Part of the house to which the wall was attached had been demolished, probably by a forty-millimetre grenade. Bloodied limbs poked out of the rubble.

It was a good question. As far as Roche could tell, the US special forces soldiers were killing everyone here for the sake of killing. Their own brief had been to stay out of the way, support as requested and search for anything unusual. The last bit, when Roche had his way, got done in silence without any bad guys waking up and shooting back. This lot seemed more interested in conducting their search in the style of the My Lai massacre.

He shrugged; Woods shrugged back then signalled towards the centre of town, picking one of the narrow alleyways between houses at random. They moved down, Roche taking the lead while Woods checked behind them. Fire was coming from all over the town now and someone, somewhere, was making a concerted effort to fight back.

Figures ran across the alleyway. Both soldiers stopped, moved into shadow and crouched, going very still, Roche facing one way, Woods the other. Two of the figures turned at the end of the alley and started towards them. Roche's headshot from the suppressed C8 caught the first, a spray of blood that looked black in the moonlight. He fell back. Roche shifted to fire at the second when a fist-sized part of the wall exploded. The .50 calibre round took the other man in the side and the hydrostatic shock all but exploded him. Roche crouched even lower and pressed himself hard against the wall. Muzzle flashes illuminated one side of the alleyway. He watched as a Growler drove by, firing.

Roche gave it a few moments and then moved up to the bodies. The dead men were locals, both of them. The one he'd shot had no face. Normally he'd have double tapped to make sure – it was good practice – but every shot threatened to give them away. He checked the small road at the end of the alleyway. It was clear both ways.

Woods covered him as he darted across the road. Now the sweat was from the tension. Roche dropped into deep shadow and covered Woods as he crossed in turn …

The side of the building next to him exploded, spraying him with fragments of masonry. He staggered back, trying to work out what had happened. Woods passed him and took the lead. Another fist-sized hole appeared in the wall next to him. Roche turned and followed. They moved fast. One of the snipers had seen them. They'd radio in a position to the soldiers in the Growlers.

What the fuck am I doing? Roche wondered.

They moved south and west, zigzagging through the town, trying to move counter-intuitively through the streets and alleys to confuse anyone searching for them and trying to keep out of sight of the snipers while they worked out where the fuckers were. So fucking counter-intuitive that it was beginning to feel like aimlessly trying not to end up dead; but then Woods stopped and made a sharp gesture: *look!*

Down the dirt track in the centre of town was what looked like a partially buried warehouse made of corrugated metal. The warehouse was in a fenced-off area topped with razor wire and the compound had already been taken by the US soldiers. About a third of them and one of the Growlers were in cover in and around the compound, engaged in a vicious firefight with the locals in the southern part of the town. Roche already knew, because they'd had to hide from them twice, that some of the US 'specialists' were roaming the streets and alleyways in two-man kill teams, executing anybody they came across, armed or not. Roche had no idea where the rest of them were.

Roche nodded and crept closer, then edged prone and with a painful slowness out onto the street, tucked in close to a wall until the wall's shadow and his own stillness was all the concealment he had. Small-arms and machine-gun fire rattled steadily back and forth, random bullets now and then exploding holes in the stone and mortar about their heads. They'd worked out three of the four snipers' positions in the surrounding hills now and Roche was pretty sure they were concealed from them. As for the fourth … Mentally Roche crossed his fingers as he took rapid pictures with the digital SLR camera. When he had enough, he turned his head to Woods and made a gesture.

Closer.

Woods made a face in the darkness, then nodded and then gestured back at the American 'specialists'.

Are they targets now?

Roche gave that some thought. The Americans in Aqar were out of control. They were on something. They were indiscriminate and they were massacring civilians. Most of all, Roche was absolutely certain that if they saw him and Woods, they'd shoot without hesitation. Anything else wouldn't even cross their minds.

He nodded. Woods raised an eyebrow but after that he only shrugged.

2 July, 0123 hours, half a kilometre south-east of Aqar

The cloned Fermat construct emerged out of the stone eight feet behind the fourth sniper. It rose silently and was out of phase with the matter of the desert air and so couldn't possibly disturb it; and yet some primitive instinct in the sniper made him suddenly turn. He was quick, impossibly quick for ordinary human nerves and reflexes, but it helped him only insofar as he caught a momentary glimpse of the Fermat before the construct shifted phase and realised itself.

There was a very faint pop as every erg of energy was sucked out of the sniper and he froze to absolute zero. The cloned construct stepped past and settled its attention on the device on the tripod set up a little way in front of the sniper. It looked a bit like a cheap barbecue with an antenna on top.

2 July, 0152 hours, Aqar

Roche stood just inside the walls of a half-destroyed house. Woods crouched beside him. They were closer to the compound now. Tracer fire from the machine-gun emplacements they'd passed on the way in was flying overhead, impacting in the southern part of the town. He tried to ignore the corpses of the family who'd once lived here. This was the shit that happened to civilians the moment there was any kind of warfare in a built-up area. He'd seen worse.

A movement on the other side of the wall. Roche heard it and froze, carbine at the ready. Woods had heard it too. Two of the US 'specialists' moved into the alley next to the house, both picking their way very carefully. The alleyway lit up with muzzle flashes, a series of short bursts from AK47s further down. The special forces soldiers staggered back and then advanced again, firing rapidly.

Roche mouthed a silent *fuck*! Both the American soldiers had been wearing body armour, and the good stuff as well. Dragonscale; but even so, you got hit by a rifle round, you fell over, gasping for breath and hoped you hadn't broken any ribs.

Apparently not this lot.

There was a popping noise as one of the 'specialists' fired a forty-millimetre grenade. The far end of the alleyway exploded. The two soldiers pushed forward fast now, firing all the time, silencing cries of pain with suppressed shots from their M4 carbines.

When they were gone, Woods checked the alleyway and signalled them clear to move on.

2 July, 0158 hours, half a kilometre south-east of Aqar

The device on the tripod was unquestionably the source

of the tachyonic quantum field. The nano-factories finished their careful invasion of it and returned to the Fermat construct. The construction was crude and certainly human. It was just fifty years ahead of their current technology.

2 July, 0212 hours, Aqar

The fence around the warehouse had been knocked down or blown open in several places. Most of the 'specialist support group' soldiers were at the southern end of the compound firing at the locals and advancing on them. They'd left a small security force behind: two soldiers at the door to the warehouse and another two out in the street to the north.

Roche reckoned that he and Woods were running out of luck. They were trying to sneak around a small town filled with soldiers with comparable training. Right now they were both lying down behind the wall of another partially destroyed house, though Roche was pretty sure this had been the result of an RPG strike. They were waiting for the two soldiers in the street to get close to them. The rest of the battle was getting further and further away, the sounds of AK47 and heavy machine-gun fire more distant and less frequent.

On the other side of the wall Roche heard the scuff of feet. Woods was up first. He moved around the wall, grabbed the nearest soldier by the face, wrapped his legs around the other man's and simply fell over. He used his grip on the first soldier to force his head up and then pushed the blade of his knife, point first, into the man's throat, severing jugular and windpipe straight away.

The second soldier turned. Woods dragging his victim to the ground confused him for a moment but even then, Roche only just caught him before he could move, wrapping one hand over the man's face and then driving the point of his knife upwards into the base of the man's skull with an audible crack. The soldier shook and spasmed; something wet coursed over Roche's gloved hand. He dropped the man, pulling the knife out, but then dropped that too and grabbed his C8 on its sling, bringing it to his shoulder.

Woods rolled the man he'd killed off him. The two special forces soldiers by the warehouse door had seen the movement and were bringing their weapons up. Years of experience told Roche where to put the sights; he stroked the trigger, a suppressed single shot. Woods was on his feet now. The soldiers by the door had their weapons up. Roche moved forwards, firing. The starlight scope flared as one of the special forces men returned fire. The other fell back as blood sprayed from his head, a bright lurid green seen through the scope. Behind Roche the night lit up as Woods fired a three-round burst. The other special forces soldier staggered slightly but merely shifted his aim and fired. Roche was moving sideways now. He felt bullets crack past him. He stroked the trigger again and the bullet's force powdered metal on the warehouse wall just to the right of the soldier's head. The man staggered again as Woods hit a second time, central mass again. *You need a headshot,* Roche thought and squeezed the trigger a third time. *Stanton told us that when he told us about Dagenham.*

The back of the man's head exploded. Dagenham, that's what this was. It wasn't Tower Hamlets Man; these 'specialist support group' cockheads were Dagenham through and through.

Woods was on his feet. Both of them ran for the warehouse now. Roche watched lights fly past him, hit the ground and bounce off. Tracer fire from the machine-gun position they'd passed. Cover or run, those were the choices. They sprinted and made it to the short flight of stairs. Roche leapt down them. He hit the warehouse door and it flew open. He heard a cry and Woods came barrelling after him. The side of Woods' head was covered in blood and so was his shoulder. Roche dragged him to the side as tracers flew into the warehouse.

'Ow fuck!' Woods shouted. The inside of the ware-house lit up with muzzle flashes. Roche felt the bullets shoot past him; then one hit and it felt like getting slammed with a mallet. It knocked him flat and the breath was forced out of him in a way that made him feel he'd never be able to catch it again.

There were bodies in the warehouse. He saw them now, lying sprawled on his back. They were hanging from the ceiling in translucent bags and there were a lot of them. They were swaying but other than that that they weren't moving.

There was light moving towards him. More muzzle flashes.

He saw one of the bags twitch. They weren't dead …

Woods fired from the ground. A short burst. The light approaching them fell backwards. Then Woods was on one knee. It was his muzzle flash that illuminated the warehouse as he fired at something Roche couldn't see.

… The bags were attached to a complicated series of tubes. The tubes ran inside and into the bodies. Like blood transfusion equipment. A dirty brown liquid was being fed into their veins and some kind of clear liquid was being sucked from the nape of the neck … Dear god, was that spinal fluid? Cerebral fluid?

There was a smell. A flash back to Brixton and the last thing he'd remembered. A smell.

Serotonin … ?

'Okay, old man, I need you to pull yourself together.' Woods reloaded his C8. He was checking all around the warehouse but the hanging bodies were obscuring his sight.

Pull himself together? What the fuck was he talking about? *I can't fucking breathe!* But Roche managed to get a grip of himself and pull a breath down into his empty lungs. The pain told him he'd almost certainly broken one or more ribs. He wasn't coughing blood though, so the body-armour must have done its job. If a broken rib was the worst he came away with from this … 'You okay?' he managed.

'No, I'm really fucking not,' Woods told him. 'The head looks bad but it's only a graze. The shoulder's a through and through and it fucking burns.' He glanced around at the bodies hanging in their bags all through the warehouse. 'And this freeze-dried-human bullshit is really messing with my head.'

'We can't do anything about your shoulder until we're out of here.'

Woods nodded. His teeth were clenched and he was obviously in a great deal of pain. Roche wondered whether even in his prime he could have taken a shoulder wound like that and still have the presence of mind to kill two well-trained soldiers immediately afterwards.

He looked up at the bodies, slung his C8 and took out the SLR camera. 'These people aren't dead.'

'Then what the fuck are they?'

'I don't know.' Roche went left and Woods went right though they both kept glancing behind them, back to the doors. They'd been seen entering. Someone would have radioed that in, but for now there was nobody else in the warehouse other than the bagged bodies. Roche took picture after picture. Compulsive. He'd never seen anything like it.

'It's like they're being harvested. Shit. But for what?'

'Roche, mate,' Woods' voice was strained with pain. Roche glanced over at him. Woods stood next to a pile of what looked like bags of sugar on a pallet. As Roche moved over to them, he noticed a trap door in the shadows at the back of the warehouse. 'That, my friend, is enough Moroccan Brown for us to retire.' Roche checked them. He'd done enough drugs interdiction work to know heroin when he saw it. He put the bags back and photographed them.

'What the fuck is this?'

'You know we're running out of time, yeah?' Woods asked and glanced at the trap door.

'You want to stay?' Roche asked.

Woods gave the question some thought.

'Fuck it, in for a penny, in for a pound,' he said. The two men nodded to one another. Woods covered the warehouse entrance while Roche lifted up the trap door enough to roll in a flashbang and a fragmentation grenade. Both of them stood well back, Roche brought up his C8.

The compression wave from the flashbang blew the trap door off its hinges. The phosphorescent flash shone through the gaps in the floorboards. The fragmentation grenade went off a moment later and the floor jumped. Holes appeared in it. Something tore at Roche's leg and he grunted as he felt an impact on his body armour from the shrapnel.

'That was a bit dumb,' muttered Woods. 'You okay?'

The hanging bodies in the bags started to shake and move and there was the sound of high velocity bits of lead impacting flesh as tracers started to fly through the warehouse. Someone was firing in through the doors again. Roche moved quickly to the trap door, saw a tattered set of wooden steps leading into a dimly lit space and started down them, fast. He took four steps and then the rest simply gave up and crumbled underneath him. The ground came up hard. He had a moment to take in the surroundings. He was in a small cellar area. The walls had a resinous quality to them. There were items embedded in the resin, screens of some kind but Roche didn't recognise the figures they showed. There was something wrong or off about the technology he could see, he just wasn't sure what. In the middle of the room was a black rectangular case …

Something moved in the corner of the room. *Christ on a bike!* It was the one of the 'specialist' soldiers. Battered and bloody but he was picking himself up and Roche didn't understand how the man could possibly have survived being in such a small space with a flash-bang and a fragmentation grenade. How he could still be alive … Moving … ?

It was the officer who'd choke-slammed the SEAL lieutenant. He was shaking his head. He saw Roche on the floor and peered at him as if trying to understand what was happening. Roche reached for his C8. Woods jumped down into the cellar. The special forces officer drew his Heckler & Koch USP sidearm …

A pale, almost skeletal, hand, its fingers too long and with too many joints, its nails all but claws, reached out from the wall and ran itself down the officer's side. There was no resistance to the movement of the hand from body armour, skin, flesh or bone. Meat fell away from bone as if it had been flensed. The soldier's eyes went wide. Blood ran out of him, over his webbing and down his fatigues like water from a ruptured dam. He sank to his knees and collapsed onto his face.

It stepped out of the wall. Tall, thin, elongated face, black eyes with no pupils, the vicious rictus grin Roche

183

had seen through the fibreoptic in Brixton. It looked down at the special forces officer. It seemed to be wearing some kind of long frock coat. Roche was transfixed. Couldn't move. Beside him, Woods howled like an animal. He triggered his carbine in a long burst at the thing. There were a few initial gouts of steam and then holes started appearing in the resin behind it. It raised its hand. Roche saw some kind of tube in its hand. He tried to shout a warning. He saw a gout of flame and heard a sound not unlike a minigun firing. Something hot and wet covered him. Where Woods had been stood there was only a pair of legs and the stump of a bloodied spine. The legs toppled over. Roche pissed himself.

The thing turned and looked at him. Roche threw his C8 away and held his hands up. As he did, he flicked the video record button on the camera still slung over his shoulder. The Scary Clown turned away and looked at the black box. Roche followed his gaze as if hypnotised. Then he realised what it was. A suitcase bomb. A portable nuclear weapon. Above him he could hear boots thumping off the warehouse's floorboards. The Scary Clown looked up before turning and walking into the wall.

Then the screaming started.

***

'Where's Woods?'
'Where's the special forces guys?'
'What happened?'

'Whose blood is that?'

Roche drove as fast as he could to the Ospreys. He was covered from head to foot in blood. He had driven the stolen Growler one handed. In the other bloodied fingers he clutched the SLR.

'Nobody's coming,' he told them. 'They're dead. We need to leave.' More questions. A one word answer: Nuke.

***

A flash. The mushroom cloud seen rising from the plane. The glare shining even through the shuttered windows on the Ospreys. It was low yield enough that the EMP didn't knock them out of the sky. They were far enough from the blast that the nuclear winds hit the Osprey as nothing worse than severe turbulence. Roche never let go of the camera.

13 – Tachyon Fields and Breadcrumb Trails

2 July, 0246 hours, Jovian upper atmosphere

'A curious choice,' commented the Fermat construct. The clones shut themselves down briefly as the nuke went off.

'They must have known a Shriven was there,' grumbled the *Irrational Prime*. 'It's the only logical reason for the tachyonic devices.' The freighter didn't think much of its own logic even as it put the hypothesis forward. A negative mass quantum field was ... unexpected. And not something the humans had shown any sign of possessing.

'Perhaps their logic is more opaque than we thought.' The Hybrid construct was as troubled as any of them.

'There wasn't any logic at all,' grumbled the *Exponential*. 'It didn't do anything useful.' The Aqar clone was bringing its systems back on-line. 'They didn't know what they were dealing with, only that they were dealing with *something* and when all you know is that you're dealing with *something*, trying to hit it with the biggest stick you can find is an absurd first response.' The *Exponential* was sounding increasingly huffy these days. 'So ...'

The *Irrational Prime* interrupted with an extensive review of human history and the application of logic to the initiation of conflict. There was a long pregnant pause and then the frigate conceded defeat. 'I don't care how common it is,' it grumbled, 'it still seems a disastrous species response.'

'We have confirmation and denial from the Shriven for their probable interference events within the timeline of various cultures,' interrupted the Fermat construct. 'The massacre of Novgorod in the local year 1570. The link is based on a single unreliable reported sighting of a "devil-like figure with a long face and arms, his fingers too long and like claws, horns upon his head and a grin that split his face from ear to ear." Unfortunately, although consistent with the appearance of diaspora Weft, the imagery is also consistent with local native mythologies of the time.' The construct laid bare the disassembled memories of the captured Shriven. 'That particular connection is now proven incorrect as we now have thorough intelligence on the movements and whereabouts of most of the Shriven Astronomers. They have interfered before. Perhaps this device is the work of those that yet remain.'

'The what? Astronomers?' asked the frigate and the freighter.

'The name used to refer to their collective selves. Please cross-reference with recorded history while I commune with the Hive on another matter.'

The construct fell silent. For a few nanoseconds, the two ships regarded one another. *Another matter* could only mean whatever outside connection the Astronomers had made.

'The massacre by the Jivaro of Ecuador and Peru of twenty-five thousand non-local settlers including the execution of one by pouring molten gold down his throat until his bowels burst,' said the *Exponential* suddenly. 'Promising? A similar devil-like figure to that of Novgorod is reported by both sides. While the non-local settlers' mythology mirrors that of the Novgorod incident, that of the Jivaro instigators does not. A Shriven was present. Am I right or am I right?'

The *Irrational Prime*, peeling back the layers of the disassembled Shriven, made a dismissive noise. 'No. They did that one all by themselves.'

'How about this: the devastation in 1646 of the Sichuan province of China. Jesuit missionaries report a devil-like figure at the court of Zhang Xianzhong. Again, the mythology of the missionaries is similar to that of Novgorod while the local mythology is substantively different.' The *Exponential* sounded smug.

'No such figure was recorded in the local mythology though.' The *Irrational Prime* found itself reluctant to encourage the frigate.

'One of the most extreme genocides in their history. I'm putting this hypothesis in the high ninety-five plus percentage points of right. Am I?'

The *Irrational Prime* paused, reluctant. 'One of the Shriven was there,' it conceded. 'The one from Naypyidaw. It was there for a year. Heads collected in piles. And noses and ears and hands … why count noses and ears separately? What's the sense in that? And he cut the feet off several hundred woman once because he got—'

'Because he had a Shriven whispering in his ear,' interrupted the *Exponential*. 'How about the one from Keetmanshoop. From 1670 to 1730 there are repeated stories of a ghost-like man with arms of snakes and a mouth of lion's teeth wide enough to swallow a man's head originating from the African coastal towns of Grand-Popo, Porto-Novo and Badagry, all of which existed primarily to facilitate the capture and transport of slaves from the local population. There's no apparent precedent for such a creature in local mythologies.'

'A devil-like figure reported to preside over a massacre on the island of Haiti in 1804 ...'

'This picture of a witch-doctor in the presence of Shaka Zulu ...'

'The Weft who stopped the Pleasure was a Shriven,' said the construct suddenly. The frigate and the freighter both stopped. 'His name was Dal. He was addicted to the chemistry of the Pleasure. It had destroyed his second part, severed his link to his soul and thus to the Hive. Others saw how he did what he did and so the Hive saw too and his secrets were shared. But because he was Shriven, no one knew how he'd come to *know* what he knew. He claimed to have dreams and visions. Madness. Yet a madness that led him to understand matter and energy and space and time more completely than any other. He destroyed our home-world and himself but he destroyed the Pleasure too. They never came back. We exist because a Shriven saved us.'

'How many of the Shriven are missing?' asked the *Exponential*. 'It's clearly not just the one that got away just now.'

'Six,' said the Fermat clones. 'But we know where to find them. The muon trail from the stutter-holes points directly to them. This one has travelled to London. It is a solid hypothesis that it has the key to the pocket dimension where the others are hiding. Logically they will now converge to either flee or fight. It would be convenient for the tau-burst detector to be functional.'

The *Exponential* seemed to grow just a little bit more tetchy. The *Irrational Prime* busied itself with some deep computation of Saturn's Rings and carefully looked the other way.

14 – Off the Books

2 July, 0330 hours, somewhere over the Libyan coast

Roche couldn't stop shaking. At first Rees and Stanton had to keep close, keeping the SEALs back, who all desperately want to know what had gone down. Then the nuke went off and put an end to any talking.

'I need to show you something,' said Roche, after the nuke hadn't killed them all. 'I need to show you what was there.' He turned to Rees and looked around the SEALs. 'I can't hide that Woods and I went in after your lot. None of the rest of you know anything about it.'

Stanton snorted. 'Right. Like that's going to fly.'

'No, *they* didn't. *You* did. You just didn't tell them. You and Rees covered for us. As much as we can, we play it as it was. It was my idea and Woods backed the play. You and Rees covered us. I came back on my own in a Growler yelling about the nuke and we cleared out and what I'm about to show you didn't happen. There was something in Aqar that none of the rest of us were meant to see, but that other lot, whoever they were, they knew. I'm sure. So I'm going to show you a few pictures. Pass it round then let me have it back.' He nodded to the SEAL lieutenant. 'I'm going to give this to you when we're done. You're going to have taken it off me as soon as the 'Sprey kicked off the dirt. Intel. It's up to you how we play it. If you want, no one looked at it. I didn't talk. This didn't happen. You need to talk about that with your guys.'

Roche passed the camera. There didn't seem any need to go into how he and Woods had entered Aqar or how the other soldiers had been tearing the place apart or how he'd shot two American special forces soldiers in the head and knifed a third in the back of the neck. They might have been arseholes but they were still soldiers. He started with the pictures of the sunken warehouse. No one paid much attention to that. Then came the pictures inside, the bodies in the bags. The air in the back of the 'Sprey turned blue.

When it came to the last video sequence, Roche showed it to the SEAL lieutenant first and no one said a word. It was jerky and dark and short and even then the creature wasn't there for half the time. But it *was* there, briefly. Just like the special forces officer was there, sliced open to glistening ribs. Like Woods was there, what was left of him.

Rees and Stanton watched it last. Rees watched it over and over. Roche had to gently pull the camera out of his hands.

'It was real then,' Rees said softly. 'In Brixton.'

'It was real.' Roche nodded and fitted a second memory card into the camera, making copies of everything. He did that three more times and then handed the camera and one of the copied cards to the SEAL lieutenant.

'Do with that as you see fit,' Roche told him. 'I don't know whether it's best for you that no one saw a thing or whether you want to report all this exactly as it happened. Your call. As far as the three of us are concerned, you're the LT, we gave up the gathered intel, and that's that.'

The lieutenant nodded. 'I'll need to have a talk about this with my squad,' he said.

'Thought so. We'll talk amongst ourselves a while.' Roche gave one of the spare memory cards to Rees and one to Stanton. 'I'd eat them and shit them out the other side,' he said. 'As soon as we touch down, someone's going to be all over us. I don't know what the fuck's going to happen down there but it won't be pretty.'

For the rest of the trip, Rees and Roche and Stanton kept to themselves, each lost in their own thoughts.

10 July, 1300 hours, Legoland

They were waiting for him when he came off the runway: Leadface, a few faces he didn't recognise and one or two that he did. The spook, whoever he was. The Americans had held him in Sicily for a week and it hadn't been pleasant but in the end they'd had to let him go. He'd had a Military Police escort onto the plane and all the way to RAF Lakenheath where the Americans reluctantly handed him over to a different set of faces in Military Police uniforms for the trip into London. He wasn't sure what sort of escort they were meant to be, whether they were keeping him safe or keeping him from running or keeping him from something else entirely. They were quiet, though. Not a word. And when they got to London and Vauxhall, there wasn't any ceremony about it this time; they simply drove to the front door, marched him in and sat him down in an interrogation room.

'This again?' he asked when he saw the rubber tubes on the table and the tea-towel and the jug of water.

The two guards stood silent on either side of the room. They didn't look at him but they were watching him. The Americans hadn't been kind about his ribs – at least, the second lot of Americans after a US Navy doctor had patched him back together. Seemed a bit pointless but it had been clear five minutes after they'd landed back from Libya that the whole base was in quiet uproar and split in two, the inevitable schism of spooks and soldiers.

Where do we fit into that? Would have been nice to have someone he could ask but all he had was himself and a pair of guards, still and silent as golems. *A bit of both, I suppose.*

Half an hour later, the spook came in. He shooed away the guards, put a plastic cup on the table, poured some water into it and pushed it at Roche. Then he threw a spread of photographs between them. They were grainy and had clearly had a lot of work done on them to enhance the contrast. They were also very

194

clearly his own pictures from Aqar. Pictures of the Scary Clown. The sense of relief knocked him sideways. He had to close his eyes for a moment and take some deep breaths.

'So, did you shoot some Americans to get these or not?'

Roche stiffened. 'Sir, if I'm being questioned about a possible friendly fire incident then I respectfully request to exercise my right to legal counsel.'

'You can respectfully request all you like, you're not getting any.'

'Then I respectfully decline to answer, sir.'

The spook rolled his eyes and leaned back into his chair. 'Christ on a bike, Sergeant!' He stabbed his finger at the photographs. 'I've got ET, someone letting off a nuke in the Libyan desert and a storm of angry Americans who want you shipped off to Guantanamo to be their play-toy. What the fuck happened out there, soldier?'

'This a debrief now, is it sir?'

'The first of many, I expect.'

'Stanton? Rees? They both back okay?'

'Yes. And no, you don't get to talk to them, not until we're done here.' He took a Dictaphone out of his pocket and set it recording between them. Roche stared at it in disbelief.

'Bloody Hell! How old is that?'

'How about you start from the beginning, Sergeant. From before you took off from Sicily. Tell me about the Americans. Both squads.'

'The briefing they gave us on the ground was to observe and record and support as requested. The mission was to be under the command of the US Navy SEALs and we were seconded to them. The SEAL LT would give the orders on the ground. They had four fire teams flying out. We were told that if we found anything strange or unusual or anything that looked like it might be nuclear material, we were to call in a specialist support unit that was flying out in the second 'Sprey.' He paused. 'When we got there—'

'When you got where?'

'Sir, when we landed near Aqar, the mission changed. The second team assumed command of the mission and told us and the SEALs to stay put. That didn't go down too well ...' Roche took a deep breath and described what had happened. The spook only nodded, so presumably he'd heard the same from Rees and Stanton.

'That sort of behaviour unusual, is it?'

'On an op? I've never heard of anything like it.'

'Anything other observations you'd like to make about this "support" group?'

Roche shrugged. 'I think they were on something.'

'Stanton in his debrief said they reminded him of the men from the warehouse in Dagenham.'

'I wasn't there in Dagenham, so I couldn't say. The crew-chief from their 'Sprey said he saw them injecting something. He thought they were on steroids. They looked to me like they were on something, right enough. Couldn't say what.'

'Walk me through what happened next.'

It turned into a long afternoon. The spook didn't say much and hardly asked any questions until right at the end.

'Did the Americans bring the nuke or was it already there?'

Roche had to shake his head. 'I don't know. I assumed it was theirs. It didn't look like anything else I saw in Aqar. But I didn't see it come off the Ospreys either.'

'Describe exactly what it looked like.'

Roche described it as well as he could remember. It had been dark in that cellar and with all manner of other shit ... He had to stop and shiver and hold his head in his hands, flashing back to how Woods died.

The spook asked more questions now, gently leading Roche in and out of the warehouse. Roche declined to answer on a few specifics, such as whether the Americans had put a guard on the doors after they'd taken the place and if so, how had Roche and Woods got inside. The rest he told as straight as he could.

'Why didn't it kill you too?' asked the spook at the end. Roche didn't have much of an answer for that.

'I put down my gun. I didn't pose a threat,' he said.

The spook tapped the photographs on the table. 'I'd have said you posed the biggest threat of all.'

11 July, 1930 hours, Legoland

They took him for a medical and x-rayed and bandaged his ribs. They let him sleep and in the morning they came at him again, this time the spook and Leadface and someone else all together, asking questions about what happened before he and Woods went into Aqar. Then the spook on his own, back over the events in Aqar itself. They seemed pretty hung up on where the nuke had come from, whether the Americans had brought it in or whether it had already been there. Roche sort of saw their point but he couldn't make himself get excited about it. Not after the Scary Clown.

When Charly took him to the mess hall that evening and started asking all the same questions over and over about that bloody suitcase, he almost lost it.

'Does it really fucking matter?' he snapped. 'I saw something walk out of a wall, Charly. Like a fucking ghost. I saw it rip one man open and half disintegrate the next. So does it really fucking matter whose nuke it was?'

Charly leaned in close. 'Easy, tiger. Was that the same something that you saw in Brixton back in January?'

Roche nodded. 'Pretty much the same, yeah.'

'So there was one of these in London six months ago?'

'*One* of these? You mean there could be more?'

'Of course there could be more. Why not? Now answer the question: was one of these in London six months ago?'

Roche nodded.

'Well then, perhaps you can see why a lot of us who happen to live and work in London just now are quite eager to know whether your suitcase bomb belonged to this … this whatever it is and whether there might be more of them. Bombs, I mean.'

Roche hung his head. 'It walked through a wall, Charly.'

'Yes. About that. Obviously the pictures you brought back don't show that part. Could you step me through it, exactly what happened.'

He talked her through it inch by inch yet again, the American officer sliced open, Woods half turned into smoke, the suitcase, how the Scary Clown had looked at him, just once, and then vanished again into the wall. The screams that came after. 'Don't the pictures show him going into the wall again at the end?'

Charly made a clucking sound. 'Sort of. They half show it. Then it just stops.'

'You've got to be *fucking* joking!'

'Easy!' Charly touched a hand to his arm. 'They show enough, Sergeant. There's no one here who doesn't believe you this time.' She patted him lightly. He looked at her closely, seeing her properly for the first time since they'd sat down together. Something had changed. Something had got to her while he'd been away.

'You've seen something,' he said. 'Haven't you?'

She smiled just a little too brightly. 'Was there any kind of smell when it came out of the wall?' she asked.

'Yeah. The room smelled like someone had just let off a flashbang and a frag grenade. Other than that?' It had smelled of iron when the Clown had flensed the American. It had smelled of cooked meat too. That had been Woods. He didn't tell her that part. Some things you just didn't tell to a pretty scientist you'd come to realise you rather fancied. He was about to say something like that which would probably have come out pitifully corny when her

199

phone rang. Whoever was on the other end was seriously pissed off. He frowned. A woman's voice, sharp and swearing and ripe with East End charm. *Linley?*

'Yeah. Yeah. I'll be right there.' Charly flashed another smile as she got up, abandoning her food half-eaten. 'Got to go,' she said. 'Duty calls.' She turned away and then stopped and looked back at him. 'Sergeant Manning, do you mind if I ask a question? Nicholas Burman – why did you go after him?'

'Because I thought that if anyone knew anything, it would be him. Well, maybe you lot, but you lot weren't talking to me back then because apparently I was mentally unstable.'

Charly's smile lingered this time, an effort at an apology. Roche figured that was as much as anyone was ever likely to give him. 'Get anything?' she asked. 'Off Burman, I mean?'

'A name.' Roche sniffed. In the midst of everything else over the last couple of months, he'd actually forgotten. 'Stylianos Evangeli.'

'The people-trafficking organ-legger?' She laughed. 'Isn't he a myth?'

Roche cocked his head. 'You're the spook. Is he?'

The smile faded. 'I'll send you the file,' she said as she left.

13 July, 0800 hours, Legoland

Roche had the file on Evangeli on the table beside him in the mess at breakfast. He'd half hoped to find it all

200

full of juicy secrets and terrible revelations but in the end there was hardly anything. Evangeli worked out of offices in Canary Wharf. He ran an import and export business, mostly dealing with goods from Greece, Cyprus and Egypt. There were a lot of rumours about a dark side to it but no one had ever found any actual evidence. Her Majesty's Revenue and Customs had been over him once or twice, looking for money laundering, and hadn't found anything. He had several domiciles across and outside of London, was clearly wealthy, frequently in and out of the country, had an interest in various nightclubs, casinos, restaurants. A playboy lifestyle. He was also a patron of the London Museum of Docklands and a substantial contributor, which didn't seem to fit the rest of his lifestyle but was hardly a cause to drag him into an anonymous dark room and get out the rags and the bottled water. The fact that the file was only stamped UK Confidential told Roche everything he needed right from the start. The spooks had nothing.

'You know the Americans legalised Bliss while we were gone.' Stanton and Rees sat either side of him. Rees was eating like he was eating for two, making up for lost days in Sicily, but Stanton was just pushing his beans and scrambled egg around in circles.

'I heard,' said Roche.

'They say the government here's going to follow suit. Make it officially recognised like tobacco or alcohol. You'll be able to buy the stuff in Marks and fucking Spencer's.'

'Op cancelled?' Roche asked. He'd heard that Task Force Hotel had been gearing up for another raid. His rib had meant he'd be missing it anyway.

'Yeah.' Stanton switched to pushing his beans around in a figure of eight.

'Stanton ...' started Rees, but Roche nudged him before Rees said anything stupid. Stanton was making a face out of his breakfast now.

'Those Americans basket-cases, the specialist support group ... they really sound like those Russian punks from Dagenham?'

'Nah.' Stanton shook his head. 'What you said about speed and strength sounds similar but the Russians in Dagenham weren't trained. Whoever those boys were in Aqar, sounds like they knew their stuff same as anyone else we play with. That's what scares me.' He pushed his plate away and gave Roche a long look. 'There's not much that makes me scared.' He shook his head. 'If they'd legalised Bliss right at the start, Red Troop would still be here. Got to ask, sometimes, what's it all for?'

Roche didn't have much of an answer for that and he was still half distracted thinking of Evangeli and the coincidence of Canary Wharf; but before he could try and think of something that was more than a dumb platitude, Charly wandered across the mess hall towards him. She looked rough.

'Christ!' snorted Rees. 'You look like you slept in those. All-nighter?'

'Something like that.' Charly's smile seemed a little more fractured to Roche this morning. Worse, even, than yesterday. She tapped him on the shoulder. 'A word, Sergeant?'

Roche followed her to another table. 'Bad night?'

'Like wanking in someone else's toilet and then finding yourself on an internet porn site. That kind of night.' Roche stifled a snort. 'I need to talk to you about Bliss.'

'Bliss?' After Aqar, Bliss seemed like it hardly mattered any more.

Charly nodded at the file on Evangeli. 'And that. Look, I don't talk about what I do and neither do you. But in the last six months I know you've seen some really fucked-up weird shit and frankly so have I. Particularly recently. I can't tell you what.'

Roche nodded. 'We're briefed. Need to know. That's the way it is.'

'What you've seen … That's just the start of the crap …' Charly stopped as a harried-looking secretary hurried past juggling three cups of coffee. 'I know. I've seen some fucked-up shit as well.'

'You have, have you?'

'Yes, Roche, I have. I shouldn't but I have. Look, it's this simple. The shit you're after, the shit you've seen, the shit I'm after and the shit I've seen, there's one thing in the middle of it. Bliss.'

'And no one has a clue where it comes from or even what it fucking is. Really?' Roche shook his head.

'I might have some ideas. But there's nothing concrete.' Charly made a clucking sound. 'It *is* exceptionally strange. Actually I was wondering if you might be interested in helping out a little on that score. Do you remember the DI who arrested you when you went after Nicholas Burman? Samantha Linley? I'm putting together a bit of an off-the-books operation. She's helping, so ...'

Roche rocked back in his chair. 'Oh, I so don't want to hear about this, I really don't.' He took a sip of coffee and made a face. 'Christ, this is shit.'

Charly put a hand over his. 'We're all on the same team, Roche. I'm trying to find where the Bliss is coming from. So are you. I did some digging about Stylianos. I've got some intel.'

'So what do you want?' Roche leaned slowly forward again, resting his elbows on the table. Stylianos Evangeli. Brixton. She was dangling the sweet scent of a few answers in front of him. Playing him with them.

'Let me take you out. Charing Cross Arches. Twelve o'clock. Maybe grab some lunch in Starbucks. Come and meet DI Linley again. And Noel.'

'Burman?' Roche took a deep breath. 'That should be interesting.'

'Won't it just?' Charly flashed a smile. She rested a hand on Roche's shoulder as she left.

13 July, 1200 hours, Europa

The *Exponential* had, it decided, quite simply had enough. It had spent weeks calibrating the Europa tau-burst detector. Months. More time than on any instrument in recent history and it still wasn't working properly. Yes, it could pick up a drone in the Kuiper belt popping off a miniscule tau-burst every few minutes and yes, it could triangulate using the baseline of the moon's orbit and get something approaching a decent bearing on cosmological events billions of light years away, but it still wasn't giving the right answers.

Unless someone had slipped around the back and invented some new physics while the frigate had been looking the other way then a star of a certain size put out a certain volume of neutrinos. So did a gas giant. So did almost everything that wasn't inert. The *Exponential* had factored all of those into its calculations. The answer kept being the same: there were too many tau-neutrinos in this system.

'The remaining Shriven are congregating,' the Fermat construct informed them idly. There were six of them left, according to the Naypyidaw Shriven. The *Irrational Prime* was already drifting steadily in-system towards the orbit of Mars. The anti-matter harvesting was done and the freighter was now towing a comet of the stuff behind it, about a thousand cubic kilometres of frozen metallic anti-hydrogen, enough to shatter a planet or just possibly detonate the largest gas giant in the system. It wasn't sure about that. The *Irrational Prime* wanted to launch the comet and let physics take its course but the *Exponential* and the hybrid had overruled it.

'There's something in this system beyond what we've seen,' the frigate complained. Fermat, meanwhile, wanted to wait until the Shriven showed themselves. It wanted the drones and the anti-matter held back in case the last few of them made a run for it. None of them quite knew what to expect if that happened but they wouldn't get very far. Unless someone had hidden a singularity in the system, the Shriven would be left to escape by the same means the *Irrational Prime* had arrived – the long slow hard way ...

Unless someone had hidden a singularity ...

A singularity could be a source of tau neutrinos. But on this scale, it hardly seemed possible. This was more like someone had parked a fairly large white dwarf star in the inner system and then somehow made it invisible in every other way ...

Abruptly, the *Exponential* wondered if it had answered its own question. What if there *was* something in the system beyond what they'd seen. What if they *were* seeing it?

The frigate decided to look at its calibration problem from the other end. It hadn't found anything wrong with the way its drones had built the detector. Now it changed its assumptions. Assume the detector is working perfectly well and there's nothing wrong with the calibration. Assume there never was. In that case it had nearly a month of data on some object that neither the *Irrational Prime* nor the hybrid construct had been able to detect in any other way.

The question became: what was it?

13 July, 1200 hours, Charing Cross Arches

Roche recognised Burman and Linley at once. Roche had only ever seen DI Linley pointing a gun at him or shouting at him across an interrogation table. She looked as pissed off today as she had then. Burman looked different, though. Burman looked haunted.

Roche waved them over, leaning against the arches. 'I'm not supposed to be out,' he said.

'Out of where?' Linley folded her arms and gave him a hard pinched look.

'Can't say.' Roche glanced at Burman. 'Surprised I haven't seen more of you around Vauxhall though.'

'He means he's working for the spooks these days,' said Linley.

'Sixteenth Air Assault Brigade, me. Anything else, I have no idea what you're talking about.' Roche wrinkled his nose. 'Saw an old friend of yours, Burden. Sergeant Stanton.'

'It's Burman, and how's he doing?'

'Still got all his bits.' Roche looked from Burman to Linley and back again. 'So what's all this about? I could tell you a thing or two but not with this civvy here.' Roche enjoyed the look that got him from Linley. Payback for taking him in.

'You remember my brother, Manning? The one you waterboarded?'

'You mean the one who deals coke and dope?'

'That's enough,' Charly stepped between them. 'We need to engage in a little bit of information gathering. Now, unless you want to strip down, oil yourselves and beat your chests for Sam and I, let's try something a little more civilised like a conversation and cup of coffee.'

'Sure,' Roche said. He turned away and they walked out from the arches and in among the tourists milling about on Embankment. Roche aimed for a designer patisserie but Linley cut him off.

'Not there. Not if you want to talk.' She led them through Embankment station instead, up over the Charing Cross footbridge to the South Bank and into the huge open space of the South Bank Centre. In the afternoon it was almost empty, a space the size of an assembly hall and they almost had it to themselves. A scattering of people sat with their laptops at a handful of tables while a solitary waitress stood behind the bar drying glasses.

Linley marched up to the bar. 'Four coffees, love.'

'So what's this about then, Charly?' Roche asked. 'You been running two ops?'

'Compartmentalised, darling, need to know, Big Boys' rules and all that. You're a big boy now, aren't you?'

Roche looked at her hard. Something was off. Something had been off since the morning. She was brittle today. His gut said he ought to walk away. Even talking out here in the open was begging to have the Official Secrets Act thrown at him, at all of them. Curiosity, though. Always the enemy of keeping secrets.

'I cry like a baby when the intelligence I need isn't available because of secrecy for secrecy's sake,' he said. From the corner of his eye he caught Burman nodding.

'Which is why we're all here,' Charly said. Sam came back and put the drinks down.

'Even though he's compromised and she's a civvy?'

'Wind your neck in, mate,' Burman said. Roche turned to look at him. Noel held his eye.

Sam sighed. She shook her head at Charly. 'You know this whole bullshit testosterone display is for you, don't you?'

'Shall we go and come back?' Charly asked. 'Pop up to Regent's Street, do a spot of shopping?'

'Not on my salary. I'll stay and watch, thanks.'

Charly said something more. Roche tuned out for a moment, distracted by what were possibly the best legs he'd ever seen coming into the centre; but a moment later, Noel brought him back.

'A name keeps on turning up,' Noel said. 'Stylianos Evangeli.' The name had Roche's attention at once. 'We've got intelligence ...'

'Highly suspect intelligence,' Linley added sourly.

'We know where he's going to be in five and a half hours.'

Roche nodded. 'I'm in,' he said.

Charly smiled at them all. 'Oh, wonderful. Now we don't have a great deal of time to plan this but I've already set a few wheels running. I'm going to leave operational planning up to the boys with the boots on the ground.'

'We need to get Stanton in on this as quickly as possible,' Burman said. Roche nodded. Rees as well, if he could be persuaded.

'The lovely Samantha will have a large contingent of the Met's finest waiting nearby,' Charly went on. 'She has resurrected a Kingship operation that never happened. I'll be based with them.'

'Now, they're going to know that there's special forces on the ground but that's not an excuse to turn Docklands into Saturday night in Basra, understand me?' Linley turned to Charly. Her face was set hard. 'That's it for me, I'm burned after this. Falsified orders, I'll be lucky if I don't end up in the Scrubs with people I've put there.'

'I know, I'm sorry,' Charlotte said

Sam shook her head. 'Fuck it, they've sold us out on this whole Bliss thing. I tried so hard to play it straight, didn't want to be like my old man. Now look at me.'

'It's for the greater good,' Charly said.

Linley shook her head. 'That's what people always say before they do something monstrous. That's how we justify all the bad shit that we do. We set ourselves up as the moral superiors of the people that we're doing this to and then commit acts that frankly aren't dissimilar. Then we give them nice euphemisms to make it okay. Rendition, Big Boys' rules, collateral damage.' The words were for all of them but her eyes never left Charly.

'You finished lecturing us?' Roche asked.

'Oh well, fuck it, it's all breaking down now. I've been pushing to hit known Bliss dealers. You'd think that them waving around automatic weapons in the streets of London would be enough, wouldn't you? But no, every single fucking anti-Bliss operation I've ever heard of suddenly got pulled in the last two days and I happen to know that the Home Secretary met with the Chief Commissioner of Police the day before. So it's not so difficult to join the fucking dots. Now you can call me naive if you want but you didn't grow up where I did.

210

There's the wrong way and the right way. The moment you compromise, the corruption starts creeping in. So you run your covert ops, put more guns on the streets of London, kidnap people, torture them in fucking Surrey of all places, and I'll help but you're all very far gone if you think that this is the way things should be.'

'I'll take a little corruption,' Roche said. Aliens disintegrating people. Suitcase nukes in Libya. Humans living inside bags, being harvested for their … fuck, he hadn't the first idea what. Fluids. 'For this, I'll do what's necessary,' he said softly.

'Yeah, that's where it all starts, isn't it?' Linley said.

Roche looked around the hall. People with their laptops, tapping away. The woman who'd caught his eye earlier. People with their newspapers. Their phones. Just doing whatever they were doing. Six months ago, Stylianos Evangeli was supposed to deal in organs. Which left Roche thinking of the people in the warehouse in Aqar, zipped up in their plastic bags. Presumably they'd been doing pretty ordinary things too, right up until someone stuffed them in shrink-wrap.

He shook his head. The others were getting up.

'Where?' he asked Charly as Burman and Linley left.

'Westferry Circus. Five o'clock.'

And that was that. Line crossed. Easy as anything.

13 July, 1700 hours, Canary Wharf, London

'Canary Wharf. You been to Docklands recently?' asked Rees. 'They done it up nice. Of course you have to shit gold to afford to live there.' They met up at Westferry Circus. Stanton and Rees came with Burman and all three were carrying big black holdalls. Roche didn't ask how Burman had got his hands on the hardware; or maybe Stanton and Rees had taken it out of Legoland. Maybe the spooks there were quietly okay with this.

'Charly's intel has the meet going down in the Docklands Museum after hours,' said Stanton. 'We need eyes on targets and recon of what's going on inside. Roche and his crew will be in the museum. Noel and I will handle security, front and back exits. Noel, we're tight on shooters. Do you want front or back?'

'Front.' Burman looked edgy. Stanton nodded.

'There's a multi-storey car park round the back on Hertsmere Road that gives excellent overwatch on the fire exits. That's mine then. We need a firm count on how many targets go in and come out, faces, pictures, if they're armed. Roche, you and Rees have the sharp end. You got everything you need?'

Roche nodded.

'I'll take you in,' said Burman. 'We've got a friendly on the inside who can give you a tour.'

'And where are you going to be?'

'On one of the boats in the dock, I reckon.'

'Yeah. Would have been my choice. Who else we got?'

'Oh, a hundred or so of the Met's finest lurking nearby.' Burman grinned. 'You relay the intel, Sam calls them in, we take them down red-handed. Cool with that?'

Roche almost smiled back. Almost.

13 July, 1730 hours, Canary Wharf, London

The Museum of London Docklands had once been a warehouse, back about two hundred years ago when the whole of Docklands had been about shipping and not about the towering glass and steel offices and flats that now dominated the Isle of Dogs and the neighbouring Limehouse Basin. The front entrance led into a wide spacious atrium that flowed smoothly into a café and then the fire doors at the back while the museum proper spread out in wings to either side. The right side was laid out as some sort of kids' activity centre while the left side opened into an exhibition area. An open stairwell in the atrium led to the upper floors on either side. Roche didn't bother with those. The meet would go down in the central area, maybe in the café, in an open space where everyone could see everyone else and everyone had plenty of places they could run if it came to it. Rees had brought a decent set of kit out of Legoland – not the firepower Burman had in his black bags but a good collection of tiny cameras and microphones. After the museum closed and the last members of the public drifted away, he and Rees set up a network and found themselves places to hide. Roche settled in the exhibition centre. They had a couple of tiny cinemas there, one running a short film about the wildlife of the Thames estuary and another running a slideshow about some old Second World War anti-aircraft forts that had been built out in the estuary and looked a bit like AT-ATs.

Roche settled under one of the benches there in the dark and waited. Five minutes later, Rees checked in from somewhere upstairs.

The last of the museum staff left and locked up behind them around seven. Around nine the doors opened again and three men came in. They were pushing a heavy wheeled crate between them. Roche started panning cameras where he could, zooming in, trying to get a clear image of each face. There were no lights on in the museum, but the sun hadn't quite set and a little twilight still crept in through the windows.

'Indigo one, you getting this?' Roche whispered.

'Check, Indigo two.' Burman.

'Familiar faces?'

'Not to me.'

The men wheeled their crate into the café. Two of them started work opening it up while the third went behind the counter and began setting two of the tables.

'What the hell are they doing?' Stanton. Roche didn't answer. He tried to zoom in on the crate. It was open now and the two men were pulling things out from inside it: oddly formed pieces of black plastic which they laid out on one of the tables. From each corner of the crate they unfolded a telescopic arm of some sort. Next, they unlatched the sides of the crate and collapsed them so they lay flat. They moved the telescopic arms and finished extending them. The arms were curved, like the pincers of some insect, all of them arcing away from the centre of the crate and then curving back in again, ending in sharp points that almost touched over the middle of the crate. It looked a little like the skeletal outline of an onion.

'Indigo Two. Anyone know what that is?' murmured Roche.

One of the men by the crate took out a ruggedised laptop and unwound a cable. He plugged the laptop into the crate and turned it on. The museum trembled. Even the men in the café paused.

'Did you get that?' Roche asked. 'I felt the floor quiver.'

'Same,' murmured Rees.

'Nothing here.' Stanton again.

'There a tube line that runs under here?'

'Docklands Light isn't far but it's overground. I've got eyes and there's nothing come past.'

'It happened exactly when they plugged that thing in,' said Rees.

'Could be coincidence.' Roche didn't believe it though.

The men beside the collapsed crate were spooling another cable away from it. They plugged in a second box, bigger than the first, and this time Roche felt the air itself jump and tense as though there was suddenly a massive charge. Like the moment before a thunderstorm.

'Anyone else feel that?'

'Something,' agreed Rees. 'Indigo one, if Charly's out there, do me a favour and ask her what the fuck that box is.'

'Mind your chatter, Indigo four.' Stanton again.

The third man was still setting places at the tables.

215

Knives and forks, plates, serviettes, glasses, a jug of water …

Whatever they were doing with the crate, they seemed to have finished. One of the men tapped his ear.

'We're set,' he murmured. Roche had to strain his ears to hear.

'Indigo one to all Indigo call signs, be aware we have two victors carrying seven possible x-rays pulling up outside. If they're armed then I can't see it,' said Burman a moment later. Roche shifted one of his cameras to zoom in on the main doors.

'See if you can get faces this time.' Rees.

A minute passed and then another. The man setting the tables finished. The other two were standing beside the crate. The air felt ready to burst with lightning.

The door opened and seven men came in. Six goons in a posse around their boss. Like the men who came with the crate, they were all on the swarthy end of Caucasian: Turkish or Greek or something like that. Israeli?

'Indigo one. The one in the middle. That's Evangeli.'

Cyprus, then. Roche checked the time. Nine fifty. Later than he'd thought.

Evangeli's men fanned out through the café. Roche studied each one, trying to see if they were armed. They weren't being careful in here, out of sight or so they thought. 'I'm seeing handguns on most of the targets,' he whispered. 'Nothing bigger.'

'MP7s?' That was Burman and Roche knew he was thinking back to Dagenham.

'Handguns only. I repeat, handguns only. Evangeli's on the phone now.' The organ smuggler was pacing back and forth between his men. He was talking fast and loud and Roche was picking most of it up. Unfortunately Evangeli was also talking in either Greek or Turkish.

'Anyone get any of that?' asked Stanton. There was a long pause, then: 'Indigo three to all Indigo call signs, I have four incoming victors on the Hertsmere Road … They've stopped outside the back door … Twenty, twenty-five … no, thirty possible x-rays, I see body armour, SMGs … Indigo two, you may want to consider getting ready to Foxtrot Oscar. Indigo one, these guys look similar to the Dagenham crew.'

Roche heard a banging on the fire escape doors at the back of the café. The goons inside were moving. Several of them had their pistols drawn. They all had their backs to the front entrance and the entrance to the exhibition hall. If he packed up and ran, they just might not see him …

Two of the Cypriots started to unlock the back door. It exploded open as two massive men in body armour smashed through. They almost threw the two Cypriots up into the air and didn't slow down. Behind them, more men poured in, MP7s shouldered and ready. One of the Cypriots got off a shot – all Roche saw was the muzzle flash – and took a three-round burst to the face that didn't so much kill him as explode his head. Roche frowned. That wasn't right. The sound of the shots was off. Odd. Not something he'd heard before. They sounded a bit like a man screaming.

'Anyone else see that?' asked Roche.

The other soldiers were simply throwing the Cypriots aside, picking them up, smashing them into tables, throwing them across the room, the sort of cartoon violence that wasn't supposed to happen in the real world. Most of the noise came from the Cypriots. Screams, shouts, curses, the snap of bones breaking. And then it was over – a handful of seconds and the sheer speed and violence of the assault had taken down everyone in the café with only one hostile shot fired by the Cypriots and one man down. The only Cypriot still standing was Evangeli. They'd left him alone. He seemed oddly unperturbed.

'You see that, Indigo?' Roche asked again. For a moment he'd been impressed. Quick and brutal and effective. Nine armed men taken down and subdued, just like that. 'That seem off to you, Indigo three?' The soldiers had been fast and strong; but the more he thought about it, the more Roche realised he hadn't seen their training. They'd burst in full of noise and fury. They'd taken down their targets with sheer speed and force but not with any skill.

'No flashbang,' muttered Rees.

The soldiers were dragging the mangled Cypriots into a group over in the atrium by the entrance doors, effectively cutting off Roche's escape. They were systematically disarming them while several others crowded around Evangeli, forcing him down into a chair.

No flashbang. That was a simple rule. You went into an unknown room with armed hostiles somewhere inside, you went in behind a flashbang.

218

'This isn't an op,' muttered Rees. 'Look at the weapons.'

'Indigo three?' Rees was right. The guns were Heckler & Koch MP7A1 4.6 millimetre personal defence weapons. Only they sounded completely wrong. Judging by the dead Cypriot with no head, they were packing the punch of a .50 calibre.

'I see them.' Stanton's voice was icy.

They weren't soldiers, then. He'd got that wrong. At least, not soldiers who deserved the name. Russian Organizatsiya. Mafia. They were shoving Evangeli over to the crate now. Roche couldn't hear what they were saying. Evangeli looked more annoyed than scared, while the Russians still looked eager, like they were gearing up for a fight even though they'd just had one. It was over, wasn't it? But from the way everyone acted, it hadn't even started.

'Indigo one, this is Indigo three. Dagenham, Indigo one. It's like Dagenham again. Same shit. Keep quiet and let Indigo two get his intel. Indigo one, confirm?'

Evangeli was getting heated with one of the gunman. They shoved him hard enough to sprawl him across the floor beside the crate. Roche didn't see what he did down there, but before he even started to get up the air changed again, more static, so much that Roche felt the hairs on the backs of his arms prickling.

'Indigo one, respond?'

The crate lit up. Sparks crackled along the four curved arms and a brilliant light bloomed between them, light-ning-white and burning steadily.

13 July, 2203 hours, Europa

'Tau-burst!' The *Exponential* had been in the middle of working out the exact mathematics of what the detector's skewed calibration was telling it when the burst came through. It paused to pinpoint the source. Two sources, as it turned out. A cross-dimensional wormhole.

The Fermat construct accepted the co-ordinates and passed them on to its three remaining clones. They began to converge on London.

13 July, 2203 hours, Canary Wharf, London

The Russians were up and covering the crate at once. Roche thought he saw the glimpse of a shape and then all hell broke loose. Half the Organizatsiya opened fire, shooting into the light in sustained bursts. He saw at least three of them toss grenades into the disassembled crate. He winced, counting down, waiting for the explosion to shred everyone in the room but it didn't come. Instead there was a blast of *something* out of the crate that threw one of the gunman several feet through the air and caught a second man, spinning him round, his arm almost wrenched off.

A shape came out of the light. It staggered, sprayed by automatic weapons-fire, then slumped. It wasn't human. It was too tall, too skinny, its arms too long for its body, its elongated face split wide open by the rictus grin Roche had seen again in Aqar only a few days ago. It was wearing the same long frock coat. It stumbled out of the light in the crate, walked into the hail of bullets and died.

'Shit ...' hissed Rees.

'Did you see ...' Roche didn't need to ask.

'Is that what you saw in Brixton?'

Roche didn't answer either. No need. The Russians had forgotten about Evangeli. He was over by one of the smashed tables and he was holding something now. One of the black plastic things. He scrambled to his feet and pointed it at the cluster of Organizatsiya men as the Scary Clown toppled. They were all staring in awe at the dead alien.

'Stop!' The gunmen in the atrium had seen him. One swivelled round, bringing his carbine to bear. Evangeli pointed the plastic thing at the soldier. Arcs of yellow-orange light twisted out of Evangeli's hand; they looped and flailed through each other as they whipped across the room. Where they touched the Russian, he simply fell apart. It was like watching someone be sliced up by a cheesewire. Blood spurted briefly and then he collapsed into diced chunks of meat and severed bone. The other gunmen opened fire on Evangeli and blew his face off. One of them didn't take his finger off the trigger until he ran out of ammunition. He stared at the ruined corpse, trying to reload. He was struggling. His partner couldn't stop looking at the pieces of his dead friend; and then four of the Cypriots threw themselves at the two Russians. Another ran to Evangeli, pulling at the black plastic thing that he'd been holding. The last two bolted for the door.

'Two coming out your side, Indigo one. Advise you wait for them to put some distance behind them and then take them. You getting all of this?'

No answer. He couldn't tell if the comms were even working any more.

The Russians at the crate were moving on the body of the Scary Clown, edging closer. There was a scream – a storm of light burst out of the crate and wrapped itself around one of them. The light seemed to swirl around him for a second. When it faded, all that was left of him was a cloud of greasy black smoke, the blackened stumps of his legs just below the knees and a few charred fingers.

Roche stared in disbelief. *Woods*. A Cypriot in the atrium pulled a gun and shot a Russian in the chest, all nine rounds, staggering him back with each one and yet he didn't go down. When the last shot fired, the Russian roared in fury and ran. The Cypriot tried to get away but watching the Organizatsiya man was like watching a leopard take down a gazelle. He threw himself ten feet through the air and caught the Cypriot round the shoulders, slamming them both into the ground. The Russian was up again straight away, screaming in fury. He grabbed the Cypriot by the nearest part of him that came to hand – his foot – and swung him through the air as though he was a rag doll, smashing his head into the open stairs, swinging him overhead and slamming him into the ground and then throwing the limp corpse into the other Cypriots grappling with his comrade. Then, only then, did he seem to notice that he'd been shot and start to slow down. The Cypriot who'd gone for Evangeli had the black ray-gun thing now. He fired it. The arcs of energy cut the Russian into pieces; a moment later, the Cypriot fell under a spray of bullets from the men around the crate.

Under his bench in the room next door, Roche struggled to keep up with it all through the chaos of shouting and motion. Something came out of the light in the crate, a shape he could barely make out except that it wasn't quite human. The Russians opened fire again, shooting in panic at something that somehow wasn't quite there. Bullets sprayed everywhere and several of them were caught in the crossfire. They were screaming at each other. Roche recognised a few words but you didn't need to speak Russian to understand what they were saying. *Kill it, kill it!* Whatever *it* was.

For a moment, caught by the light, Roche saw the outline of a Scary Clown. It was barely there, translucent at best, and yet he saw its clawed hand reach out and slice a man diagonally from collar bone to ribs. There was an explosion of blood and then the Russian fell apart, cut right through to the spine.

'Indigo one? Indigo three?' No answer from either of them.

The Russians were running now. Most of them ran for the back. A third Clown came out of the light from the crate. It aimed a tube like the one Roche had seen in Aqar. He didn't hear it fire over the shouts but one of the Organizatsiya thugs simply disintegrated. The others scattered, terrified.

In the atrium, the Cypriots had all fled. A last Russian was still there, too damn crazy to be scared. A fourth creature came out of the light. The Russian picked up the gun that the Cypriot had used. Curling streamers of light twisted out of it. They struck the Clown and wrapped themselves around it. It seemed to struggle and then threw aside the arcs of light as though they were physical things. It turned and pointed its tube at the Russian. The Russian dived out of the way. A large hole appeared in the wall behind where he'd been standing.

'Indigo two, this is Indigo three. I have more targets coming your way.' Almost all of the Russians were running now. The ones who could make it out of the fire escape had already gone; the rest were scattering, bolting for the main door. One of the aliens had gone outside the back. The other two had half-vanished, walking through walls as though they weren't there. They were like ghosts. As best Roche could tell they were heading out the front now.

'Indigo one, multiple targets heading your way. Heavily armed targets juiced on steroids or something being pursued by …' By what? By what, exactly? 'By a pair of I don't know. By fucking aliens. Do not engage, I repeat, do not engage.'

No answer.

The museum was suddenly almost empty. He couldn't see anyone in the atrium or the café any more but that didn't mean much when the Scary Clowns could simply walk through walls. How did anything walk through fucking walls, for Christ's sake?

'All Indigo call-signs, this is Indigo four. Someone just picked up a Mercedes Sprinter and threw it at something that looks like a bad Halloween costume.'

Rees? 'Where the fuck are you, Indigo four?'

Couldn't be sure there weren't any Russians still here either. Bliss soldiers. Whoever they were.

'Upper level window. Opposite where Indigo three was supposed to be.'

'And where the fuck is Stanton?'

'Right where he's supposed to be, Indigo two. Okay, and now Bad Halloween Costume Guy just walked through a hail of bullets and ... holy fucking shit! Indigo two—'

Roche had been about to close the laptop and take his chances slipping out of the exhibition room when the back doors exploded and a Scary Clown came flying back into the museum. It was like an overblown piece of wire-work from a wushu movie – he didn't just stagger back through the doors, he was hurled about fifty feet through the air, straight through what was left of the café and into the open stairs, cracking the banisters. The Clown crashed to the floor but it landed on its feet and threw something back at the door. Roche had time to catch a glimpse of a shape there – a human shape – and then everything in the back half of the museum exploded. He felt the shock through the floor, felt the whole building shiver. All the cameras whited out and died.

'Indigo two. If any of you are still listening out there, I lost eyes. I'm looking for a way out.'

'Indigo four. I can't recommend the back, Indigo two, not at the …' There was the sound of something metallic smashing into something else and a lot of shattering glass. 'Just don't come out this—' A hideous screeching sound ripped through Roche's earpiece, painfully deafening until Roche ripped it away. The building shook again from another explosion in the café. Roche shut the laptop and slipped it back into the pouch over his back. He picked up the suppressed C8 Burman had found from somewhere and rolled carefully out from under the bench in the tiny exhibition screening room. Not that there was much need to be quiet.

The building shook again. Roche crept out into the corridor. There was hardly any light in here, no windows, only what filtered in from the atrium and they were well past sunset now.

He sensed more than saw the Bliss soldier hiding in the exhibit beside him. It wasn't that he moved and Roche couldn't be sure he'd heard anything over the destruction of the atrium. But he felt the air change, or maybe it was the smell. He lunged forward as the Bliss soldier launched himself and Roche felt the knife whisper past the back of his neck, so close it might have cut a hair or two. He spun around in the air as he moved and fired the C8 into where the man ought to be. The muzzle flash lit up the room, garish photographs of the Thames estuary scattered all around the walls and a single diving figure rolling away.

Dagenham. Aqar. Now here. He needed a head-shot and he couldn't see shit.

'Indigo two coming out the front, fast.' He dropped a frag grenade behind him and raced out into the atrium.

What was left of it.

13 July, 2207 hours, Canary Wharf

The first hybrid construct clone to reach Canary Wharf north dock phased through the subterranean foundation structures and emerged into the water of the dock itself. It took a moment to assimilate the data available from the surrounding infosphere. Paramilitary units were scattered all around the north dock, some of them engaged in exchanges of small-arms fire, others simply hiding out of the way, observing or in flight. At least four Shriven were present. Their previous efforts at concealment had fallen aside in the last few minutes.

They were fighting for their lives. That was … unexpected. And something had already terminated one of them. The clone was reasonably sure there had been six altogether at the start. That wasn't right. The technological base simply didn't exist for the native sentients to offer any kind of threat to a Shriven, even ones armed only with diaspora technology.

The clone rose out of the water and hovered in the air, half in-phase with the ordinary matter of the world around it, half not.

An explosion wrecked the frontage of the brick building in front of it. The clone's particle detectors registered a spray of unexpected muons and a tiny gamma-flash; then a Shriven burst out through the wreckage. It tumbled across the docks, still rising, and into the tower block across the water. It was functional enough to have the presence of thought to phase out as it struck the building and flew on through it as though the tower block was vapour. Its phasing wasn't perfect. It left behind it a mosaic of tiny cracks in everything it touched.

The clone carefully adjusted its own phase, making itself as good as invisible to the local sentients, swivelled and flew after the Shriven; but as it did, a second figure emerged from the plasma wreckage. Amid the litter of broken stones and tiles, a human form raised its arm towards the clone and the arm wasn't a human arm but a quasi-organic nano-grown plasma cannon. Fiercely flickering balls of metallic light spun around the weapon.

Also unexpected, since the clone had considered itself to be invisible. It fired a fine spray of anti-protons at the human. Fierce tiny flashes of nuclear annihilation detonated in the air around it, vaporising a thin layer of stone immediately under the human and liquefying the earth beneath its feet. The human vanished in a cloud of hard radiation and exotic short-lived particles. The clone turned its attention back to the Shriven, hunting for the muon tell of another phase shift.

The blast from the plasma cannon caught the clone squarely in the back of the head, apparently far less of the human having been converted into high-energy photons than the clone had anticipated. The human, who should have disintegrated, was now surrounded by the glitter of a coherent energy field. The plasma shock confused the clone momentarily. It phased as a second discharge shattered the air and narrowly missed taking off the top corner of a tower block. The heat blast of over-shocked air passed through the clone and smacked into the water below. It watched the shockwave speed across, a rippling ring of white.

'What are you?' it asked, excreting the question as a sequence of exotic particles while at the same time phasing back to fire a sustained spray of coherent mesons at the energy shield.

It didn't see the thing that came down from above it which sheared it clean in two despite its phase state and simultaneously infected it with a corrosive nanite set that overwhelmed its own regenerative capacity.

'Never mind that, what are *you*?' asked the thing. It ripped the clone to pieces until it was shredding atoms and spraying mists of naked coloured quarks. 'What are you?' it asked, over and over. 'What are you?'

13 July, 2207 hours, Thames Estuary

'What was that?' asked the Fermat construct. It adjusted the modulation and intelligent adaptation of its own coherent energy shield and began dispatching microscopic drones. 'Can any of you answer me? Because that shouldn't have been possible.'

13 July, 2207 hours, Europa

The *Exponential* checked through the mathematics a second time but there wasn't any room for doubt in the Europa detector results. Not if you assumed it was working.

'We're not alone out here,' it told the others.

The *Irrational Prime* came to have a look. The Fermat construct and its various clones were a touch busy but the construct assigned enough of its attention to at least get the gist of what the *Exponential* was saying.

Which wasn't particularly much. Just that there was another spaceship in the system and that it was invisible and that it had been here with them all along, right from the start, and that, if its neutrino signature was anything to go by, it was really quite big.

15 – The Crossfire

13 July, 2207 hours, Canary Wharf

Rees was saying don't go out the back. On the other hand, there were a couple of problems with going out the front. The first problem was the Scary Clown that had picked itself up after being thrown back in through the fire exit. The second problem was the Organizatsiya man who'd come racing in through what was left of the doors behind it, jumped through the air like he was Spring-heeled fucking Jack and landed in the atrium. Right now, right where Roche wanted to go, the Shriven was trying to kill the Russian with those claws it had. The Russian was surrounded by some sort of glittering translucent bubble and had one arm fitted into a lividly luminous sleeve that looked vaguely like an organic version of a rocket launcher for anti-tank missiles. Balls of vivid green light spun in patterns around and up and down that arm. The Clown's claws sliced into the glittering bubble but never very far, while the soldier kept trying to kick and punch and push the Clown away to bring its glowing arm to bear.

Despite what he was seeing, Roche stopped for a moment and stared. That was no Russian. Fuck! *Shaw? Lewis Shaw?*

Yeah, and he'd just dropped a frag grenade behind him. Snap decision. He needed another exit. He ran three paces and threw himself forward before the pressure wave from the grenade detonating back in the exhibition room knocked him flat. He rolled and fell among the smashed remnants of the café tables and chairs, kept rolling, letting his momentum take him on and back to his feet and half ran, half stumbled into some dark part of the museum on the other side. The interactive children's zone. When he looked back, half the front of the museum was missing and the soldier in glittering light was heading through the ruin of the museum entrance and outside.

He ought to run; but again, Roche couldn't help but watch. He had a good clear view now as the soldier raised his arm. It *was* Shaw. Lewis Shaw. They'd had pints together back in the Bell in Tillington.

'Fuck. Me!'

A claw-fingered shape emerged from the floor. Shaw spun around and a torrent of blinding white fire spewed across the open space of the museum. It hit the Scary Clown square on and hurled it clean across the museum, into the back wall and straight through. Roche's eyes grew wider. The brickwork of the wall was still there. The alien had gone through a solid wall as though it was made of mist. He'd seen it before, in Brixton and Aqar, but that didn't make it any better. *How? How is that possible?*

He had barely a moment to take it in. Shaw, silhouetted in the entrance, erupted in a fury of light that seemed to wrap itself around him, bright as a nuclear flash. Roche turned and stumbled away. Outside wasn't looking good either way. Somewhere round here were some other stairs. He found them and bolted up, away from the shredded atrium and glad to have good solid brick around him again. Up top, he ran for the nearest window and skidded to a stop. Outside the back of the museum Hertsmere Road squeezed between the old warehouse brickwork and the dirty white concrete cliff of the multi-storey car park and cinema complex where Stanton was on overwatch. There were great gouges in the concrete around the second floor. A mangled black Sprinter van lay on its side up against the wall. It looked as though it had been thrown at the car park. Two more vans, riddled with bullet holes, were parked close to the museum's rear fire exit. Several of the Russians had taken cover behind them and were firing up at the multi-storey. The car park had chunks bitten out of it all over. Roche could see sections of crumbling masonry and exposed metal supports. He raised his carbine to fire on the men around the van and then stopped as he saw what they were looking at.

There were sirens in the distance.

'Position, Indigo two?'

'Heading your …' He had to stop. A flat staccato hammering filled the air. From up in the car park, Stanton had opened up with a minimi para, a cut-down carbine version of the squad automatic weapon used by the regular army. The men around the other vans started yelling and screaming and firing back. Roche fired two bursts, headshots, taking one Russian with each and then ducked well out of the way as they turned to fire on him as well. A good solid brick wall was supposed to make a decent piece of cover but the next thing he knew, pieces of it were exploding in his face. He scrambled further away. Whatever rounds those MP7s were firing, they were chewing the masonry to pieces. What he needed was …

'Am I going stupid or was that Lewis Shaw?' Rees again. The chatter of Stanton's SAW fell silent. The screaming howls of the high-velocity MP7s faltered. Roche snarled something and peered back again.

'Fucking Legoland,' he growled. 'You're not going stupid. It's a fucking op.' A black one, black as pitch. Shaw had entirely vanished six months ago, him and Martin Collins, so what else could it be? But then … but then what the *fuck* was Charly playing at? Or didn't she know … ?

Changed things, though. He ran back down the stairs. For a moment the museum was quiet, the ruined café and atrium empty except for rubble and the remains of the fight. Evangeli's crate was still there, its telescopic arms bent and mangled. Roche ignored it. He ran to the atrium. Shaw was gone. There was another man standing out there on the wharf, though. Someone different. Something about him felt off. He wasn't armed.

'Indigo one, respond?' No answer. He had no way to know what had happened to Burman and Linley and Charly out there but he'd heard a lot of shooting and a good few explosions and the pop of 40mm grenades. Grenades on an op in Docklands, for fuck's sake. 'Indigo three, have you had any contact from Indigo one?'

'Negative, Indigo two.'

Half the front of the museum was missing. Outside around the north dock he could hear more sustained gunfire and more explosions. There were flashes of light, muzzle flashes and ... longer flares that he couldn't so easily explain. It was moving away, though. Not his problem.

The man out on the wharf was still there. He hadn't moved. There was something very wrong about that.

He found the corpse of the last Cypriot. The black plastic thing was still clutched in the dead man's fingers. Roche prised it free. It fitted comfortably in his hand, soft and slightly slick, almost as though it was altering itself to the contour of his grip. It felt more rubbery than plastic. He took it and ran back up the stairs, looking for Rees and a good position over Hertsmere Road that would let them and Stanton trap everything in a crossfire.

As he reached the top of the stairs, he heard Stanton open up with the SAW again, followed shortly by the sharp detonations of two grenades in quick succession. The air shook and the walls and floor of the museum quivered. A burst of silver light erupted from below and the museum shook again, hard this time, knocking Roche flat. He glanced back but all he saw were screams of slashing silver light, lashing around a Scary Clown. Roche pulled out a camera and started it filming, strapped it to his arm, shouldered his C8 and fired. He saw the bullets hit, saw the alien reel back as gouts of steam popped from its coat.

The Clown whipped around and pointed a small tube in his direction. Roche dived back. A man-sized chunk of brickwork disintegrated where he'd been standing. He moved position. Down in the exhibition hall, something else had emerged out of the wall. It looked like another Clown except instead of being dressed in a frock coat it was covered in a mirrored chrome-like finish, even its face. Streamers of silver light sprayed out of its chest, cascading through the café, tearing at the Clown. They whipped like ropes, cutting brick as they flailed as though the walls were made of smoke, sparking as stray ribbons flared off twisted metal.

A movement behind him snapped at Roche's attention. He whipped around, raising the carbine, but it was only Rees.

'Fucking hell,' said Rees. 'I thought you were gone.'

'Look, mate, you didn't see what was going down out the front. Take this.' Roche passed the camera to Rees and then pointed the black rubbery thing from the atrium at the Clown and fired it. Ropes of golden light launched through the air; but as he did, two more Scary Clowns emerged from the walls. They came at the chrome thing from each side and slipped their claws into it. The silver light died. Roche fired again and hit one of the Clown aliens. It flickered and lurched and pieces of it fell away. The other two picked it up and seemed to dissolve into the air. They drifted, ghost-like, into the atrium and away towards the North Wharf. Rees stared at the thing in Roche's hand.

'What the fuck is that?'

Roche shrugged. 'Does anyone know—'

The SAW opened up again outside.

13 July, 2211 hours, Canary Wharf

The Fermat construct arrived as a second clone ceased to function. The last one was still rushing to catch up from its observation position in North Africa.

'What sort of spaceship?' it asked. Its concentration was largely dedicated to the local situation. The Shriven shouldn't have been able to break its clones. Something else was doing it.

'Not one of ours,' replied the *Exponential*.

'Send a drone to investigate.'

'I'm not sure that's wise. Won't that give away our presence?'

The Fermat construct didn't answer straight away. It flew cloaked between the towers of Canary Wharf, looking for the entity that had destroyed its first clone. Outside the entrance to the Docklands Museum, something that looked human but clearly wasn't snagged a pair of de-phased Shriven as they came out into the open. One lurched away. The other seemed held fast. It lashed, writhing violently as it shrank into itself. The Fermat construct ejected a cloud of tiny pinhead drones. Inquisitive nanites swarmed through augmented flesh, looking for signatures and traces. The human-shape barely seemed to notice. Its fingers dug into the Shriven deeper and deeper until the Shriven crumbled to ash. The nanites abruptly ceased to exist. The human-shape, meanwhile, stubbornly refused to disintegrate. It stared straight at where the Fermat construct was hidden in the air.

13 July, 2211 hours, Canary Wharf

Roche scrambled to his feet and to the nearest window looking out over Hertsmere Road. The SAW had stopped and he heard the sharp cracks of pistol shots. Double taps. There was another crash and an explosion from the front of the museum, from by the door. Down on the street, Roche saw Burman walk past a van, shooting anything that moved with his Sig. He looked like he'd lost it, completely lost it. A van started to pull away as he passed. Burman emptied his clip into the side of it. Roche shouldered his carbine and fired into the roof as it picked up speed, long sustained bursts. Rees did the same. So did Stanton, still up in the car park on the other side. The van screeched around the corner past the entrance to the multi-storey, heading for the main road.

Burman had a grenade launcher out now. A 40mm HE grenade caught the rear left corner of the van, exploded, lifted the back of the vehicle up and sent it tumbling onto its right hand side.

'Noel!'

Stanton was on the street now. None of the Russians immediately below were moving. Roche ducked back, ejected his spent clip and slotted another into place. He snapped back up to the window in time to see Stanton roll a frag grenade into the back of a van.

'Frag!' He ducked back.

The wall behind Roche shuddered. The floor buckled. Much more of this, whatever the fuck was going on around the front, and the whole warehouse was going to give up and fall down. Another explosion blew the last vestiges of the museum façade to pieces.

Rees grabbed him. He clearly thought the same. 'We need to get out of here.'

'Front or back?' Roche dashed for the stairs, what was left of them, and jumped. In the ruin of the museum's façade, shaking off a mound of rubble, something was stirring, fast and angry. It threw aside a piece of masonry that must have weighed as much as a small car and started to struggle out.

'Back!' yelled Rees. They bolted for the hole in the wall that had once been a door.

'I hope to fuck Burman and Stanton cleared the street out there!'

'Bugger that – Burman's gone fucking rambo. I just hope to fuck he doesn't shoot us simply for moving!'

13 July, 2212 hours, Canary Wharf

The thing that was pretending to be human smashed into the remains of the museum, apparently in a fit of some emotional passion the Fermat construct didn't understand. The impact demolished most of the rest of the façade

239

and it didn't seem to care that most of the stone crashed around and on top of it as it clawed and tore its way free. The construct tossed an implosion singularity into the rubble. The bomb went off and sucked in most of the matter of the museum and some of the surrounding buildings and then spat them out again. It probably wasn't enough to make the other entity even pause but the detonation filled the air with enough noise and smoke for the Fermat to reconfigure and construct a small hyper-velocity neutronium cannon for itself. It considered firing on the other creature and then held back. The human wasn't really human at all. Its structure held the idea of the shape of one but underneath it seemed to be made of exotic matter and a swarming and constantly changing collection of quantum possibilities that the construct simply couldn't pin down into a consistent state in order to annihilate it. The thing, whatever it was, had dispatched the first clone simply by not being what anything was supposed to be.

Whatever it was, it was a significant threat. The construct calculated whether the other entity had suffi-cient data to deduce the presence of the Weft Hive. The answer appeared irritatingly inconclusive.

Best to get rid of it.

The construct ejected a second cloud of drones that swarmed around the entity and, in a small localised area, sucked away the background energy of the universe. Rather to the construct's surprise and alarm, the entity didn't simply disintegrate like it was supposed to. It drew what the construct recognised to be an

M1911 Colt .45 from inside its jacket and fired a tidal wave of naked quarks and clustered strangelets. The construct phased rapidly through different matter-resonances as they passed and then assessed the damage. Considerable. What was worse though, was that it didn't quite understand how the entity had done what it had done; and now it had vanished, and the construct had to accept a perfectly probable hypothesis that the entity wasn't dead.

We withdraw. It didn't need to add anything more. The Hive, always in the construct's thoughts, concurred.

Superficially.

The construct looked harder.

Deep within the Hive they were calculating. The Pleasure. That was the most probable conclusion and now the Hive didn't know what to do. They were afraid. The construct could feel the ripples of it running through them. Five hundred years since the diaspora and in all that time the Pleasure had never returned. Five hundred years of preparing for a war that never came and now it had.

Maybe this is something else. But they all knew it wasn't.

13 July, 2213 hours, Canary Wharf

Roche sprinted across the street and hurled himself at the entrance to the multi-storey. Behind him, the entire back wall of the museum bulged inward. He felt himself sucked backwards, had enough time to throw himself to the floor and kick out, rolling out of the way up the entrance ramp before the London Museum of Docklands simply shattered and exploded. Something vaguely human-shaped shot through the collapsing wreckage and slammed into the car park three storeys above along with a hail of fractured bricks. A deluge of falling rubble sprawled out across the street, covering the wrecked vans and cars and the numerous bodies on the floor in a thick cloud of reddish dust. Roche slowly picked himself up. He coughed, choking in the brick dust. He was covered in pieces of broken stone, in crumbs of mortar and glass.

'Rees?'

'Yeah.'

'You okay?'

'Yeah. Kinda. What the …' There was a rustle of sliding gravel as Rees sat up. The entrance to the multi-storey was half blocked with rubble that spilled down the ramp.

'Christ.' Roche spat out a mouthful of red dust. This was London? It looked more like Fallujah during the worst of the fighting.

'Roche … What the hell?'

'What the hell do you think?' Through the settling dust, Hertsmere Street looked still. The sounds of gunfire still rattled down the canyon of the street. 'Did you see Burman? Stanton?' Roche couldn't quite tell which way the fighting had moved.

'What I *think* is that there are some things Charly didn't bother to mention, because if I'd known what was *actually* going down then I'd have brought the whole rest of the fucking Rebel Alliance with me. We got some X-wings parked in the underground car park in Vauxhall just sitting there, just waiting. I mean, point me at the Death Star and let's … Roche, what the fuck is this shit?'

'Do I look like fucking Mulder?' Roche pulled himself to his feet and dusted himself down. Most likely the shooting was coming from the police roadblocks on West India Docks Road and Aspen Way. He started jogging along the ramp. Stanton had taken his position up here because it gave arcs of fire over both as well as over the back of the museum. 'You remember Lewis Shaw and Martin Collins?'

'I didn't know them. I heard they went missing. When was it? Last year?'

'January sometime. I wasn't there but I knew them both well enough.' Roche nodded back to the bottom of the ramp. 'He was here. I'm sure it was him. You said so too.'

'I thought …'

'You still got the camera?'

Rees howled with laughter. 'Did I fucking tape it, you mean? Christ! I was trying not to die and completely go fucking mad. But yes, I did indeed tape that episode of fucking Pacific Rim or whatever the fuck it is that was going on in there.'

'I got some from the museum but not when it went batshit crazy.' Roche whispered into his radio mike. 'Indigo two to all Indigo call-signs. Respond?' He shook his head. 'Comms went shit the moment that fucking crate opened up. For all I know, nothing got out.' They rounded a corner onto the third level of the multi-storey.

'I'm certain that was Shaw.' He looked over the edge of the car park into the street below.

'That was the thing you saw in Aqar?'

Roche nodded. Hertsmere Road was covered in rubble from the collapsed warehouse and museum but otherwise it was empty. Nothing moved.

'Only here there were three of them.'

'Five. Maybe six. Come on. We need to follow Shaw. You were up at the window. Which way did he go?'

'Back through the rubble, and no we fucking don't!' Rees walked over to the other side of the car park, then waved Roche over. The roads running past the West India Docks were empty now except for a handful of police cars, parked with their lights flashing. Level with the storey below, an elevated section of the Docklands Light Railway ran past. Roche went back to the other side, searching for Shaw. Sporadic bursts of gunfire echoed from further down the road where Linley's men had set up their roadblock.

'There!' Rees pointed into the ruin of the museum. There was a soldier down there, racing through the debris in impossible leaps and bounds.

'Shit! He's going to get away.' And they'd never catch him on foot. Roche ran back to the other side, looking for a quick way down. The gap between the elevated DLR track and the car park was only a few feet but from there it was a long way down. He started running among the cars, looking for an old Ford, because nothing hot-wired as easy as an old Ford.

'Got one.' Rees was ahead of him. Thirty seconds later they were tearing through the car park, looking for the exit. Thirty more and they were out. Rees turned the Ford up Hertsmere Road towards the police road-blocks and then slammed on the brakes. The road was a sea of rubble. He shook his head, screeching the tyres as he shifted into reverse and stamped on the accelerator. 'Even a fucking Mastiff couldn't get through that shit.'

'Just get round the other side!'

Rees executed a perfect reverse handbrake turn and screeched around the side of what had once been the London Museum of Docklands. The North Wharf itself was still hidden behind the remains of the museum but now Roche could see the tower blocks behind it. They were scarred. Canary Wharf tower was missing pieces of its glass roof. Flashes and booms still echoed around through the darkness. He thought he could hear a helicopter somewhere overhead, low, but he couldn't see its lights. *Bloody idiots getting close to this ...*

'The fucking ground is shaking!' bawled Rees. 'Can you feel it?' Across the North Wharf, flashes of small-arms fire fractured the night. Rees turned sharply again and crashed up through the open barrier into the pedestrianised space towards the front of the museum. They shot past a pub and screeched to a stop at the edge of the rubble. The remains of some rather nice and expensive Audis lay crushed under a mountain of shattered Victorian brickwork.

'Where the fuck is Shaw?' Roche strained his eyes, trying to make out any movement. A couple of wankers with phones were hunkered down in what was left of the pub's beer garden, filming them. Roche suppressed the urge to shoot them.

'Priorities, mate! We still got men under fire!' Rees jumped out of the car and crouched beside it, shouldering his carbine, already scanning for targets.

'These fuckers were the same ones who shredded Burman and Stanton in Dagenham, right?' Roche jumped out after him, covering the remains of the museum. 'But Shaw was ours. You want to go fuck about with some pissy drug-crazed pusher dickwads, you go do that, Rees!' He was shouting now. Screaming almost. 'There!' Across the docks, ropes of fire shot over the water. A sphere of glittering light flared as the light enveloped it. Roche leapt to his feet. 'There! If you want to know what the fuck this is all about, we go after …' He stopped. Something leapt out of the museum, tall and thin and translucent. It had too many limbs and something about it suggested it was armoured. Roche tried to get a bead on it but it was too quick. The air around it shimmered. It landed next to the water and rolled in and was gone. It didn't make so much as a ripple.

'Er …' started Rees. 'How many arms did that have? Because I'm sure it was more than two.'

Across Docklands, all the lights went out.

13 July, 2218 hours, Canary Wharf, North Dock

The Fermat hybrid construct sank into the waters of the North Wharf and watched. The Shriven were stuttering southward, out of phase with ordinary matter-resonances and passing through everything as though they were ghosts. The Fermat's surviving clone scattered a net of exotic quarks across the path of the Shriven, forcing them to phase back into mundane matter. As soon as they did, the clones scattered a handful of anti-matter bomblets that would have vaporised most of the West India Docks and annihilated the Thames waterfront from the Limehouse Basin right across to the other side of the Isle of Dogs.

The construct neutralised them. *Let them go. Withdraw. Do not expose our presence.*

Dazzled by gluon-flashes, the Shriven hosed the spaces now and then occupied by the two clones with a broad spectrum of exotic particle states and high-end radiation. It didn't do very much but the lights were pretty if you had the psychology to appreciate such things. The first of the Shriven reached the underground bunker beneath One Canada Square and activated a device that flashed an electro-magnetic pulse over most of Millwall and the East End and drained ever erg of energy out of every electrical device within a radius of approximately half a mile.

13 July, 2219 hours, North Dock

Everything went dark. The street lights, the lights in all the buildings around him, everything. The bubble of light around Shaw vanished. Flickers of what looked like sparks flashed momentarily across the pyramid roof of One Canada Square. The Ford's lights went out, though the engine kept running. Rees tapped his radio and shook it. When Roche looked, his own was dead. Even the battery charge light was out. He swore.

'Electro-magnetic pulse?' He stared hard at Rees. Rees took out the camera, looked at it and shook his head.

'Dead.'

A light grew over One Canada Square like a faint Aurora. Dim curtains of green and violet shimmered above it, rose and faded. The wankers back in the wrecked beer garden were pointing their phones at it and fiddling with them, trying to work out why they suddenly weren't working. They probably thought it was some sort of publicity stunt. After the laser show from the Shard last summer, maybe it was.

'Take the car round the other way.' Roche abandoned Rees and the Ford and ran on foot, south on the pavement alongside the water, the C8 slung over his shoulder, heading after Shaw and clutching the black rubber weapon he'd taken from the dead Cypriot. At some point there were some questions to be asked there about who this Evangeli was and where his connections went and how the fuck he happened to be cosy with half a dozen Jack-the-Ripper crazy bastard aliens. Yeah, but not now, and anyway Evangeli was dead. Shaw and the answers he had. That was what mattered.

13 July, 2221 hours, approaching Mars orbit

The *Irrational Prime* was in a holding orbit, waiting to be told what to do. Behind it a comet sped, carefully shepherded by magnetic fields, tiny and almost impossible to see. It was only a few kilometres across. Not the sort of thing you wanted hitting your planet if you happened to be anywhere near the impact site but otherwise nothing to fear; and besides, most likely it would hit any decent planet's atmosphere and bounce off or else break up into a shower of much smaller pieces that would burn up and hardly do any damage at all.

Except, being made of anti-matter, what would actually happen was the sudden explosive release of energy equivalent to the moon hitting the earth at about three times the speed of sound. It would crack a planet in two, strip it of its atmosphere and cause shockwaves through the crust that would shake every structure to powder. For any planet that happened to be made mostly of hot molten rock, the comet would cause the crust to shatter, set up resonances and standing waves that would distort the shape of the world by tens, even hundreds of kilometres. At the very least it would extinguish all life on any planet. Almost as certainly, it would destroy all further possibility of life. If they were lucky and the planet was a reasonably small one, the impact might actually shatter it. That last possibility was speculative and the freighter and the frigate had been exploring the mathematics on and off for the last few weeks, trying to work out an answer. In the end, sometimes the only way to know was to try a thing out.

'So are we going to use it or not?' asked the *Exponential*.

'Apparently we wait and see what happens.' The Hive had held back on the comet. The *Irrational Prime* thought

249

that might be about to change. It was a nice easy clean way to solve the problem, after all.

The *Exponential*, meanwhile, had been dabbling with human figures of speech. It had decided to make a study of them while there were still some humans left.

'Shall we get popcorn?' it asked.

13 July, 2221 hours, North Dock

Roche raced along North Colonnade, ignoring a fire-fight in Cabot Square to the south. The flashes of light had stopped. He felt the ground tremble under his feet. Under the arches of the Docklands Light Railway beside Canary Wharf station, he slid to a stop. One Canada Square was right in front of him, surrounded by thick smoke or vapour. There were sparks running up and down it. A pane of glass near the top exploded and rained shards across the street. Then another pane exploded and then another and then suddenly they were shattering everywhere, from top to bottom. Roche ducked sharply round the corner into the narrow shelter of Chancellor Passage underneath the railway lines. Needles and shards of glass were flying everywhere. He could still hear weapons firing in Cabot Square. He could hear people screaming.

One Canada Square was shrinking. Narrowing. The ground shook again. The tower shuddered and started to sag and buckle as though its walls were being sucked inward. The same thing he'd seen at the museum. He hurled himself away and threw himself flat, sliding across the pavement as the building imploded in a thunder of shattering glass and screaming metal. A wind reached around the corner and under the railway and blew him down the street like so much tumbleweed. He fetched up in a doorway. Pieces of shattered glass and tortured steel and savaged concrete rained around him. They peppered his body armour and he felt a sting in his shoulder.

A severed hand landed with a wet smack on the concrete beside him. For a moment he lay still and stared at it, too battered to move. The ground was shaking. A pulse shuddered through him, through the wall beside him and the paving slabs underneath him, hard enough to make him grunt. He hauled himself painfully back to his feet, checking everything still worked. His rib was agony again.

Something was coming out of the wreckage. A glittering bubble, constantly bright under the deluge of the white energy beam.

Shaw?

Another pulse shook the street. Roche stumbled and looked for anything that might pass as cover, clutching the weapon he'd taken from the museum. The next pulse came, strong enough to shake mortar dust out of the bridges over his head and almost knock him off his feet. A pair of dead Organizistya lay sprawled further down the passage. With each pulse they jerked and danced. It reminded him of those biology lessons at school where they took electrodes to dead frogs and made their legs spasm. He caught a glimpse of another shape, too tall, arms too long, drifting among the shadows in a long frock coat. Shaw lifted his arm and a burst of fiery yellow shot from the alien weapon towards it. The creature in the frock coat made no effort to get out of the way. It seemed to swallow the fireball.

The pulses were coming more quickly now. Roche could hardly stay on his feet.

An explosion under the ground shook the rubble. Bricks and slabs of concrete jumped around the street. The bridge above him groaned as it flexed. Roche stumbled away. He pointed the weapon from the museum at the shadows where he'd seen the Clown and squeezed, holding it tight. Ropes of golden light twisted through the choking dust, wrapping themselves around the darkness. They lit it up and now Roche could see the shape of it. Almost but not quite human. Its head snapped towards him but before it could move, before Roche could think to stop firing and run like fuck for some cover, Shaw raised his arm again and a series of darts flew like tracer fire, each one flashing as bright as the sun. Roche turned and staggered away, holding his hand over his eyes. He stumbled into the relative shelter of an overturned van and took cover behind it.

The ground was shaking like a drumskin now, like an earthquake, a pounding so hard and so rhythmic that everything lying loose on the road kept jumping an inch up into the air. Roche staggered and then fell and gave up. The light, the noise, the shaking, the …

With a last shudder, the pounding stopped. The bubble around Shaw vanished. Flickers of what looked like sparks flashed across the ruin of One Canada Square. In the sudden quiet he heard screaming from the square behind him. Gunshots. The pop of a 40mm grenade and then the explosion that followed and then the sustained rattle of a squad support weapon. Ahead of him, the man who might have been Lewis Shaw suddenly jumped and tumbled and rolled out of the rubble. An instant later, an explosion came from where he'd been. Pieces of shrapnel or debris flew like bullets, zipping and fizzing through the air. Puffs of dust flew up where they pock-marked the surrounding blocks. A loud bang a few inches from Roche's face made him jump where something hard and fast punched right through the van, puncturing the metal and leaving a hole surrounded by jagged aluminium petals. Roche slumped back. The Scary Clown was out in the open now. He reached for his camera, then remembered Rees had it, that it didn't matter anyway, that his radio was dead, that some fucker had let off an electro-magnetic pulse.

The Clown fired two more shots at something Roche couldn't see. Damn thing was right there in front of him, a dozen yards away and in the open, clear as anything now that there was no one here to see it. As it turned away, it drew out some sort of device about the size and shape of a rugby ball, twisted it sharply and vanished – no, not *quite* vanished – Roche thought he caught a flash of movement and pieces of rubble twitched and shifted on the street. The Clown had suddenly moved impossibly quickly, that was all.

All? He almost burst out laughing at the absurdity of it. *All?* And the glittering bubble around Lewis Shaw? Some sort of force field, that was *all*. Nothing special, although he was fucked if he knew how *that* worked. Yeah, and aliens that walked through walls and …

From the ruin of One Canada Square, something was rising up into the sky. Bullet shaped and maybe as tall as a house. Roche stared. It simply hung there for an instant, lightning playing along the steel spirals of its outer skeleton; and then the base pulsed with a circle of brilliant white light and the earth shook and everything jumped and the thing suddenly shifted further up into the sky in the blink of an eye, and hung there. The back end of it pulsed again and with every pulse it jumped further away. Like watching something in stop-motion. Roche stared, transfixed. The pulses grew steadily more frequent.

Observe and report. Trust your eyes. It's about what you see, not what you *think* you see.

All that training. He really did burst out laughing this time. Hysterical, which was no use. He took some deep breaths. Twenty years doing this. Twenty years and he'd seen some seriously fucked-up shit in that time, starting with Kravica. That had taken some beating but Somalia, Afghanistan and Iraq had all given it their best. This, though … Nothing had made him ready for this. Nothing could.

He had friends who'd started families. Ketch had said the same about having kids. *Nothing makes you ready for it. Nothing can …*

Get a fucking grip!

Shaw was standing in the rubble, clear as day, wrapped up in his bubble again and firing into the air. No one anywhere, ever, was going to believe any of this except for the fact that it had happened and tomorrow morning it would be all over the news and there would be a thousand and one clips taken from the mobile phones of the people like those idiots back in the beer garden, because that was what you did these days. You didn't run for your life or scream your head off for the nearest policeman, you ducked for cover and then turned around and filmed it with your phone, right … ?

Except you didn't. Not when someone set off an EMP and fucked everything with a battery across a half-mile radius.

Shit! The laptop! He hadn't got a damn thing to show for any of this except what he'd shot in the museum. If the laptop still worked. If the fucking Clowns hadn't pulled what they'd pulled in Brixton.

Very slowly, Roche dragged himself up. Shaw had stopped shooting at the sky now.

'Shaw? That you?' Roche waved.

The figure in the rubble didn't respond at first. Roche walked slowly closer, wary. Six months, thereabouts, since Shaw and Collins had vanished. Same sort of time he'd seen the first Scary Clown back in Brixton and gone mad. And they'd not been away on some op or disappeared in some messy little fracas in some country far away. They'd been out on the piss in Hereford and simply hadn't come back. Or so the stories said. And now here they were.

'Shaw?' Special programme? That sort of thing happened now and then. What was with the arm, though? 'Shaw? That you?'

At last Shaw stopped looking up at the sky and turned to look at Roche instead. Quick as a snake, he fired.

16 – Life on Mars

13 July, 2225 hours, Low Earth Orbit

The *Fermat* construct latched on to the side of the Shriven ship as it stutter-warped out of the Earth's atmosphere. Once the ship reached a comfortable orbit, it detached. It picked a defunct nuclear-powered satellite and latched on to that instead, powered down most of its systems and settled for hiding and waiting. The *Exponential* was already reconfiguring all the drones that had been collecting anti-matter and weaponising them to attack the cloaked space-ship that the Europa detector was now tracking

'They were here before we arrived,' it said.

The construct flinched. 'The Shriven should have destroyed this world when they found it.'

'Some part of the Hive already knew of this world before we came here,' observed the freighter. The consequences of such an appalling revelation were beyond calculation.

The *Exponential* continued weaponising the drones. 'Whoever they are, they might not know that we've found them. We should stay quiet.'

'Yes.'

There was a flaw in that plan, of course, and they both knew it. A one-hundred-and-seventy-mile-long flaw called the *Irrational Prime*.

13 July, 2225 hours, approaching the orbit of Mars

The *Irrational Prime* drifted through interplanetary space, pretending as best it could to be a dead and inert lump of rock. It zoomed its optical and ultraviolet sensors up to the limit of their magnification and began piping the feed through to the Hive and the Fermat construct and the *Exponential*. The last few Shriven had stutter-warped out of the Earth's atmosphere in a makeshift ship cobbled together from nano-factories. It shed bits and pieces that weren't part of the core structure and weren't taking the strain. The freighter calculated how long it would take for the Shriven to build an Einstein-Podolsky-Rosen drive (what the humans would have called it if they had one) and how far that might take them. Short of drawing on the underlying zero-point energy of the universe, the Shriven would be limited to total mass conversion. It was busy working out exactly how far that might get them when space around the Shriven ship burst into blossoms of light.

13 July, 2225 hours, City of London

Shaw moved so damned fast that Roche barely even saw it. He threw himself sideways as a ball of fire shot down the street. Shaw leapt into the air, jumping maybe fifty, sixty feet up and straight down the street to where Roche had been standing. Roche fired the museum gun. The bubble around Shaw shivered golden but that was all. Shaw came down and landed ten feet down the road from Roche, hitting the tarmac so hard it cracked around his feet. Roche fired again, this time at the entrance to the tower block beside him, Brodies Bar and Restaurant, carving his way in. Any way out would do but he wasn't going to have time.

'Roche? Sergeant Roche Manning?' Shaw had his arm raised, the arm that wasn't an arm any more but merged into some sort of organic plasma cannon. For a moment, he looked almost confused.

'Shaw?' They stared at one another.

The flicker of recognition faded from Shaw's eyes. He snarled. Roche dived through the entrance to the restaurant and sprinted through the abandoned tables, out the other side, through the kitchen. The lifts wouldn't be working, wherever they were, but there would be stairs …

Shaw raised his arm and fired a series of plasma bolts. They were smaller than the ones he'd used on the Clown but they came a lot faster. They seemed to chase him. Roche ran, putting distance between him and Shaw, pointing his own weapon back behind him and firing it continuously without even looking to see whether it was doing anything, slamming the first door he came to shut behind him in case that spoiled Shaw's aim at all. The wall shuddered. He saw a face, cringing, curled up in a corner. 'Run!' he screamed. He glanced over his shoulder as he turned the corner. The walls behind him were disintegrating. Shaw stood in the entrance, the shield like a halo around him, but he didn't come in.

Roche found some stairs and ran up them as fast as he could, then raced across the next level of the building, kicking through doors with a frantic violence, driving his way to the windows right in one corner. He got there in time to see Shaw stand back amid the rubble of One Canada Square and raise his arm and fire.

The walls disintegrated. Roche curled up and pressed his hands over his ears. The three topmost floors erupted upwards, blown off by the force of the explosion and then collapsed down. A scalding wind picked up monitors and printers and scanners and threw them like rocks from an angry giant. Flimsy plasterboard partition walls snapped, metal posts bent and buckled, chipboard doors were torn off their hinges and thrown through the air. Roche cringed in his corner, hiding under a cheap desk. Most of the front of the building erupted outward from the force of the explosion. Most of the rest fell to bits. Three feet away from him, the floor collapsed.

The rumbling seemed to go on and on. Roche didn't move, waiting for it to finish or for the last piece of the building frontage to finally give up and collapse, taking him with it, but it didn't. The noise of falling concrete finally stopped. He peered back out through the hole that had once been a window.

Shaw was back where he'd been before. He had a substantial part of the building on top of him now but that didn't seem to be troubling him. He pulled himself steadily out of the rubble, picking up twisted girders and huge slabs of masonry as though they were pieces from a fallen theatre set and tossing them away. When he was clear, he paused for a moment to look at the wreckage around him and then walked slowly off. Roche watched him go.

'Indigo four,' he whispered. 'This is Indigo two. Shaw's heading your way. Be advised, Shaw is not fucking friendly. Do not approach. Do *not* approach.'

Then he remembered the radio was dead.

13 July, 2237 hours, approaching the orbit of Mars

A string of explosions peppered space around the Shriven ship in flashes of hard white nuclear light. The *Irrational Prime* let its particle detectors tick over, watching the flurry of x-rays and gamma rays. It was odd watching the fight from so far away, with several light minutes of separation between them. Everything it could see was already finished for the ships themselves, the fight three steps further onward. For the Fermat construct hiding in its satellite, it must be even stranger. It would feel the flux of particles but it wouldn't see the explosions that made them until minutes later, until the *Irrational Prime* picked them up and spread everything it saw across the infinity of entangled pions that was the Hive.

261

A series of new lights flickered around the Shriven ship. A swarm of much smaller ships, sweeping in from somewhere. They sprayed the Shriven ship with loops and arcs of white and golden energy which shimmered off the Shriven shields. Then they came closer in, as if they were nuzzling up to it, as if they wanted to board it. The *Irrational Prime* tried to up its resolution on the attacking drones to see who they were. It was hard to be sure but they seemed to be constantly changing.

In a flash of light the Shriven finally activated their EPR drive and shot suddenly to exactly twice the speed of light. For a handful of minutes, the *Irrational Prime* lost track of them.

13 July, 2241 hours, City of London

Roche lowered himself down to the ground and picked his way through the rubble littered across Canada Square. When he finally walked out of the dust of fallen buildings, coughing and wheezing, the fighting had died away. Already he caught glimpses of a few people here and there, the crazy and the stupid and the insanely brave. Young, mostly. They were gathering in little clumps and clusters, half of them holding their phones and shaking them, staring at them, cursing them, talking about them. People stared at him as he staggered past. A part of him still wanted to shoot them for that. Another part was long past caring.

'Indigo two?'

A police siren burst into life somewhere ahead of him. He didn't know quite where he was going. Shadowing Shaw, that was all.

'Indigo two, do you copy?' Still nothing. Still down from the EMP. At least the idiots with their phones couldn't take any pictures.

Shaw was a hostile then, was he? 'I have to follow him. Find out where he goes.' Except Shaw was already gone. He'd already lost him. 'We need their intel. We need to know who they are.' He was talking to himself, muttering under his breath. Not a good sign.

An old Ford pulled up on the corner ahead of him, the one Rees had stolen from the multi-storey. The passenger door flew open and Rees beckoned from inside. Roche was barely in before Rees pulled away with a screech of rubber.

'Just saw Shaw getting into a police car. He's heading for Commercial Road and the City. You want to tail him?'

'Oh fuck yes,' growled Roche. Rees caught his eye as he turned into West India Dock Road and floored it.

'If that was Lewis Shaw then this is someone else's op,' he said. 'We shouldn't fucking be here. We should never have fucking been here.'

Roche growled. 'If it is then they've known for some fucking time that there are things that aren't fucking human in the world and whoever they are, I want to find them and break their fucking necks!' His legs hurt, his shoulders hurt, his arms hurt, his back ached, his head throbbed where something had caught him just above the left ear ... 'Ketch saw one of them in ninety-five.

Discharged on medical. I saw one in January. Discharged on medical. The Yanks, when they went out to Aqar, they knew what they were looking for and they nuked the place. I can't believe it was a total fucking coincidence that someone this end found a way to get us out there with them. Someone *knows*, Rees. Someone's known for months.' He caught his breath, trying to find some calm. 'It *was* Shaw, Rees. He saw me. He recognised me. He said my name and then he tried to kill me.'

The Ford tore along Commercial Road, weaving maniacally between the erratic scatter of stationary cars strewn askew across the tarmac in the aftermath of the EMP. The Ford's speedo was all over the place, the dial flicking madly from zero up to a hundred and back again.

'The engine never died. No electronics.' Rees grinned. 'Fuck your Audis and your Mercs, nothing beats an old Ford in a pinch. Was some weird fucker of a pulse though. The battery's as dead as a doornail. Doesn't make sense.' Rees dodged around a neat queue lined up in front of some traffic lights that weren't working any more. People were standing by their cars, talking to each other. Presumably they'd gone past the point of trying to phone for help. After a minute, Roche started to see cars moving again, a few warily coming the other way. The skyline of the City of London ahead was still bright with lights. Rees braked hard as they reached the junction at Aldgate. The cars here were still running but the traffic lights were out and nothing was moving. A lorry, trying to turn across the traffic, had been blocked by two cars coming the other way who were now stuck on the yellow hatching with the enormous 'Keep Clear' written across it. Audis. It was always a fucker in an Audi or a Merc. Used to be BMWs that were driven by cunts but apparently they were richer now. Roche wanted to get out of the Ford and drag them to the side of the road and maybe shoot them in the knees.

'There!' Rees pointed. Fifty yards ahead, blocked in by the traffic, was a police car.

'You sure?'

'Get the plates!' Rees tossed him a small spotter's scope. As Roche read the plates, Rees nodded. 'That's him.'

'Hold back then. Hold back. See where he goes. He's got to report in after this but for Christ's sake don't let him get wind of us! He thinks I'm dead.'

Rees snorted. 'Hold back? I'll be lucky to move.' He had a point. Monday night traffic in central London was shit at the best of times, the Aldgate junction was already in gridlock and Roche could hear the distant sirens. As soon as word got out about Docklands, the City would be swarming with armed police and road-blocks going up left right and centre, diverting people away from the square mile. The City of London police were a bit fucking quick like that. There'd be helicopters too and the media would storm the place at the first hint of what had happened.

'He's moving,' said Rees suddenly. Shaw was out of the car. Roche moved to follow.

'Rees, you take point. I'll cover from the sides. He's seen me and he knows me so I can't get close.'

The glittering bubble had vanished and Shaw's arm looked like an ordinary arm again. He was still nigh on six foot six, though, and even in civilian clothes he stuck out. He was an easy mark to follow. Rees trailed him most of the way down Mansell Street and past the Tower and St Katharine Docks. Roche switched in when Shaw crossed the river at Tower Bridge.

'He's heading for Vauxhall.'

Rees took over again down the Albert Embankment. By the time Shaw walked in through the back doors into Legoland, neither of them were surprised.

'Well that answers that, then,' grumbled Rees, 'What the fuck now?'

'Shaw and I have some words, that's what. I go in and you watch my back and remember that he tried to kill me, that he's working for fuck-knows-who and you don't go anywhere near him. If it goes south between me and Shaw, let it. Pretend you know fuck all, right. Brief Charly and Stanton. Tell them all of it. As far as anyone else goes, you were never here. Or maybe, more to the point, you never left in the first place.'

Rees nodded. 'Got it.' He tapped the webbing pocket that held Roche's camera. 'Got this.'

'This too. If it's not fried.' Roche handed him the laptop he'd taken into the museum.

13 July, 2241 hours, Mars orbit

The *Irrational Prime* had no way of knowing where the Shriven were or what was happening to them for as long as they had their Einstein-Podolsky-Rosen drive engaged. It could, however, deduce that the only useful destination for the Shriven was Mars. By then they'd use up half the mass of their improvised ship as fuel to drive the entanglement engine.

The Pleasure, on the other hand, clearly didn't worry about that sort of thing and simply mined the vacuum energy of empty space. As soon as the Shriven popped into existence in close orbit around Mars, they had drones harrying them from all directions with more forms of energetic attack than the *Irrational Prime* could make into any sense. The Shriven ship manoeuvred violently but it didn't make the first jot of difference. The drones were playing with the Shriven – showing off, even competing with each other. They changed their shape as they dived into the fight, morphing back and forth between various baroque ideas of spaceships drawn from human myths. They were playful, gleeful, joyful even. Gaspingly inefficient, but they didn't seem to care and it wasn't going to make any difference. As the Shriven ship plunged towards the Martian surface, a large piece sloughed off the back. The stutter-warp drive fell to bits. The ship began to tumble.

The waiting Martian surface lit up with plasma flares. A network of primitive defence satellites surrounding the planet awoke from their energy coma and started firing on the drone ships. Hundreds and hundreds – thousands – no, *tens* of thousands of tiny warheads launched themselves towards the onrush of the Shriven, scattering around them and attacking the Pleasure drones. The first bursts of accelerated anti-particles, high energy x-ray lasers and focused gamma bursts damaged a few but then the drones adapted. Thermonuclear light flashed, blinding the *Irrational Prime*'s sensor arrays. Energy spikes erupted from the planet from high-end gamma bursts. A few seconds later, the first streams of exotic particles were registering on the *Irrational Prime*'s detectors. Drones exploded into thousands of tiny sub-munitions. As the satellites died, the surface of the Red Planet lit up in a glorious light display.

'Please monitor more closely,' requested the Fermat construct. The *Irrational Prime* was still watching everything happen with almost a full minute delay.

'Me?' The *Irrational Prime* spat out a particularly venomous sequence of exotic particles. 'Why me?'

'You were constructed by the Shriven. Your presence is not out of place. You belong here. I do not.'

There was also, the *Irrational Prime* had to accept, the small matter of the Fermat construct not being particularly well equipped for independent inter-planetary travel. There were still the *Exponential*'s drones though.

'They are clearly technologically distinct,' said the frigate quietly. 'The Pleasure, if it detects them, will know that the Hive are here.'

The *Irrational Prime* irritably adjusted its orientation and angled itself so its main drives were pointing towards Mars. 'You realise that if I do anything other than blaze in at full acceleration, it's all going to be over before I get even close?'

Of course they realised.

'You realise this isn't going to end at all well.'

But yes, they realised that too. Just as the freighter understood the real reason for the construct's request.

The *Irrational Prime* muttered an irritable excretion of heavy mesons, lit its fusion torch and screamed off through space on a one-way trip towards Mars.

13 July, 2344 hours, Legoland

'Shaw!' Roche caught up just as Shaw crossed through the inner security screen. He didn't make any attempt to follow him any further. If it hadn't been for the military policemen manning the checkpoint, he'd have shouldered his C8 and pointed it at Shaw's face. As it was, he held the alien weapon from the museum. 'Shaw. Hold the fuck up, mate.'

Shaw stopped. He stood for a moment with his back to Roche and touched his ear. Calling for help? Calling for something. *Well go on then, you tosser. I've got my back covered too, thanks for asking.*

'Hello, Roche.' Shaw turned around and walked slowly towards him. He kept his hands out where Roche could see them, palms turned up, showing how harmless he was. Roche didn't buy it for a second. 'Tough one, eh?'

'You care to explain what the fuck that was all about, Shaw?'

Shaw shook his head.

'What about where you've been for the last six months?'

'You know better than that, Roche. Sectioned out into a classified compartment that no one else knows

269

exists. I'd have thought you'd figured that out after tonight.' He glanced at the three military policemen. 'Look, after what you've seen, someone's going to have to read you in one way or the other. I can give you a little. Not a lot. You want to go out for a pint?'

'It's pushing one in the fucking morning, Shaw. Where the fuck's open on a Monday night? And no.' He raised the black rubber light-gun and pointed it at Shaw. 'No, I don't want to go out for a fucking pint. An hour ago you tried to kill me.'

The MPs had their sub-machine guns shouldered and pointed at Roche in a flash. 'Put it down!' 'On the floor!' 'Get on the ground!' Give them credit, they knew a weapon when they saw one, just from the way Roche had been holding it. Roche raised his hands and then dropped to his knees, moving very slowly so they didn't …

Shaw's movement was so sudden and so fast that it was a blur. In one moment he was standing at the checkpoint, in another, in the blink of a single eye, he'd moved ten feet sideways. His arm lashed out and he smashed one MP's throat and then he moved again; before Roche could even understand what Shaw was doing, he'd snapped the second man's neck. The last one swung his MP5 around but he didn't have time to pull the trigger before Shaw snapped out a crescent kick and knocked it flying so hard that he bent the gun and shattered half the bones in the soldier's hands. The soldier's cry was cut short by a vicious throat-punch. Half a second later his neck was broken. Roche twisted, levelling the alien gun; but before he could bring it to bear, Shaw moved again with blistering speed. He kicked the gun out of Roche's hand, grabbed Roche by the throat and pinned him to the ground. Roche couldn't help thinking of the SEAL lieutenant in Aqar, how that shouldn't have been possible, but Shaw had the speed of a mongoose and the strength of an elephant and nothing Roche could do made the slightest bit of difference.

'What. The fuck. *Are* you?' Roche gasped.

Behind Shaw two more soldiers were coming, picking their way over the bodies of the dead MPs.

'What am I?' Shaw laughed. 'Shit, Roche. You want to know what's been going on, is that it? Is that all it is?'

13 July, 2344 hours, Mars orbit

The *Irrational Prime* shot through space, accelerating all the time, dead straight towards Mars. There wasn't really any other way to do it. It lined itself up on where the Shriven ship had crashed in the Noctis Labyrinthus, since that seemed to be the centre of the conflict. The last few satellites were still firing on the stuttering drones, simple high-energy x-ray lasers, gamma bursts and accelerated anti-particles. It was all desperately primitive and, while it made for a great deal of light and some picturesque particle sprays, the drones attacking the Shriven simply shrugged it off as though it wasn't there. Now and then they killed a few of the remaining satellites as though passing the time while they thought up something more interesting to do. The drones remained high above the Valles Marineris for a while, bombarding it with beams of plasma, creating lava-falls and geysers of molten rock. Most of it didn't look like it had anything to do with the Shriven. They were doing it because they could. Because it was art. Not that the Fermat construct or the Weft would ever understand that.

After a while they switched to massive thermonuclear bombardment of the canyon instead. The *Irrational Prime* had no idea why. They were wiping out their creations before they'd even had a chance to cool.

'Those satellites are diaspora weapons,' observed the Fermat construct.

'Yes.' They would hurt the freighter, though, because the *Irrational Prime* was, beneath its borrowed cloned mind, a very simple piece of technology of the same age as the Shriven and with almost no means of protecting itself from a meagre solar flare, never mind a directed beam of anti-protons. It could see what all the fuss was about now. On Mars, the Shriven had built something. They'd tried to hide it but now it was out in the open, all its cloaks stripped away.

The *Irrational Prime* adjusted its course and flew straight at it, as hard and fast as it could.

14 July, 2345 hours, Legoland

'You just can't leave it alone eh, Roche? You want to know the truth? Fine, here it is: that thing that your mate Ketch saw in Kravica? The same thing you saw in Brixton. The same thing you saw in Aqar. The same thing you saw today. They're fucking aliens, mate. Fucking aliens!' Shaw's grip on Roche's throat was slowly tightening. Roche tried rolling, tried kicking Shaw's legs out from under him, anything to break the hold. Things that should have worked against anyone, no matter how strong they were, but Shaw was something else. Roche brought his feet up into his chest and kicked as hard as he could and Shaw didn't even flinch. Shaw's fingers around his throat were as tight as they wanted to be, Roche realised, not as tight as they could be. Shaw could crush his neck whenever he wanted. It was like fighting the fucking Terminator.

'What. Are. You?'

'Aliens, Roche.' Shaw shook his head and for a moment there was a flicker of disbelief, of horror, of shock, of a man lost and overwhelmed by what he knew and what he'd become. 'Do you know how long they've been here? Since Columbus discovered America. We call them the Astronomers. That one in Brixton, he was Copernicus.' He smirked. 'Always made me laugh when I was a nipper, Copernicus. Copper knickers. Then there was Brahe. Kepler. Galileo. Newton. Herschel. Herschel was the one in Aqar. Five hundred years. They've been feeding off us. They're like fucking parasites, bleeding us dry, keeping us exactly where they want but that's all going to change now. They're not the only ones out there. There are others.' For a moment the grip on Roche's throat relaxed. 'Me and Collins. We were pissed. We met this guy …' Shaw laughed. 'We were just walking down the path beside the river looking for a fucking kebab ...' Shaw paused again, somehow lost. 'I told him I was going to shoot him. He said okay.' Shaw laughed. 'Can you believe that? He said okay. So I did. I nailed him between the eyes. He just stood there. Said he wanted to know what it felt like, being shot in the head.'

Shaw's eyes changed. He picked Roche up by the throat and slammed him into a wall. 'And then you found the fuckers in Brixton, and that's when we knew where it all went wrong. But not any more.' He tightened his grip. Roche kicked. He gouged at Shaw's face but nothing made any difference.

'Sorry Roche,' hissed Shaw. 'But the chosen are chosen.'

Roche's vision started to collapse. He heard the roaring of the sea in his ears and felt his kicks and punches lose their focus, and everything went black.

14 July, 0015 hours, Mars orbit

'It's been sort of interesting being you for these last thirty years,' the *Irrational Prime* told the *Exponential*. It turned off the fusion plume and slowly spun the massive freighter lattice around, putting as much sheer bulk as it could between its core and the orbital defences around Mars. It detached its sensor arrays and extended them to peer, on long fibrous monomolecular arms, around its mass. 'But don't let that go to your head. You'd be more effective if you permitted a greater variance in your pseudo-random instinctual responses and gave that part of you a little more autonomy too.' The drones swarmed over the Shriven construction, pouring out seeds that grew into a menagerie of armoured insectile soldiers.

'Says the ship who's about to crash into a planet,' grumbled the *Exponential*, but without any trace of mockery.

'You'd be doing this if you were here.'

'I'd have better sensors. I wouldn't need to.' They both knew it wasn't about the sensors.

There was a pause. The *Irrational Prime* hurtled on towards Mars. The nearest of the orbital defences was starting to notice and preparing to engage. It was small and weak and barely dangerous to anything at all but the only defences the freighter had were bulk and speed.

'There's an expression,' said the freighter as the first anti-protons began to shred its forward structure, annihilating little chunks of its lattice in firework flashes of light and colour, 'that I've learned from the humans.' Its cannibalised sensor array was picking up everything from the surface. Constant plasma flares. Nano-assembled bug-creatures that died and melted and simply resurrected themselves. The Shriven were still functioning but they were being overwhelmed while their structures dissolved around them, constantly eaten away by ever-evolving pico-machines. There were drones everywhere, raining like a swarm of meteors. Some became distracted by the *Irrational Prime* and latched on to it, burrowing into its metal skin and pouring out bizarre creatures into its insides.

'Is it "fuck you, dick-gobbler"?' asked the *Exponential*.

The *Irrational Prime* didn't answer. In the chaos of light and energy, of drones fighting against drones, of weapons hastily forged out of the Martian landscape by nano-factories working overtime, between the flashes and tears of the freighter's own destruction, it was beginning to see through the Martian surface to what lay underneath. The *Irrational Prime*, as its body began to break up around it, infested the last of its sentience into the nanite swarms and automated conscious algorithms that were dying as they dutifully defended the Shriven base. They were old, diaspora-descended and technologically retarded. It slipped inside them as a friend, unnoticed as they corroded and unravelled before the storm of drones, nanophages and wild twisting conceptual intelligences wrapped up in code the likes of which even the Weft had never seen. It watched; and as it watched, it peeled back what the Shriven were defending.

The Shriven had built themselves a dimensional vault. They were trying to lock themselves away for a hundred years, a thousand, however long they thought they'd need before they could come out again and be safe. They weren't going to reach it but it waited for them, hanging open. The vault was filled with vats. Lakes and lakes, all carefully labelled and categorised: epinephrine; corticotropin; norepinephrine; endorphin; dopamine and acetylcholine. Serotonin. A sea of it. Five hundred years of harvesting. Enough to make a Shriven of every Weft there was.

'You have to destroy that,' said the hybrid construct and the *Exponential* and the Hive all at once and together. 'You *have* to destroy it!' Yet the freighter could hear the dissenting voices in the Hive already. *Do we? Can it really be so bad? Isn't there a way around the shriving to keep the pleasure? Perhaps we can alter the chemistry … ?*

The Shriven were dying. They had no escape left. The *Irrational Prime*, too, was past doing anything more about its own trajectory. It only had a few seconds. It carried out a last few calculations and then closed the vault, sealing it shut so that nothing from the outside would open it again. At least, not in any hurry.

'I've given you a few days,' it said to the Fermat construct. 'Figure something out.'

14 July, 0016 hours, Battersea

The two men hauled Roche out of the boot of the car and dumped him on the ground. He couldn't tell where he was except that it was a building site somewhere. His head pounded and his neck ached. Not that it was going to matter for much longer. Whoever had tied his wrists and his ankles had known what they were doing.

'Shaw,' he croaked.

The two men dropped him on the ground and kicked him in the stomach. When he curled up, they kicked him in the kidneys instead. What made it worse was that he knew these men. He knew their faces. He'd seen them in Hereford now and then. 'Jones,' he gasped.

He was fairly sure one of them was called Jones. He didn't know the other one's name. They were SAS, both of them.

'Which squadron?' he asked. Which earned him a stamp on the shoulder.

'So you're supposed to be a tough man, are you?' There was a familiarity about these men, about the way they moved, fast and slick. Like the Organizistya from the museum. Like the Americans in Aqar. They were on something.

One of them drew a pistol from his jacket. With a slow deliberate movement he fitted a suppressor to it. He watched Roche all the time. 'You lot always did think you were something special. Bloody Special Recon tier three arseholes.'

He raised the pistol. The other soldier stopped him, shaking his head. 'I'll get a rock,' he said, and vanished into the darkness.

'Why, Jones?' asked Roche. 'Why are you doing this?'

'Why do you think? Because the lords and masters say so. Because you're in the way. Can't let you—'

He finished with a strangled noise as his face burst open in a shower of blood and mangled bone, spattering across Roche's boots. He collapsed. Rees stepped over the body, pointing his suppressed Sig out into the darkness.

'I counted two. Any more?' he hissed.

Roche shook his head and held out his hand. Rees cut him loose and hauled him up.

'Let's get you out of here.'

14 July, 0016 hours, Mars

'I had in mind something with a bit more depth. A little pathos. A touch of nobility,' said the *Irrational Prime*, a nanosecond before what was left of it smashed into the Martian desert at a relative velocity of several hundred thousand kilometres per hour. 'But actually, *fuck you, dick-gobbler* sounds about right.'

PHASE FOUR

17 – The Irrational Prime

The drones belonged to the Fermat hybrid construct now. Strictly they belonged to the *Exponential*, but the *Exponential* was close to four thousand light years away and had gone very quiet since the *Irrational Prime* had smashed into Mars. The freighter had come up with the right idea, though.

Most of the drones were still around Europa or between Jupiter and Saturn, harvesting anti-matter from the quantum fluctuations of empty space. The Fermat construct called them closer. They aligned themselves so there would be a star behind their own position as viewed from Mars, as seen from the hidden spaceship that the *Exponential* was tracking with its tau-burst detector and from Earth too. The mathematics were easy enough. Each drone simply waited for the alignment to be right and then flared its engines. No one who was looking out into space would see anything different or unusual. The tiniest variation in the energy output of particular stars now and then, perhaps, but nothing outside the possibilities of instrument noise and variations of the stars themselves, or the haze of interstellar gases drifting through the galactic plane.

It would be possible, the construct thought, to carry out a statistical analysis on the observations of all stars in all spectra and spot an anomalous jump in the apparent statistical noise of the data. A perceptive mind might conceivably see that; but the Fermat construct had no idea how the Pleasure thought. None of the Weft had encountered them since the diaspora and no one had understood them even then.

They're not like us.

The construct made the drones' movement as hard as possible to see. It did it with the logical precision of the Weft. They converged on the comet of frozen anti-hydrogen that the *Irrational Prime* had shepherded into the inner system. They began to nudge it, shifting its trajectory little by little, speeding it on. Turning it. The mathematics was all there. The *Irrational Prime* had worked it out in the last second of its existence and had shown the Fermat construct how it would work. It had locked the Shriven vault for exactly the length of time it would take for the anti-comet to be turned and set into the right orbit. It had worked the timings down to a few micro-seconds.

When the construct was done with that, it set the drones back to harvesting anti-matter to build a second weapon; but the thoughts from the Hive were somewhat different.

We are coming, they said, and showed it what that would mean.

18 – Bliss

14 July, 0145 hours, The Travellers Inn, Chelsea

Rees practically had to carry Roche into the car. Now he had a little more time to look around him, Roche could see the familiar towers of Battersea Power Station. Shaw's men had carried him inside it, into the middle of the building site it had become and looked set to stay for a while. Some new development that had looked glorious and wonderful until the company behind the venture went bust.

'We go to Leadface,' Rees said. 'This is fucked up.'

'Leadface?'

'Major Lledwyn-Jones. Shaw was SAS.'

'Fuck's sake, I know who he *is*. Those two were SAS too.' Roche groaned. 'We don't go to Leadface. He's compromised. Everything is fucking compromised. First thing we do is go to ground. You know how this works. We're on an op in hostile territory. We've got the intel but the enemy know we're here and they're looking for us. What do you do?'

'Run like fuck to the extraction point and bug out.'

'Extraction points are all blown. Contingency plans are all fucked.'

'Figure out new ones.'

'Right. Except *you're* not blown,' growled Roche. There was a silence as Rees turned onto Battersea Bridge and crossed the river heading north. 'Shaw didn't see you. You go back, you take the bodies, you dump them in the river, you put yourself up in a cheap hotel and in the morning you go back like nothing ever happened. You were out on the waz. That's that.'

'No one's ever going to buy that, Roche.'

'You so sure? All hell must be going on in Legoland right now. Tomorrow is going to be utter fucking chaos, more shit hitting more fans than in the entire history of shit and fans. Do you realise what happened tonight? I suppose the morning headlines are going to say terrorists, not that a bunch of fucking aliens duked it out between them all across the Isle of Dogs, but even so. Christ! Last I saw, bits of Docklands looked like they did back in the Blitz. They brought the fucking Canary Wharf tower down, for pity's sake! They took out the power across half the fucking city! Do you have any idea how fucked up that's going to be? *Any* idea? People are going to be absolutely shitting themselves. Everyone. Whoever Shaw is working for, they're either running with their heads right down or this is just the start. They've left more loose ends than a builder's string vest.' Roche paused, gasping for breath. 'In the morning, you go back. You find Stanton. You find Charly. Burman if you have to. We're not in this on our own.'

Rees shook his head as he drove into Chelsea. 'That's pretty fucking thin, Roche.'

'Look, it's your call but you might still be good. If you can … I need one of you to go back to the Docklands Museum. Get in with the forensics team trawling the wreckage. Maybe Charly can do that. That thing I showed you in the car? There are more of them. Get hold of them. As many as you can.' Roche coughed. Spasms of pain seared his ribs. The one he'd broken in Aqar had never had a chance to heal. 'Get one to Charly. Oh, and ask her about anything that can make an electro-magnetic pulse that isn't a nuke. Tell her to go tap up "Q" or whoever the fuck deals with shit like that because we're going to need *something* before we face Shaw again.'

Rees pulled up outside a Chelsea hotel. 'Yeah. I'll put in a request for a Klingon cloaking device and a pair of light sabres too. Anything else? Ring of power? Iron Man suit?'

'Oh fuck off. You know what? Actually, yes, I'd like an Iron Man suit please.' He cracked a smile.

Rees looked at the hotel. He looked at Roche, then sighed and fumbled for his wallet. 'This is really going to cost a fucking lot, isn't it? And it's going to have to be on me.'

14 July, 1230 hours, Limehouse

Chelsea wasn't going to fly – that much was obvious. Rees paid for one night in advance and maybe he could claim later that he and Stanton had stayed there after an all-nighter in Kensington. Maybe. Roche helped himself to as much breakfast as he could force down and then checked out and moved across London. He stopped in the West End to draw out as much cash as he could, bought a handful of burner phones, some cheap surveillance equipment and a new laptop from the tech shops on Tottenham Court Road, then took the bus out through Smithfield and Wapping past Limehouse. The West India Docks were sealed off by a huge police cordon, helicopters up, cars and vans and traffic cones and black and yellow tape all over the place. Roche counted four helicopters hovering or circling. One of them looked police, the other three looked private. Journalists, probably. One BBC, one Sky News, one maybe CNN? He hadn't listened to the news yet but he knew it would be Docklands and nothing else. It would be that for days. The whole country had woken up to it and now everyone was wondering what had hit them. The roads were quiet. A lot of people had stayed at home. He could feel the fear, the uncertainty, in the people he passed, the few Oxford Street shoppers, the old men on the bus, the normally cocky Indians behind the Tottenham Court Road tech counters.

He got as close as he could to the West India Docks, close enough to see some of the scars for real, then turned back and walked through Limehouse. Parts of the Thames Path were taped off. He had no idea why. In the Limehouse Basin, several of the boats were burned-out husks.

The Holiday Inn, when he found it, was still open. In contrast to the rest of London, it seemed oddly busy. No one looked askance at Roche as he came in to the foyer, battered as shit and clutching a big black bag, and asked for a room.

'Journalist?' asked the receptionist when he went up to the counter. Roche shook his head.

'Government,' he said. 'Structural engineering specialist.' He didn't mention that his own specialism was more in making things fall down than in putting them up.

The receptionist nodded and then bit her lip. 'Got any ID?'

Roche shook his head. 'Bit of a rush on this morning,' he said.

'I'm going to have to charge you the full rate.' She puffed out her cheeks and looked him over. 'I'm really sorry about this. You've obviously had a rough night.'

Roche smiled as best he could. 'You could say that, yes.'

'Look, I'm going to have to charge you the full rate but if you can drop by some time with some ID to show you're not a journo ...' She smiled brightly. 'We can sort it out then.'

The full rate turned out to be slightly more than the five-star Chelsea hotel had been the night before. Roche pursed his lips. 'Closest hotel to the docks?'

The receptionist smiled back at him. 'Closest that's got any rooms left.'

He paid in cash and then spent an hour with the laptop and the various cameras, sorting out how everything linked together and synchronising them with his own kit from the night before. He stripped and cleaned the HK417 Rees had left for him – point of principle that, to strip and build up a weapon yourself before you trusted it to work. When he was done, he found the hotel fire exits and made his way up to the roof with the scope from the gun. From up there he had a clear view over the north bank of the Thames to the West India Docks. Apart from the pyramid peak of One Canada Square, the rest of the skyline was still there, the tower blocks still standing. A column of smoke or maybe steam rose from roughly where the London Museum of Docklands used to be. At least it had happened in the night. At least the offices had mostly been empty. That was about the only consolation.

He went back to his room and turned on the news at last, watching for a while. Talking heads came and went, speculating over what had happened the night before while footage played in the background. Shaking mobile phone shots of men with automatic weapons running through the streets, taken out of office windows. Talk of D-notices slapped onto some film of what looked like a man floating in the sky. For a while they switched to a report on a series of explosions in Brixton. More shaky phone-cam footage, this time. A soldier, kitted up, carrying what looked like a SAW. Burman? The soldier moved awkwardly, obviously hurt and equally obviously running away. Then someone else. Screaming. Flashes of light and fire. Footage of damaged buildings, shop frontage that looked as though it had been half-melted and then blown apart. After that they cut to the Aurora Borealis over One Canada Square. Eye-witness reports only, this time.

'So these "mysterious lights in the sky"? Are we talking lasers, Mike?' The voices drifted in over the images but Roche had no time for them. He was only interested in seeing what had happened.

'No, Trevor, I don't think so. You see, the thing about lasers, as I'm sure everyone who's ever used a laser pointer will know, is that you don't actually see them unless there's smoke or vapour in the air to scatter the light beam. Otherwise all you see is a spot of light. Here, let me demonstrate ...'

In the background they had film playing of a Scary Clown. Only a moment of it, fuzzed and blurry but definitely there for half a second before vanishing again. They had it on a loop. Too tall, arms too long, face too narrow in its long frock coat. The sounds from the video had been muted but not silenced. He could hear the screaming, the almost hysterical shouting and swearing. He wasn't the only one to have seen them any more. How many others?

'So what are we talking about then, Mike?'

'Well, we could be talking about some sort of electrical discharge, Trevor, but most likely at this point – and of course we can only speculate – we're looking at some sort of ...'

291

Roche hit the mute button. Talking heads talking shit. None of them knew what had happened except that some buildings had fallen down and a lot of people had been shooting at each other. No one knew who the Scary Clowns were so of course they were terrorists. They'd probably be Muslims too before the end of the day. There were pictures of what appeared to be special forces soldiers now and then, running through the ruins, and also of some very distressed police armed response units, so of course it was terrorists and Muslims. People would be asking what mosque they went to soon. It made him want to throw things.

A bit later he saw a blown-up still from the same footage and the caption: *costumed terrorists strike Docklands*. Costumed terrorists? They made it sound like some corny super-hero movie, like London was waiting for Batman to sweep out of the sky. Made him laugh. *And what's London got? Bojo on his bicycle ...*

When he was done checking his kit and then checking it again, he went out and took a walk past the Limehouse Basin and down the tow-path beside the Limehouse cut. There were a lot of people out now, clustered together, talking quietly, subdued, looking about. A lot of people who hadn't gone in to work. The roads, where they weren't closed, were congested. Roche cut north and walked around as far as Mile End stadium and then back through Tower Hamlets. He hadn't put it together before but all of this was a stone's throw from the tower block they'd staked out a few weeks back where Spiderman had been. Maybe it was thinking of superheroes that made him put it together.

He walked back to Salmon Lane and the Red Lion Pub and bought himself a late lunch, then called Rees from one of the burner phones.

'Remember the day we saw Spiderman. Remember the pub?'

14 July, 1900 hours, Prince Regent Pub, Salmon Lane, Limehouse

Rees came bang on time, eyes everywhere, tense as a drumskin. He spotted Roche but didn't show any sign of recognising him until he'd checked everyone else. He went to the bar and ordered a beer. Roche left him be. After another minute, Rees came and sat across the table.

'Clear enough?' Roche asked.

'I thought maybe Shaw picked you up in Chelsea.' Rees couldn't keep his nervousness out of his eyes.

'Just being careful. You get anywhere?'

'Kind of.' Rees put a small backpack on the table and surreptitiously opened it. There were three of the weapons from the night before, a squishy black rubber pistol grip under an elongated disc, and two black rugby-ball things like the one he'd seen the night before.

'What are those?' Roche poked at the rugby balls.

'My source was very helpful with those,' growled Rees. 'She called them "mysterious black ovoids" and suggested that, given what the other things did, we should leave them well alone. The best bit is the EMP gun in the car. One shot and about the size of a suitcase but apparently it works.'

'Your source is Charly, right? She okay?' Roche felt an irritating surge of jealousy. What was the sense of that?

Rees shook his head. 'No idea. Haven't seen the delightful Miss Whelan-Hollis since the op. No idea what happened to Stanton or Burman either. But the whole of Legoland went mad as a bag of spiders as soon as the news broke, so who the fuck knows. Got any sense, they'll all be keeping their heads down and looking about switching identities and emigrating to South Africa. You and I might have a think about that too.'

'I want to set up surveillance on Shaw. He comes out of Legoland again, I want to know where he goes.' Roche pushed a pair of burner phones across the table. 'This is off the books so far it's off the fucking table. You know that, right?'

'I know.' Rees bared his teeth in a vicious grin.

'Seemed to me that last night you weren't so keen.'

Rees shrugged. 'Seemed to me last night there was still a chance Shaw might not be a cunt. Seems to me now that I was wrong.'

'With a cherry on top,' Roche laughed.

'What?'

Roche shook his head. 'Old man's joke, mate. Old man's joke.'

'Got him. He's moving.' Rees's words were short and clipped and reeked with a venomous enthusiasm. 'I'll take him first.'

'I'll be in position in two minutes.'

'He's on the Lambeth road heading for Southwark. You know he's going to the docks, right?'

'I'll know he's going to the docks when I follow him there,' said Roche sharply. 'Okay, I'm coming up Kennington Road.'

'Black Audi.'

'Got it.'

'I'm pulling back. Going to drift north. I'll spell you again in a few minutes.'

Roche was in a Ford Mondeo, taking it in turns with Rees to tail Shaw across London. He thought Rees was probably right about Shaw heading back for Limehouse and Docklands but when Shaw finally crossed the Thames at London Bridge he went on north into Tower Hamlets instead. He stopped and parked up outside the Prince Regent and went into the tower block where Spiderman had been.

'That's a bit of a coincidence,' muttered Rees. Roche had already pulled up around the corner and was rummaging for a laser-mike.

'Sixth floor, second window from the left,' he said. 'Got to be worth a try.'

Rees parked up on Blount Street. They walked into the little apartment block on the end of the road where

Roche had been on overwatch the night the nuke had gone off in Damascus. They ran up the stairs and hammered on the door at the top. When there wasn't any answer, Roche kicked it in. He opened the window over Salmon Lane and then moved away out of sight while Rees set up the laser-mike.

'Apparently there's an emergency session of the UN security council kicking off later.' Rees was still fiddling with the mike. 'They say President Greenwood is hauling his fat arse out of the White House and flying over to see the damage for himself. We've got Iran speculating that it's all a hoax, a piece of elaborate Hollywood theatre, that we did it to ourselves to give the US an excuse to steamroller across the whole of the Middle East. The Chinese have gone very quiet but rumour has it their ambassador has already been out there. Oh, and the Pope's said not to worry, the Second Coming and the Apocalypse aren't due, but Christ, you should have seen how packed it was in St Peter's Square this morning. It's all over the world now, Roche. Damascus, Myanmar, Namibia and now this. People are shit-scared.'

'It's been all over the world a while,' Roche muttered. 'We just didn't know about it.'

'Here we go.' Rees moved to be out of sight of the window too.

'... *pull in the rest of your sellers until it's sorted.*' The voice faded in and out as Rees tuned the laser-mike. There was what sounded like a chorus of dissent.

'Was that Shaw?' Rees asked. Roche nodded.

'*I don't give a fuck about your pissy little problems. Trip says you do this so you do it.*'

The other voices were indistinct, still objecting to whatever it was Shaw wanted. There was a sudden shout and lot of swearing and the crash of upturned furniture and then the smash of glass. They didn't need the laser-mike to hear the scream. It lasted about a second. Roche ran to the window.

'Did he just ...'

The sixth-floor window next to the one Rees was lasing was smashed. There was a body on the ground below. Down on the road, a car screeched to a halt.

'*You know where you need to be and you know you need to be there tonight.*' Shaw's voice crackled through the microphone full of fury. '*You want some of the good stuff? Then come and get it. You can be one of the soldiers in the new fucking army.*'

There was silence and then the sound of a door slamming.

'I think he's coming down,' said Rees.

'Go! I'll clean up!'

Rees bolted out. There were two people beside the body beneath the window now, one of them crouched down beside it, the other talking into a mobile phone. Two more people were heading over from across the street. A few seconds later Shaw came out. He ran to the body and pushed the crouching man out of the way, then rammed a syringe into the dead man's chest. For a moment nothing happened and then the dead man turned out not to be dead any more. He sat up very suddenly, flailed his arms for a few seconds and then stood up. He followed Shaw to the Audi and got in.

'You on him?' Roche asked Rees. He was almost done packing up the mike.

'Aye … Oh, shit!'

In the distance, Roche heard sirens. The Audi pulled out of the car park with a screech of tyres and shot off along Salmon Lane towards the bridge over the Grand Union Canal.

'Fuck.' Rees again. 'Get your arse moving. Shaw's burning rubber.'

Roche threw the last cables into the bag and raced out to the Ford. He pulled away as a police car came screeching round the corner, sirens blaring, passed them and pulled to a stop outside the tower block. Roche watched through the mirrors as two policemen got out of the car and looked about. One of them stared after the Ford but he didn't start writing anything down. They went over to the knot of people who'd gathered, the ones who'd seen Shaw bring a dead man back to life, and that was all Roche saw before he turned a corner and they were out of sight.

'He's on Commercial Road heading east,' called in Rees.

'West India Docks?'

'No. He stayed on the A13. He's heading out into Essex and he's going some.'

By the time Shaw reached the turn-off for the City of London airport, Roche had almost caught up with

Rees in the Audi, pushing the Ford past a ton and triggering every speed camera they passed. That was someone's licence fucked, then. He passed flashing signs warning him that City Airport was closed. All flights over and out of London suspended. Heathrow was closed. The government had stopped short of calling a national emergency and turning out the army but it was close.

Shaw passed Newham and then took one of the Dagenham exits, heading towards the river.

'I'm not liking this,' grumbled Rees. 'Pull back.'

'What's up?'

'I've been here before. We scouted this place … Yeah, he's going back under the A13 and onto Courier Road. There's nothing there except one vast container warehouse. It's a distribution centre. It's massive. When you come off, turn under the main road and take the exit for Marsh Way. I'll meet you there.'

Five minutes later they were standing on the grass verge, taking it in turns to peer west through the scope from Roche's HK417. All Roche could see was an immense concrete field with vans and trucks in neat lines and, closer to the river, ranks of shipping containers. There must have been more than a thousand of them.

'You want to know the kicker?' asked Rees when they'd both had a good look. 'That Dagenham warehouse Stanton kept banging on about? The one they hit back in April? That was less than half a mile up the river from here.'

15 July, 2200 hours, Dagenham

'Quiet, isn't it?' They took it in turns watching through the scope through the day, waiting for Shaw to come out or for something to happen, but nothing did. They didn't see anyone at all.

'Everyone's staying at home,' muttered Rees. 'Can't say I blame them. I mean, what would you do?'

Roche snorted. 'Me? I'd come and spend the day lying stretched out on a stinking piece of Thames wetland with a scope watching nothing happen. You?'

'Sounds good to me.'

Early in the afternoon they repositioned themselves into the edge of the Bean River, a narrow strip of trees around a shallow sluggish smelly waterway about ten feet wide that sliced the warehouse complex in two. On the west side were the actual warehouses. On the east side, the container park, endless lines of Mercedes Sprinter vans and some offices. Shaw's car was parked in front of the offices along with a dozen others. Nothing moved. No one came out and went off for lunch. No one left the building to go home.

An hour after dark, when they still hadn't seen anyone and Shaw's car was still parked out front, they settled on Roche going in while Rees set himself in the undergrowth with the HK417 and a night sight. Roche headed downriver to the container park.

'It's just a hunch.' Roche took a bolt cutter to the first container. He had a bit of a look at how the container was locked, swore, put the bolt cutters back in his bag and took out a line of cutting charge instead.

'Well, that'll be quiet,' hissed Rees. 'Shall I let off some flashbangs for fun?'

'Roll with it.' He set up the charge. 'At least this way we'll know if Shaw's really here or not. If that doesn't bring him out then nothing will. If he does come out, don't bother shooting him because it won't work. Hit him with that EMP thing and leave the rest to me.'

He took cover behind another container. As soon as the charge blew, he ran back. 'Any movement?'

'Nothing.'

Roche hauled the container doors open and stopped, stunned. The container was rammed full of Bliss. Vials must have been stacked some fifty rows high, fifty wide and hundreds deep. He turned on the phone's video so Rees could see for himself.

'Holy Mother!'

Roche shook his head. 'That's something like a million pops.'

'You pick that container at random?'

He nodded.

'You got enough for another?' Roche picked another container and blew it open. Same again. 'Fucking hell. You got any way to get in touch with that Linley bint? Make her day this would.'

'Met police directory enquiries, mate. Christ!' Roche looked about him. He guessed around a thousand shipping containers were parked out here. If they were all full of Bliss then that was about enough to keep the entire country happy for a month; and they were about to make this shit legal? 'Rees, Shaw's dropped the wrong side of the fence,' he whispered. Not that he'd had any doubt before. 'He's turned to the dark side. We need to get eyes in there. Move up.' Roche dropped to his knees and shouldered his carbine, giving cover as Rees darted closer. It was instinct to use the carbine but, as he squatted there, he wondered if he should be quietly throwing that away and using the gun from the museum instead. Although even that hadn't stopped Shaw in Docklands.

Close to the door, Rees took up a position to cover Roche as he ran up. They closed in on the offices. There wasn't much to them, a large prefab building mostly made of corrugated metal walls with a few windows around the front. They circled it, looking for any other way in and came up with a fire exit around the back, closed and locked. Roche shook his head. They crept back and tried the front. The door swung into an open plan office space, a few desks arranged around a square of filing cabinets. Everything looked neat and abandoned, as though whoever worked here had quietly gone home and tidied up before they left. Exactly the way an office was supposed to be after hours.

Rees started sweeping the area with his HK417. Roche tapped him on the shoulder and shook his head. He slung his own C8 across his back and took out the weapon from the museum instead, then gave a second one to Rees. Rees looked dubious but he took it and slung the 417 across his back.

'Shit, Roche, this is like holding a rubbery banana. I feel a total fucking lemon.'

302

They finished their sweep. Along the back were four private offices, two either side of the fire exit. They were as empty as the rest. Nothing. No sign of Shaw, no sign of anyone. Rees beckoned Roche to the square of filing cabinets. All the drawers were shut except for one, half an inch open. Rees cocked his head.

Roche eased it open. The drawer was empty but as he pulled it right back as far as it would go, there was a click from inside. Roche jumped back, adrenalin-spiked, half-expecting something to explode; instead, the cabinet shimmered and disappeared. Or rather, it *almost* disappeared. Roche could see it still there but he could see through it too. It existed in outline like a ghost. Like the Clown alien in Aqar and back at the museum. He touched a finger to the surface of where the cabinet ought to be and felt nothing. No resistance at all. He pushed his hand inside it and still felt nothing. For a moment, he paused. Then he took a deep breath and stepped through. Nothing happened. Inside the middle of the square of filing cabinets was a hole in the ground wide enough to swallow a man. There weren't any steps, no sign of a ladder or a winch-cage. Just a hole.

'Shit. I have a bad feeling about this.' He beckoned to Rees.

'You sure you don't want me on watch out here?'

'Shaw didn't leave. No one's come or gone for the whole day.'

'This stinks,' muttered Rees. 'I'd call it in if I knew who to call.'

'Yeah.' Roche went back to the hole. He turned on a torch and dropped it into the hole and then watched as it didn't fall so much as float down. It stopped after about a hundred feet.

'Fucking hell,' hissed Rees.

15 July, 2230 hours, VY Canis Majoris, 3900 light years from Earth

The *Exponential* had arrived at last, via a sequence of singularity jumps, to one of the largest stars in the galaxy, a red hypergiant that the humans would recognise as lying in the constellation of Canis Major. The *Exponential* had seen a lot of stars over the course of its life and red giants were something of a speciality. The hypergiant, though, earned a moment of its attention simply from its size, being some two billion kilometres across. In human terms – and the *Exponential* had spent a lot of its time trying to think of things in human terms now – the star would have swallowed all the inner planets in that system and both the larger gas giants too. Europa would be deep inside the chromosphere and the rings of Saturn would have been skipping through the corona. In a few tens of thousands of years it would evolve into a yellow hypergiant, getting hotter and hotter and blowing off huge volumes of its own mass as it did.

There were a lot of Weft ships gathering around the star.

The *Exponential* casually measured the star's neutrino output and compared it against the theoretical models, although hypergiants were sufficiently uncommon that theoretical models of their structure and behaviour were tentative even among the Weft. The neutrino count was off. Deep inside the star, someone was messing with gravity and time. The *Exponential* wondered how long it would take. It could see the theory. A star like this would explode as a supernova in the normal course of things. Messed with, it might easily turn into a hypernova with a gamma ray burst capable of causing mass extinctions half a galaxy away on any planet unlucky enough to be caught in the beam. The beams of a gamma ray burst were narrow, though. You'd have to be very unlucky, the *Exponential* thought, to be on a planet that happened to be in the way.

It quietly calculated what planets were.

15 July, 2230 hours, Dagenham

Roche dropped a clip into the hole in case the torch was somehow a fluke. When it did the same, he swore under his breath and jumped. Gravity let go almost at once. He floated most of the way down until he started to fall again for the last few feet. It made him lose his balance as he landed. He rolled. His hand pressed down into something sticky.

The only light was the torch he'd dropped. It shone across the floor. The floor glistened. He sniffed at his hand. Iron.

Blood. *Christ!*

He waved to Rees to follow him down. They each lit a torch.

'What the fuck is this?'

They were at a crossroads between four tunnels whose walls and ceilings were as smooth as glass, seamless and perfectly square. They were pleasantly tall. A strip of dull red light glimmered above them, leading off into the shadows until each tunnel opened up into darkness. There was no way to see what was waiting for them.

The floor was black. Wherever they shone their torches, it gleamed.

'That's a fuck of a lot of blood,' whispered Rees. 'Too much for one person.'

Four paths and only the two of them. They each picked one. Roche couldn't help noticing how his feet stuck to the floor just a little with each step.

'Radio check?' Roche jumped. Rees, from the walkie-talkie on his belt, sounded tinny and alien.

'Loud and clear.'

The passage opened up ahead of him; but before Roche got there, lights suddenly flared from the walls and the ceilings. The light was soft, not the harsh of fluorescents, and came from everywhere. Warm and with a tinge of yellow like sunlight.

'That was me,' said Rees. 'At least I think it was. I might have found Shaw.'

'What?'

'I'm in a square room,' said Rees. 'I've got exits left and right. Looks like a situation room. I've got a large table and a whole wall full of monitors. The monitors are blank. I've got papers on the table and I've got at least seven corpses. Human. I think. They're in bits.

They've been torn to pieces. One might be Shaw. Or maybe not – frankly it's a bit fucking difficult to tell. They've been dead hours, not days. Fuck! I think this happened while we were watching.'

Roche eased forward. 'I've got another square room. Exits left and right. I don't know what this was. I've got … Whatever used to be in here, it's been smashed to pieces.' He crouched and looked at the smears of blood on the floor. Underneath a mangled desk was a severed human hand. It looked like it had been torn bodily off an arm. 'I've got blood here too. Human remains.' He crept further into the carnage around him. Upturned aluminium tube tables, smashed monitors, tangles of cables, scattered hard drives. Here and there, Roche saw metal table legs and computer cases sliced in two with the knife-edge precision of a high-powered laser.

Something caught his eye. A fragment of chrome. It was a finger with a blade instead of a finger nail, sharper than any razor. Roche crouched beside it and picked it up, then ran the edge over the bent aluminium leg of what had once been a trestle table. The fingernail cut through the metal as though the metal was made of candyfloss.

'I've think I've got a piece of one.' He turned the finger over in his hand. The skin was brilliant and metallic. It felt warm. The inside was hollow except for the tiniest trace of a brown powder.

'You need to see this,' said Rees. 'There's a nationwide distribution network but that's just the start of it. There are connections to the US, to China, to Japan, Germany,

Russia, Holland, Italy … fucking hell, it's all over the place.'

A faint noise from the room off to Roche's left brought him up sharp. 'Rees, have you moved?'

'Turn around.'

Roche turned. He could see Rees standing at the other end of the glass-walled tunnel, looking back at him, silhouetted by white light. Roche tapped his ear and pointed. *Contact.* He gestured for Rees to hold his position, levelled the alien gun at the exit to his left and eased his way closer. Pieces of mangled plastic ground the floor under his feet. It was like trying to walk through dry autumn leaves, impossible to be silent. The light pissed him off now. Sure, it made it easier to see what he was dealing with, but this was a sterile square place with nowhere to hide. The light left him exposed. Running straight into Shaw or some alien thing down here would be short, shitty and messy.

'Rees, have you still got that EMP thing?'

'I got it.'

There wasn't any sort of door. The tunnel beyond looked the same; seamless, square, glass-walled, lit by a red glow. It ran five yards then turned sharply towards Rees's position. Roche crept to the corner and peered around with a tiny periscope. The lights were on in the other room but it still took him a moment to realise what he was seeing.

The room was trashed like the one he'd left. Worse, as if it had seen the bad side of a couple of grenades. Half a human corpse – the upper half – hung from the far wall, somehow embedded into it. A leg and a foot and half an arm protruded from the ceiling. The walls were covered in blood and glistening pieces of white that might have been bone. Shattered metal and plastic littered the floor. Most of it looked like computer equipment, mangled beyond recognition. Sitting in the middle, very still, was a pile of chrome. It took a moment for Roche to see it as more than a heap of scrap metal; but then it twitched, very slightly.

Roche backed away. This time he made damned sure he was silent.

'Rees,' he said, when he was back in the other room. 'We've got company.'

19 – The Pleasure

15 July, 2310 hours, Dagenham

They took it from two sides at once. Roche held his position while Rees picked his way through the litter of entrails and pieces of corpses that had once been human. The twitching pile of broken chrome didn't seem to notice. Roche hesitated. He could have kicked himself for that – you taught yourself not to, to take the shot when it was there to be had, to make sure the enemy never saw you coming, never had a chance to look you in the eyes, never had an opportunity to defend himself. But that had been the days when things were black and white, or had tried to be.

The chrome thing shifted. Its head snapped around and Roche felt a searing pain up his left arm. He screamed. Rees fired at once – ropes of golden light twisted through the room and wrapped themselves around the chrome. It flickered like a bad television, turning translucent and then so thin it was almost invisible and then snapping back to solid again. As the pain eased, Roche fired his own weapon. The chrome thing staggered to its feet. Great swathes of it were missing.

It had lost an arm from halfway above the elbow and the chrome side of one leg had been sheered away from hip to ankle, leaving an angry scar of writhing brown and flickering sparks. Its one remaining hand had a finger missing and a hundred thin wires like fishing lines running out of it, spreading all across the room, diving into every single piece of computer equipment, broken or not.

The flickering came faster and faster. The hand with the wires fell off. The golden ropes wrapped around it squeezed tighter. There was a smell of ozone, of scorched metal. The metal around the chrome shoulders suddenly burned white hot and started to spark. The creature's face changed, its features running like molten wax.

Whatever resistance it had abruptly failed. The ropes of light snapped taut. The chrome was sliced in a moment into a dozen white-hot pieces. Wherever they fell, everything they touched burst into flames.

'Crap.' Rees backed away.

'Grab what you can!' snapped Roche. He jumped into the room and grabbed at the hand with its wires then snatched his fingers away with a yelp. Burning hot. He cast his eyes about for a fire extinguisher but couldn't see one.

'Already done. How do we actually get out?' shouted Rees. 'Clues for the clueless?'

Roche dropped his bag and slipped the C8 off his shoulder. He pulled off his shirt.

'Never mind! You just jump and it carries you …' Rees's voice faded. Roche wrapped his shirt around his fingers and picked up the severed chrome hand. He didn't have time to look at it. The flames were spreading. He ran back to the shaft. Rees was peering down from the top.

'Jump!' he said. Roche jumped. As he did, the air in the shaft took hold of him and lifted him up. Gravity hadn't forgotten him – he still felt heavy; but he was rising.

'Shit!' Rees suddenly looked away and then looked back. 'We've got company!'

It took a few seconds for the shaft to carry him to the top. By the time he got there Rees was gone. The ghost-shape of the filing cabinet was still …

A series of explosions shattered the offices. The blast smashed into the filing cabinets, tumbling them down. The noise left him dazed. He staggered on, tried to keep moving, pushing the cabinets as they fell into him, wriggling out of the way but there were too many and there wasn't enough space. One of the cabinets crashed across his back. He heard a staccato burst of gunfire and the familiar sound of a C8 with a suppressor. Another blast of white light raked the offices. It cut through the walls as though they were paper. With a groan he pulled himself out from under the fallen cabinets. His rib was killing him again. His ankle hurt too. Twisted at the very least. If it was broken then he was fucked.

'Rees?'

A machine gun opened up outside, a steady spray of bullets hosing through the office, churning the cheap furniture and chipboard partitions into splinters and sawdust. Rees came hurtling back, skidded across the ground and dived behind the cover of the filing cabinets.

'Fuck!'

'What's out there?' Roche tested his ankle.

'I don't fucking know. More of those fucking Russian Mafia idiots I think. At least a company with heavy weapons and more of this alien shit.'

'Back door?'

Rees looked at the fire exit. 'Fucking crazy.' He offered Roche a hand. 'You good?'

'Ankle. I'll be slow. You go, I'll cover.'

They crawled for the fire exit. The machine-gun fire stopped. Whoever was out there, they'd be coming through the front door in a few seconds. If they had any sense, they'd start with a grenade or two. Whoever they were. More of the men who'd hit the Docklands museum, Roche supposed. As soon as they reached the fire door, Rees jumped up and kicked it open. He bolted out, sprinting as fast as he could, jinking from side to side. Roche crouched, C8 shouldered, firing three-round bursts into random places. He didn't even know if there was anyone out there; then he saw two men run out from behind a van, raising what looked like M16s. He took the first one down with a head-shot. The second took a three-round burst centre mass. It staggered him and the head-shot that followed finished him and now Rees was almost at the vans and Roche would have to run while Rees covered him in turn …

Another figure stepped out, slow and deliberate. Roche put a three-round burst into him without thinking and then lined up a head-shot but the soldier didn't even flinch. The air shimmered around him.

Shaw.

He didn't shoot Rees. Instead he jumped in front of him and swept his legs out. As Rees sprawled across the concrete, Shaw jumped back up. He was absurdly fast, quicker than a snake. He picked Rees up and disarmed him as though he was taking a toy from a child, then took him and held him up by the throat.

'I know you're in there, Roche. Give it up. You and Rees here, you could join the army. You'd be good. Come out and I'll let him live. Otherwise I crush you both. You can help me find that little shit Burman. Whelan-Hollis. I know you fancy her, Roche. We've got her. You can be the one to …' Whatever else he'd been planning to say, Roche shut him up by shooting him in the face. Not that it did anything useful while he had that force field around him but at least it stopped him talking. The only reason he didn't open up with the ropes of golden light was he had no idea how to make sure they didn't slice Rees to pieces.

'Bad fucking call, Roche.' Shaw threw Rees aside. He raised his left arm. Flesh and bone morphed and changed, flowing into the shape of a gun. Lights started to glow around his wrist, brighter and brighter, then detached from his arm and started to spin around the barrel. Roche ducked back into the shredded remains of the office, not that the flimsy walls would make a blind bit of difference. He'd tried the alien gun. He'd tried the old-fashioned bullet in the head. He'd thrown

314

a flashbang and a fragmentation grenade into a room in Aqar and a soldier like Shaw had lived through it even without a force field.

Which left the black rugby ball things.

'Last words, Roche?'

Roche took one of the rugby balls out of his bag. It was heavy. He twisted it the way he'd seen the Clown by the Gherkin twist it. Nothing happened. He threw it at Shaw in case it was about to explode.

15 July, 2311 hours, Challenger Deep, the Western Pacific

The Fermat construct watched its last clone end. It could build more, it thought. It could use the drones left in the system, the ones that had once belonged to the *Exponential*. It could build a small army but it couldn't build anything that would stand up to the Pleasure. The Hive would have to see to that. The Hive was already mustering its forces. A singularity bridge wouldn't be long in coming and then the Weft and the Pleasure would come face to face once again, hard and bad.

The construct considered its possibilities. The most useful course of action, it concluded, was to proceed on the basis that the Pleasure didn't know it was there, didn't know the Hive was coming, and do nothing to jeopardise the surprise when the Hive appeared through the bridge. The safest course, then, was to simply disassemble itself.

It made one last call to the drones guiding the comet of anti-hydrogen towards Mars. It spoke through the entangled pions that each drone carried captured in the tiny proto-sentience that powered its thoughts. The drones dissolved into elemental matter and dissipated into inter-planetary space, traceless.

It considered its own disassembly one last time, noted what had just occurred and considered another possibility. It noted there were other means of agency. It thought perhaps it might examine them more closely.

15 July, 2320 hours, Dagenham

For a moment, Roche waited for something to happen: either an explosion from outside or else Shaw firing his plasma cannon or whatever the fuck it was his arm had turned into and that being pretty much the end.

When neither of these things happened, Roche peered back outside.

Everyone seemed frozen. Shaw was standing there, arm raised, a huge halo of fire around his fist, plasma fire gathered and bursting out of him, only for some reason it was moving incredibly slowly. Roche watched it flying towards him at a steady walking pace. Shaw wasn't moving at all. Roche half ran, half limped out into the car park, firing. Everything around him was still. The wind, the air, everything. 'Come on then you cunts, finish the fucking job!' There was something strange about his own weapon too. The ropes of golden light crawled out and jumped through the air with an elderly lethargy. They almost couldn't keep up with him.

He was wrong about Shaw. He saw that as he got closer. Shaw was still moving, he was just moving incredibly slowly …

A sudden rush of air and sounds flooded him. He was most of the way across the car park, firing and shouting and everything else had been silent and suddenly wasn't. The ropes of golden light from his own gun wrapped themselves around Shaw and sparked across his bubble of glittering light. Shaw's fireball found its energy and raced through the air. The detonation thumped across the car park. It lifted Roche off his feet and staggered even Shaw. The office building vanished in a cloud of super-heated plasma. It was as though everything except Roche had paused for a few seconds and ground almost to a stop and then picked up again. Everything. The whole world.

'There!' roared Shaw. He seemed taken aback, as though Roche had simply appeared out of nowhere. Roche reached the first row of vans and threw himself behind it. He scrambled in a low crouch for the next just in time as the first exploded in white-hot fire, catapulting one mangled Sprinter spinning into the air. It smashed down on top of the rest. Roche kept moving. Something as basically crap as a Sprinter wasn't going to offer much cover. He'd need a tank. He wasn't sure even that would do it. The *USS Missouri*, maybe …

He couldn't see the rugby ball he'd thrown but he had another one.

Shaw jumped straight up into the air. Like Spiderman back in Tower Hamlets only about five times higher.

Roche gaped. Couldn't help himself; and Shaw was looking right at him. He could almost hear Shaw's voice. *There you are. Now fucking die already.*

He twisted the rugby ball, readied himself to throw it, then stopped himself. It was already working. Shaw was hanging in the air. Moving, maybe, very slowly, towards the apogee of his leap. Hard to tell. A brightness was gathering around his arm but watching him was like watching high clouds against the sky, trying to work out whether they were moving or whether they were simply there.

Frozen in time.

The EMP device. Rees still had it. Roche ran back to where he lay. He couldn't tell whether Rees was alive or dead. How long did he have? Twenty, thirty seconds? He opened the suitcase. There wasn't much to it. An arming switch and a timer. He flipped the switch and set the timer as low as it would go. Five seconds. He pulled all the grenades from Rees's webbing and yanked the pins and scattered a few in among the vans, then dropped the last couple where he thought Shaw would land. He hauled Rees over his shoulder and started to run as best he could, as best his howling ankle would let him. It was pathetic, really. He was hardly going—

The world came rushing back. Shaw, up in the air, fired his cannon at where Roche had been half a moment earlier. A line of vans exploded. Roche didn't look back. Didn't dare.

The first grenades went off, one after the next, shredding the vans and setting off a series of secondary explosions as their fuel tanks burst and caught fire. Light flared across the car park. Shaw, back on the ground now, stood in furious silhouette, wreathed in flames as Roche staggered away.

Roche turned to face him. 'Come on then! Finish it!'

Shaw raised his arm. Roche watched as the EMP went off. Shaw's shield flickered and died. The last two grenades detonated a moment later and blew shreds off him. When that wasn't enough, when there was still something moving, Roche levelled the alien gun and squeezed. The writhing ropes of light cut what was left into chunks.

'Fuck you, Shaw.'

He didn't look back as he stumbled away.

20 – Singularity

16 July, 0200 hours, Clacket Lane Services

The further Roche got from Dagenham, the more the burn on his arm troubled him. He couldn't think what he'd done to himself. He stopped halfway home at a service station, pulling into the car park in some stolen car, wondering if he might change it for another. Probably not at two in the morning when there was hardly anyone there except a few truckers. He managed to get himself a coffee and a place to sit and counted himself lucky. Luckier than Rees. Rees was pretty fucked up. He had broken bones and a half-crushed throat and he wasn't breathing right. At least he wasn't dead. Given time, he'd mend.

The rib was giving him gyp. The ankle was a sprain and he'd be over it in a few days. The arm, though … he pulled back his T-shirt and peered at it.

There was writing. Writing on his arm. Writing tattooed into his skin: *We knew them as the Pleasure. They will give you everything you desire and take your freedom and your soul. Many of you will want this but in the end they will devour you. We will help you.*

Roche went to the bathroom and tried to scrub it off but it wasn't written so much as etched. He had no idea what it meant or how that shit-bastard of an alien or whatever the *fuck* it was had put it on him. Either way, it wasn't going away any time soon.

They were running the news in the service station, a single solitary television playing to an audience of empty waxed cardboard coffee cups, crumpled crisp packets and sandwich wrappers. It was all still about Docklands. Talking heads talking shit about terrorists and Muslim fundamentalists and Al Qaeda, as if Al Qaeda would have nuked a Damascus mosque. People slowly coming to terms with the notion that the world had fundamentally changed and yet, at the same time, banging on about how life would continue as it always did. Politicians on both sides saying the same. Keep calm and carry on. The spirit of the Blitz. Remember the IRA, remember 7/7. We didn't let the terrorists change us then and we won't let them change us now. Don't let them *win*. Parliament had been recalled from the summer recess until the current emergency was resolved. That was all. No need for martial law or a state of emergency. London would pick itself up. The city would come back stronger because that's what it always did.

The news bulletin ticker-tape that always scrolled across the bottom of the news these days quietly let everyone know that Parliament would also be voting to legalise Bliss later in the day. Amid the litter and detritus of passing late-night drivers, Roche shook his head, wondering how many Westminster fat boys had the first idea what was coming.

16 July, 0200 hours, Mars

The anti-matter comet was a little under a million kilometres away from Mars, travelling with a relative velocity of around a thousand kilometres per second. Deep inside, electric currents ran through the tiny atom-thick slivers of inert frozen hydrogen that striped its insides. The hydrogen vaporised and annihilated with the surrounding positrons and anti-protons. Tiny flashes of energy broke the comet into thousands upon thousands of fragments. The pieces spread apart, all of them aimed for the Hellas basin, an ancient impact crater resulting from something about the same size striking the planet some four billion years ago.

16 July, 0220 hours, Clacket Lane Services

'Hey, Rees.' There were aliens in London. Someone was making the drug called Bliss that no one understood or could even test. He had his theories about that now, but not much evidence. He had the footage from the museum, though. That ought to be enough to wake everyone up.

'We have to go public, Rees,' he said. 'Make copies. Send it to every national newspaper. The BBC. Maybe CNN and Al Jazeera for good measure.'

Rees didn't answer. Right now he couldn't talk. He nodded though. Faintly.

'Shit, mate. You need help. I can't take you with me.' Roche took the chrome hand out of the bag and looked it over. It wasn't hollow like the finger had been. It seemed to have some sort of interface but it was like nothing he'd ever seen before. The hand had been wired into everything down there. You had to wonder how much it knew, how much of the Bliss network it had unravelled.

Not that that was any use to him now. He drank back the last dregs of his coffee.

'Give me ten more minutes, mate.'

He helped Rees out of the car and into the service station, gave him a last burner phone so he could call himself an ambulance and then drove off into the night alone.

16 July, 0317 hours, Mars

In its last moments, the *Irrational Prime* had worked out with cold mathematical precision when to allow the Shriven vault to re-open. Several higher-order dimensions peeled back on themselves and the vault phased back into existence. A fraction of an instant later, the first pieces of the comet hit the surface of Mars, scattered around a diameter of two thousand kilometres. In the normal course of things, each fragment would have punched twenty kilometres into the planet's crust, carrying with it the equivalent energy of several million hydrogen bombs. The resulting crater would have been a hundred kilometres across. It was the sort of thing that happened every few tens of millions of years. The sort of thing a planet took in its stride and shrugged away.

These fragments came in thousands and were made of anti-matter. The first strikes punched straight through the Hellas Basin and vaporised everything in a thousand-kilometre radius. Shock waves started around the planet's crust, pulverising it. They started to travel into the planet's mantle but were almost instantly overtaken by more fragments which super-heated as they came through the fireball of vaporised crust and punched even further towards the planet's core. The second set of shockwaves reduced the planet's crust to so much dust and then the fireball reached critical density and the plasma of annihilating matter and anti-matter detonated with the force and brightness of a miniature supernova. For a few seconds, the Hellas basin flared brighter than the sun. Mars shattered.

16 July, 0320 hours, Camberley

Roche drove slowly past his house and kept on going. The front door was open. When he parked a street away and came in through the back, he found three dead men inside. On his bed was a small package and a note. The package, when he opened it, looked like some sort of tablet only with a bizarre socket on the back. It took him a second to realise that the socket was an exact match for the chrome hand. He plugged the two together and the tablet sprang to life. A message popped up on the screen:

Download data?

The note was somewhat more straightforward. The note simply said: 'Run.'

Outside, through the curtains, there was a light so bright that it looked like lightning but wasn't. The night sky lit up brighter than a midsummer day, the brilliant white light of Mars dying. Roche stuffed the tablet in his bag and grabbed a few things. By the time he went back to the car, the light was already fading. By the time it had gone, he was on the road again, heading west. He didn't really know where he was going.

They were coming. Whoever *they* were.

16 July, 0320 hours, VY Canis Major

The *Exponential* drifted in a close orbit around the vast bulk of the hypergiant star, flitting in and out of its outermost layers. The Weft were manoeuvring one end of a singularity bridge into place, injecting linear and angular momentum in carefully controlled doses into the exposcd singularity, adding matter and bleeding it away through accelerated Hawking radiation.

The *Exponential* watched the Hive settle the singularity in place and begin to feed it. Very soon it would be ready to become a bridge across the stars.

TO BE CONTINUED ... ?

Read the other side of the invasion in:
Empires: Infiltration, by Gavin Deas
Available now!

Acknowledgements

Empires grew out of conversations with my agent, Robert Dinsdale, and with Simon Spanton at Gollancz. It started with Robert's enthusiasm for shared worlds, faltered on the stones of my scepticism, and then flourished with Simon's suggestion of a way to go about it. Simon also suggested Gavin Smith as a collaborator, which pretty much me sold on the idea and was how Gavin Deas was born. So thanks go to Simon and Robert for spawning this and not minding too much when what Gavin and I wrote didn't turn out to be quite what we talked about during those first conversations.

Simon then neatly managed to pass the editing (for which read cross-checking between the two books) on to someone else, so thanks to Marcus Gipps at Gollancz who edited this and to Colin Murray for his work rearranging my words into coherent sentences.

In particular, thanks are due to Gavin 'who needs physics?' Smith, who was managing perfectly well as an SF author without some fantasy writer showing up and throwing Maurice Broaddus books at him. Gavin put up with my impatience, a brief deviation into writing something that was starting to look like another Transformers movie, and even wrote part of a chapter for me. We learned a lot about how not to do collaborative writing and we're still talking.